It's immensely liberating to read this grotesque novel far out on the fringes of fiction. It has been many years since Danish literature has produced such a phantasmagoric novel that brushes so closely to plausible historical reality.

Niels Houkjær
Berlingske Tidende, Denmark

A very good novel ... sad, hilarious, profound. Like life itself.

Jon Helt Haarder
Jyllands-Posten, Denmark

Like *The Elephant Man* by David Lynch, Peter H. Fogtdal's novel celebrates the life and the dignity of those who were considered sub-humans. It's a wonderful novel where the pursuit of human dignity is narrated with a masterly mixture of drama and humour.

Sergio Luis de Carvalho
Lisbon, Portugal

Library of Congress
Cataloging-in-Publication Data

Fogtdal, Peter, 1956–
    [Zarens dværg. English]
The tsar's dwarf / by Peter H. Fogtdal;
[translation by Tiina Nunnally]. —
1st ed.
p. cm.
ISBN 0-9790188-0-3
(alk. paper)

I. Nunnally, Tiina, 1952–
II. Title.

PT8176.16.O38Z4513 2008

839.81'38–DC22

2008002346

Hawthorne Books
& Literary Arts

9   1221 SW 10th Avenue
8   Suite 408
7   Portland, OR 97205
6   hawthornebooks.com
5   *Form*:
4   Pinch, Portland, OR
3
2   Printed in China
1   through Print Vision

    Set in Paperback.

    First published as
    Zarens Dværg by
    Peoples Press in 2006.

    First American
    Edition, Fall 2008

To Marie Huda Fogtdal and Choul Wou—
with special thanks to Marianne Miravet Sorribes,
Janne Breinholt Bak, and Sandra Freels.

**DANISH TITLES
BY PETER H. FOGTDAL
INCLUDE:**

Skorpionens hale
Jupiters time
Lystrejsen
Flødeskumsfronten
Drømmeren fra Palæstina

The Tsar's Dwarf

A Novel
Peter H. Fogtdal

TRANSLATED FROM THE DANISH BY
Tiina Nunnally

HAWTHORNE BOOKS & LITERARY ARTS
Portland, Oregon | MMVIII

THE TSAR'S DWARF

I   The Russian Guest

NIGHTSHADE
Atropa belladonna

1.

MY NAME IS SØRINE BENTSDATTER. I WAS BORN IN 1684 in the village of Brønshøj. My father was a pastor, my mother died in childbirth.

When I turned six my body decided not to grow anymore.

I don't care for the term "dwarf."

As a rule, I don't care for dwarves at all.

2.

THE FINE GENTLEMEN HAVE BROUGHT ME HERE TO Copenhagen Castle. They've set me on a carpet that feels as if I'm treading on seaweed. Now they're looking at me in that jovial manner they favor—their heads tilted, their lips twitching—but I stare right back at them. I *always* stare back, because they're uglier than I am. The only difference is that they don't know it.

"Do it again," says the finest of those gentlemen.

His name is Callenberg. He's a smug cavalier with red cheeks. His legs are bound with silk. I put my hands on my hips and stare at his multiple chins, which are quivering with mirth.

Callenberg spreads his legs and smiles. I move across the soft floor, duck my head, and walk between his legs. I do it four or five times, back and forth, like some sort of obsequious cur. And now they're all applauding; now they're cackling contentedly in their perfumed chicken yard. Of course I could have bumped my head into Callenberg's nobler parts, but that would have been foolish. And you can say any number of things about a wench like me, but I'm no fool.

"Splendid." Callenberg draws his legs together with a satisfied grunt.

The courtiers once again stare at me with a condescending expression—the same way that everyone looks at me, with a despicable mixture of contempt and joviality. But they could just as well have been staring out the window. They could just as well be gazing up and down the length of the Blue Tower, because they don't see me, those people. How could they see me when they're as blind as bats?

ALL AT ONCE I catch sight of my figure in the mirror. I'm small and withered, with deep furrows on my brow. My eyes are tiny and green, my lips thin and sardonic. My nose and my ears are a bit too big, my hair is long and graying. The veins dance up and down my bowed legs, but there is *nothing* ridiculous about me. That's something they're all going to learn.

Callenberg sits down on a scissors chair and snaps his fingers. A moment later a glass of clove wine is brought to him along with a plate of Flemish chocolates. His hands are fat and pink, his nails look like shiny seashells. That's how a human being is. Loathsome and vain, with habits that increase in cruelty the more the person eats.

"Ask the dwarf what sort of tricks it can do."

The First Secretary turns to me. When he speaks, he does so slowly, as if he were talking to an idiot. I choose to ignore him. I'm familiar with the fine gentlemen. I have more experience with them than I would care to admit. I know how they think and how they behave. They can't fool me with their vulgarities.

"Can the dwarf perform tricks or read fortunes in salt?" Callenberg asks.

"I can both read and write," I tell him.

Callenberg tilts his head back and laughs. He would howl with laughter no matter what I said, because dwarves are so droll, dwarves are entertaining in the same way that parrots are entertaining. We are creatures who serve only one purpose: we exist so that human beings can feel superior.

Callenberg rubs his hand over his chins.

He is the Lord Steward at the castle. Not just the Lord Chamberlain but the Lord *Steward*. That's the sort of thing that the nobility care about. Their whole *raison d'être* lies in titles. The higher the title, the greater the reason they have for existing.

"I can both read and write," I repeat with annoyance. "I also know German, Latin, and a little French."

"And where has the dwarf learned these things?"

I let my eyes survey the chamber. Exquisite portraits of Frederik IV hang on the walls. The drapes, which are a golden peach color, flutter in the breeze. There are chromium-plated mirrors with sullen looking angels. The strong scent of Hungarian cologne permeates the wallpaper. All very elegant, for those who have a taste for elegance.

"I suppose the dwarf is also knowledgeable in Russian?"

The Lord Steward looks at me with a condescending expression. Then he snaps his fingers and a chamberlain opens the lavishly embellished doors.

"Tell the dwarf to come back tomorrow."

The First Secretary nods. He has a weak chin and a timid face—the sort of face that confirms the amount of time he has spent in submission to his master's fury.

Callenberg disappears down a long passageway lined with Venetian mirrors.

The last I see of him are his hands behind his back and his thin legs beneath his stout body. After that he is swallowed up by the castle—and by the specters of all the kings who refuse to let go of the past.

A FEW MINUTES later I'm escorted down several narrow staircases intended for the servants. The stairwell feels damp and clammy, and I very nearly slip on the high steps. Two dead bats are lying on the stairs. The archways are draped with cobwebs.

The footman opens the door to the kitchen. In front of me is a vast room that goes on and on, as far as the eye can see. There are people everywhere: master cooks, footmen, errand boys, and pastry chefs. They're rushing back and forth, armed with marzipan and mackerels and mulberries.

I stare at the wooden spoons that are almost as long as I am tall. And at the pots containing saffron, the tubs holding Iceland cod and whiting in brine.

We start walking.

The kitchen makes me uneasy. There's a strange mood in there, as if the kitchen were *waiting* for something. I pass two assistants who are making a pigeon pâté. A royal taster is sampling a sour burgundy. They are all in their own meaningless world; they are all *waiting*.

The footman leads me over to a back door and opens it impatiently. When I turn around to ask him a question, he gives me a swift kick. Involuntarily I gasp with pain. Then the footman points to the moat and the high castle bridge. He points to the slum quarters, the flatbed wagons, and the flea market. When he slams the door, I angrily wipe my mouth and start walking.

It's still a hot summer day. The towers of Copenhagen are sweltering in the sun, and the barges gleam like silver in the canal.

I head across the High Bridge to Færgestræde. A horse-drawn cart loaded with wine barrels almost forces me into the water. A moment later I vanish into the crowd among the coaches, soldiers, and loudly shouting fortune-tellers.

3.

I LIVE ON VINTAPPERSTRÆDE IN THE MIDDLE OF THE KING'S city. It's a narrow lane where violence hangs in the air. Not even our watchman dares make his rounds in that section of town. There are six distilleries, four taverns, and a couple of miserable whorehouses. But I take pleasure in the atmosphere; it keeps me on my toes. The human being is an animal that fights to survive. Nowhere is this more apparent than in the part of town where I live.

I share a wretched cellar room with my poor scoundrel Terje. His path through life has taken him from pub to prison, with involuntary stays at Bremerholmen. We've been together for four years. Before that I lived with another scoundrel who was also fond of misshapen females. In a way I'm in charge of my own curiosity cabinet. Each morning I haul myself out of the cabinet, brush myself off with a damp cloth, which is enough to turn the stomachs of many goodfolk—and then I listen to their comments.

They say that I have an ancient face, that I'm descended from a demonic race. They think my head is deformed, that my fingers are stunted, that all the parts of my body are out of proportion. But who decides what is out of proportion?

According to other wise folk, I belong to a noble race that has lived on earth longer than human beings—a race that has mysterious powers and can see into the future. That may be true, but I don't really care. I have the same problems as everyone else. I eat, I shit, and one day I will die.

WHEN I STEP inside my cellar room, I find Terje curled up on the straw pallet. He is unwell, as usual, his body burrowed in day-old vomit. He is shaking with fever and a cold sweat. His face looks like mauve porridge speckled with yellow beard stubble. The Scoundrel looks up at me, his expression reproachful.

"Where the devil have you been?"

I ignore him and go over to one of my stools. I have three of them. The Scoundrel made them for me so that I could reach things in the larder. I don't live in dwarf lodgings like other dwarves. I have no use for a dollhouse with sweet little dwarf doors. With a few objects to help me, I can manage to get by in the world—without extra assistance. There's no reason to feel sorry for me.

Right now I open the larder, which once again is half-empty.

A rat leaps out with a scrap of cheese in its mouth. A moment later it darts through the wood shavings on the floor.

I look at my scoundrel.

"I have work at the castle."

Terje laughs scornfully and spits into the straw. He's one of them—a human being. He's tall and redhaired, with a chest like a Scanian rebel. He is usually quite handsome, but ever since Candlemas he has been sick with consumption. Now he looks shrunken and withered; his smell has taken over the whole room. I ought to be used to it. There are all sorts of different smells in the world when you live between the legs of goodfolk.

I go over to Terje and study his face. I see the dull look of his eyes and his hair, which sticks out in greasy tufts. Then I wipe the fever from his brow. Sickness is Our Lord's way of rooting out His children. The Devil is more merciful. The Devil has always been more merciful.

"Don't you want to hear anything about the fine people in the castle?" I ask.

"No."

"They have chairs made of gold in the offices, and there are mirrors on the walls—even on the inside of the doors."

"What for?"

"So they'll have a good view when they scratch themselves on the ass."

Terje laughs hoarsely. I stretch out my hand to him, but he knocks it away. Then I go over to my little box. It's filled with herbs and healing salves: amanita, swallowwort, and mustard plasters. There is also a secret compartment containing tinctures. I open the box using a rusty nail that hangs around my neck. Then I select the herbs for a miracle-working elixir. And as I work, the voices come to me. They're like birds flying around my head, birds that demand to be heard.

I turn around to look at the Scoundrel.

"You'll be dead by tomorrow," I say.

Terje nods, slowly and sadly. Outside the dogs are baying, and a drizzle settles over the city like a delicate silk coverlet.

WHEN TERJE CROAKS, he'll be the third scoundrel that I bury. Scoundrels don't last very long, especially when they've been thrown in irons at Bremerholmen. But they're needed in the house, particularly for a wench like me.

"What the hell did the king want with you?"

Terje has a malicious look on his face. I ignore him and pour beer into the birchwood tankards.

"He probably wants to use you for a footstool."

I slap his face. Terje puts his hand to his cheek but is wise enough not to say anything more. He makes do with giving me a glare, but a glare that doesn't seem to belong to him.

I go over to the fireplace. The elixir is brown and bubbling; a bittersweet scent spreads through the room. I light another candle. There is only a small peephole in the cellar, because who would want to look out at Vintapperstræde? And who would want Vintapperstræde to look in at us?

"Sørine?"

"Yes?"

"You're a good sort."

I smile sadly. A few minutes later Terje starts to snore. It's a familiar sound. I don't like to admit it, but I'm fond of the sound. Terje's snoring makes me feel calm. I don't know why.

I PUT THE box of herbs away and take out my diary. Writing is my solace. When I write, I have control over the world. Then all that exists are the letters of the words and myself. Then I can speak the truth about human beings. I can study those peculiar creatures as if I were a *mathematicus*. And that's a necessity, because they would never dream of doing it themselves.

I learned to read and write at an early age.

My father brought in a castigator when I was eight years old. He was an elderly man with bloodshot eyes. Like all castigators, he was more interested in chastising than in teaching. I had my lessons at the parsonage, in a dank little room where I was supposed to stay so as not to frighten the parishioners. Slowly I began to catch on. I was taught the Bible and Luther's catechism. It was tedious reading, but the words fascinated me; they were like building blocks. Words could become sentences, sentences became pages, and pages became gospels. When I write in my diary it's my spirit that hovers above the waters. Then I'm the one who gives names to the world. Then I'm the one who becomes Our Lord.

I cast another glance at Terje and take off my homespun jacket. It's much too hot in the cellar. There are bugs everywhere, laying eggs in our hair and in the goat milk. I have always preferred winter. It's less filthy, more callous.

I decide to lie down in the straw for a moment.

My body aches all over—in the bones, in the joints, and in my crooked legs.

I close my eyes and say a prayer. It's a prayer that I've often repeated.

The next morning Terje is dead.

A SPIDER'S WEB of slime fills the Scoundrel's throat. His mouth with the three teeth gapes open all the way down to his guts. His lips are blackish blue.

I study him with curiosity. Terje's gaze is fixed on eternal heavens. The Devil, not God, has come to get his soul, because the Scoundrel belongs to the Evil One. It's in Hell that a man will quench his thirst. It's in Hell that he meets buxom gypsy women and enjoys the most fiery liquors. Hell can only be a solace after Bremerholmen and consumption.

I try to roll Terje onto his side, but he's too heavy. So I stick a hand under his body, down into the straw, down to the mice and the rats and the vermin. And there, as I thought, I find a little leather pouch. It contains no less than twelve gold *rigsdaler*. A fortune to me.

I give the Scoundrel a reproachful look and try to close his mouth, but it keeps falling open. As if Terje is trying to say something, as if there's a drinking song that he wants to sing before he loses his audience. Or maybe it's just something that he wants to complain about—the way everyone complains in this rathole called Copenhagen.

I shove an angry hand under Terje's jaw.

Suddenly something gives way. I let loose a sob. No more than one protracted howl, before I pull myself together again.

I look around the cellar. Soon I have to go up to the castle, but first I need to find the night-soil man so that he can come and get Terje. It usually costs three *skillings*, unless the body is especially heavy.

The cellar has changed. You would think that something had been removed, but instead something has been added.

When I step out into the street, I sense that Terje is going with me, that he's lurking near my left shoulder, and that he's looking at the world with a more blissful form of disgust.

4.

I MET MY SCOUNDREL WHEN HE WAS WORKING AT TORVET, the marketplace square, with the executioner. He had just started as the executioner's assistant and was carrying out his work with great zeal. There was plenty of variety for a restless soul like his. Some of the poor wretches were beaten with the bat; others were flayed or broken alive on the wheel. It was hard work, but well-paid. A branding paid four *rigsdaler*, decapitation by sword brought ten *daler*, breaking on the wheel paid twelve, while drawing and quartering on the post and wheel paid no less than fourteen *rigsdaler*. A man could live well on wages like that.

I couldn't stand Terje's occupation. The performances at Torvet were sheer barbarism, but as any knave knows, people must have their entertainment. Even the respectable towns-women turn up when the body of some poor wretch is put on the

post and wheel. And when the executioner holds up the severed
head, they cheer along with the most bloodthirsty rogues.

I don't know what's wrong with goodfolk. Do their own lives
have meaning only if other people suffer? Is that what it means
to be a human being on this earth? I find all forms of bloodletting
abominable. Nothing in my soul wishes to watch the dismem-
berment of poor folk.

I should say that Terje was not a bad scoundrel. He took no
joy in the suffering of others. Beneath his hard surface was a
sensitive scoundrel, but you had to know him well to realize that.

One day Terje had finally had enough of his work at Torvet.
It started one November night when things began to haunt him.
A pauper appeared before him and began zealously pursuing
him—not just at night but also in the daytime. More of the
executed appeared, all of them threatening the torments of Hell.
The apparitions showed him their split-open skulls, they pointed
to their broken wrists and crushed hips.

I tried to help the Scoundrel as best I could. I brewed
elixirs and whispered incantations, but I was up against forces
that I couldn't control.

One fine day in January a shadow settled over Terje. It
crept inside of him at night, and from that moment on he suffered from consumption. And something else took hold—
something that grew even bigger with his visits to the taverns.
The Scoundrel turned into a real scoundrel. The goodness
was sucked out of him until only a hull remained—the hull of a
person who was barely even alive.

I turn around one last time in Vintapperstræde. I suddenly know that I'm not coming back, and that I'll never see this
pit again. The realization fills me with incomparable elation—
and fear.

I walk along my street, heading for the castle, wearing a
hat, a homespun jacket, and short men's trousers. The farther
I get from home, the more people stare. I always make my face
into a mask—a mask to show the goodfolk that I'm anything but

adorable and that I don't want to be picked up and shown around. That I would prefer to be keelhauled than to be chucked under the chin. That I refuse to hide under bureaus because children find it so charming. I can't abide toddlers. The only thing we have in common is our small size. That's the mask that I wear. It's my salvation.

I turn another corner. Two calves peer at me from their stall. The street is littered with piss and paper. Mostly piss.

"A little turd," shouts a shopkeeper. "Look at the little turd."

I swing my cane and manage to avoid slipping. Who knows what the day will bring. Nothing good. That much I do know.

5.

I'M BEING ESCORTED THROUGH THE NARROW, CLAUS-trophobic passages inside Copenhagen Castle, up and down stairs that put a strain on my deformed limbs. The passages are lit by meager wax candles that go out at the slightest provocation. The candles have been stuck in holders along discolored walls. Here only servants are admitted. No member of the royal court would dream of frequenting this desolate part of the castle, where the inhabitants are sweaty and where knives sit loosely in the sleeves of toadies and flunkies.

We pass footmen, master cooks, carpenters, and chamberlains—all of them with faces rigid with importance. Most of the court puppets cast sidelong glances at me and smirk. Afterward they rush onward with their tankards, documents, and ivory trays.

The footman accompanying me is the same one as before. His face has a chronic stupor to it; a paltry little wig sits askew on his head. He opens the door to a chamber, and to my surprise I see an enormous cake, the biggest one I've ever seen in my life. The cake is shaped like a big church with red spires and golden cupolas in the form of onions. It's decorated with candied fruits, marzipan, and icing, but it doesn't look like the churches here at home. In front, in an elaborate courtyard, rest snowbanks made of whipped cream and macaroons. Little marzipan soldiers are lined up next to opulent sleighs.

The door shuts behind me, but I hardly hear it. I keep staring at the huge monstrosity of a cake. It's not yet finished, but the monster is taller than I am. Looking closer, I see that it has been adorned with all the details: gables, archways, and gilding. Even the doors look real, down to the last door handle, hinge, and doorframe.

At that moment Callenberg appears with some of the courtiers. They offer no greeting, just look me over with an expression of curiosity. I put my hands on my hips and stare them down, like the milksops they are.

"Put the dwarf inside the cake," says Callenberg.

Before I manage to say a single word, a servant lifts me up. I try to scratch his face, but the servant is too strong. He laughs and drops me into a big hole. I land on my feet and can just barely see over the edge.

The men laugh like idiots. I stare back at them and try to climb out of the hole, but the servant pushes me back inside.

"Careful!" says the pastry chef. He's a thin man with a battlefield of warts on his face. The cake smells like glue, and I wonder how much is decoration and how much is actually edible.

"Tell the dwarf to crawl down inside the cake."

The footman turns to me and repeats the command, but I don't care for his tone of voice. At that instant Callenberg nods. The footman shoves my head down. I try to resist, but it's pointless.

Now the hole is covered with a lid. The world disappears, and I find myself in the heart of the world's most ridiculous cake, inside a hole big enough to hold only a dwarf. I gasp for breath and pound on the cake. There's no air. I feel nauseated. I'm going to die. And as if that weren't bad enough, I'm going to die inside a cake!

In a sense it would be appropriate to be buried under candied fruits, to be weighted down by God's marzipan-infested hand. My life is worth nothing. I'm a parrot without plumage. No one will remember me the day after I'm dead. At most they'll remember my body. They'll remember my height, my back, and the ape-like appearance of my hands. But they won't remember me.

Because there is no me. I am my body—I have no soul. There is no place for me in God's kingdom. But there *is* a place for me in the void. In the void I'm allowed to take my place.

"Can it breathe?"

"Jump up!" a second voice commands.

I crouch down as I wait for the moment when there will be nothing more to wait for. Then the lid is torn off. The world is back—the world and the Lord Steward.

Slowly I stand up. My body is still asleep. It feels good to breathe the air again; it's something to which I've grown accustomed. I peer over the edge of the cake. To my surprise more courtiers have arrived and more footmen. Some of them are snickering loudly, others are staring arrogantly, as if confronting a phenomenon of nature that they cannot comprehend.

"Get up on the roof, poppet."

I gape at the Lord Steward.

"Crawl up between the towers. Do you hear me?"

I sigh. I'm just about to explain to him that not even a dwarf can fly, that I can only get up there if he brings me a stairway, but I decide not to say a word. I just look at the Lord Steward, at his fat body and double chins that quiver with every consonant he speaks. And suddenly I know that something has gone wrong. I'm important to the Lord Steward. I'm his last hope.

The royal house has use for a dwarf.

The royal house has use for *me*.

I cast another glance at the high-born people. Utter silence. But the silence of the fine folk is always too good to be true.

"We'll have to make a staircase," sighs the pastry chef.

A moment later a footman lifts me up and carries me down to the cellar. On the way he makes sure that I hit my head against the doorframe. When he tosses me into a cell, I'm no longer conscious.

6.

WHEN A DWARF IS BORN, IT WOULDN'T DREAM OF REVEAL- ing its secret. The dwarf infant wails like a human being. It breathes with the same tenacity. It suckles milk and sleeps the slumber of the innocent, its cheeks flushed pink. There is nothing demonic about a dwarf baby. It doesn't have the number nine imprinted on its scalp, it doesn't howl at the full moon. And many years pass before the human being discovers that she has suckled a snake at her breast.

I'm quite certain that my father had a serious conversation with Our Lord when he realized that I was deformed. It hap- pened when I was six years old—when my body stopped growing. My father felt that I was God's punishment for the sins of his youth. Before I was born he had written a wish list for Our Lord— a list of demands, everything that he wished from his first- born. The first item was the most important: The child had to be a boy. Next came a list of talents, none of which I possessed. But the list had no significance as soon as my father discovered that I was deformed. From that moment on, he dropped all his demands and lapsed into a divine despondency.

I can see him before my eyes, the way he looked back then: young and blustering, a ruddy barrel of a man, filled with anger at the Creator, talking to himself and the marsh. There's no doubt that he felt himself persecuted and that he was keeping accounts which would be presented to God on Judgment Day.

I don't know when my father found himself again. Whether months or years passed, or how long it was that he suf- fered under his defeat, but at some point he decided that I should be hidden away and protected from the world, since I was too little to manage on my own. I was wrinkled and hideous—a little but old person, the size of a *skilling* coin. Not a child that could be presented after a church service, unless the purpose was to terrify the congregation.

Of course I was the only dwarf for miles around. I found my playmates not in the parish but in nature, at the marsh— and in the darkness, which became my best friend. Because it was there that I found protection. It was in the dark that I could feel safe and loved, while the light deceived the eye.

The light exposed every abnormality of my physiognomy. The light was merciless and unrelenting.

AFTER A WHILE the door opens. At first I'm unsure what door it could be, but then I remember where I am. A big rectangle of light floods the cell, and a man is standing in the doorway holding a tallow candle in his hand. I don't recall having seen him before. He is dressed as a cavalier, wearing the obligatory powdered wig, an elegant silk coat, and elegant shoes that gleam in the dim light.

"Sørine?" he calls.

I glare at the rogue without answering. As far as I know, there's no one else in the cell but me. It's clear that his eyes have not yet adjusted to the dark, but that doesn't matter, because I haven't yet adjusted to the light.

"Are you there, Sørine Bentsdatter?" The man clears his throat. "My name is Rasmus Æreboe. I am His Majesty's *notarius publicus*."

The cavalier's voice is soft and pleasant. He has a bit of a lilt. He must be from the islands of Fyn or Falster. Yet there is something finicky about him that I find irritating, something that invites a good slap.

A cautious little smile appears on his face.

"Oh, there you are, my dear. I have to talk to you about something important." He smiles again. "But you haven't put on the dress."

I notice a dress lying on the floor of the cell. The footman must have tossed it in when he locked me up. I pick it up. It's a gown with rose-colored embroidery and a stomacher, an insert covering the stays on the bodice. Elegant but tasteless. The gown has obviously belonged to a child, and it's too big for me.

"We don't have much time. Do you understand?"

"Time for what?" I retort.

"Time before the big banquet."

Æreboe turns around and speaks a few words to a man I can't see. Then he gestures for me to follow. I don't move from where I'm sitting. A moment later a footman appears. He comes toward me with an unyielding expression on his face. I hiss at him angrily. The footman sweeps me off the floor, grabbing me under the armpits, as if he were picking up an infant. Then he holds me away from his body, as if hanging me out to dry. As we move along, I dangle helplessly between Heaven and Hell. The footman turns left, going past a workshop where sedan chairs are made. Finally we end up in a small room with a window and a table. The *notarius* is already sitting there. He looks friendly and at ease. We're talking about an idiot.

The footman sets me down so hard that pain shoots up from the balls of my feet, through my ankles and knees, and into my lower back. I always feel pain whenever a human being wants to display his propensity for power, but I never show it. I wouldn't give a varlet like that the satisfaction.

"Now, now, show a little restraint," Æreboe says.

The *notarius* is a man of average height with big, guileless eyes, a sensitive mouth, and a straight nose, belying a generous but fussy nature. His complexion is transparent, but an ugly scar on his forehead lends him a certain gravity.

"We want you to sing a song," he says.

At first I have no idea what the *notarius* is talking about, but then I happen to think about the cake, and about my role in that ridiculous episode.

"...for His Majesty the Tsar. You will be an important part of the banquet."

"What banquet?"

"For Peter Alexeyevich. The tsar is coming here tomorrow to dine at the castle. The plan is for you to jump out of the cake and sing a song in Russian! I have no doubt that it will be greeted with cheers."

Again I glare at this ridiculous *notarius* who has taken over Callenberg's role. What sort of an eye-servant is he? To my chagrin, I have no idea what a *notarius* does. I know only that it sounds miserably dreary—a position that allows admittance to the castle and the opportunity to practice the art of arse-kissing.

"…because you see, the Tsar loves midgets!"

I can feel my face wincing.

"Or dwarves, if you prefer that term."

"I'll be damned if I'm going to jump out of any cake. Do you think that I'm some kind of performer at the flea market?"

The footman grabs me by the scruff of the neck and throws me against the wall. There is something impersonal about his action—as if he has never done anything else in life but toss dwarves about. I peer up at the human beings and get to my feet. My shoulder feels bruised, but nothing is broken. It's a good day.

Æreboe smiles.

"You're a feisty midget."

"And you're a mama's boy who thinks he can control me!"

The footman reaches out for me again, but this time I'm too fast for him. I flee under the table and hide behind a leg.

"Leave us for a moment," says Æreboe.

The footman nods and goes out the door.

Rasmus Æreboe stares at me. His lips are pressed together in fury.

I crawl out from under the table.

The human being always wants to exert his will. There is only one thing of interest to him: submission. That's why it's impossible to trust this reputable *notarius* with the reputable silk tongue.

I smile and await his malice.

"You'll end up in the stocks or condemned to hard labor. Do you realize that?"

"Ha!"

Rasmus Æreboe regards me like a castigator who doesn't dare castigate me.

"You ought to be proud, Sørine. You have been chosen to perform for the king. At the same time you will have the opportunity to meet His Majesty the Tsar—the most splendid of all sovereigns in Europe. When I was stationed in Russia, I met him several times. First as private secretary to the Danish envoy; later as emissary extraordinaire for His Royal Highness Frederik IV."

"I won't perform for the Muscovites' tsar."

"Why not?"

"Because I refuse to denigrate myself before a flock of over-stuffed spendthrifts. I am not a court jester. Laughter doesn't come easily to me."

"But it's so amusing to look at you, Sørine."

I cross my arms and glare at the rogue.

"You'll earn a couple of *skillings* for your performance," he says kindly.

I laugh loudly.

Rasmus Æreboe gives me a look of disappointment. I sit down on a footstool and peer up at him.

A dwarf is always looking up at human beings, but only in a physical sense. Never anything more than in a physical sense.

7.

DUSK SETTLES OVER THE HARBOR LIKE A SHADOW. IT slips quietly through the sports hall, the rope works, and the windows of the castle. The last rays of the sun cling to the church towers, dance across the red rooftops, slide over the ramparts, and disappear. But the sun will be back. Everything repeats itself. Everything repeats itself.

Outdoors the city prepares for the night, for the arrival of the stars.

My life is about to change soon; there is nothing I can do about it. Everything is out of my hands. That ought to make me feel calm, but I'm anything but calm.

I look at the congenial *notarius publicus*—or rather, the apparently congenial *notarius publicus*, because no one can truly know a human being. No one has any desire to know a human being.

Rasmus Æreboe keeps on talking about his days in Russia— how cold and raw it was, how everything froze solid during the long winters: the rivers, the poultry, the Hungarian wine. He talks about the barbaric inhabitants, about the funereal language that sloshes in the mouth like pea soup.

I watch Æreboe. I see how his eyes grow bigger when he speaks of the beautiful Church of the Ascension in Moscow, after which the cake has been modeled; about the flickering of the pine torches over the nighttime snow; about the decorated sleighs that were pulled by Siberian tigers. And suddenly I have the feeling that Æreboe could keep on this way for hours, that he can't be stopped once he gets started. The past turns to tears in his eyes as he speaks of the mighty tsar, who is both cultivated and barbaric. A giant of a man who can drink any foreigner under the table, an awe-inspiring despot who keeps a collection of molars he has pulled from the mouths of his own soldiers. And the more Æreboe talks, the more I have the impression that he's bored in Denmark, that he misses the frozen steppes of Russia. And I wonder yet again what a *notarius publicus* actually does. Maybe it's a post that is just as dreary as it sounds.

"Nowadays I work at the stock exchange, so there's no time to keep up my Russian," says Æreboe, as if he could read my mind.

I nod.

"But right now the plan is for me to teach you a song or several verses of poetry that you can recite for His Majesty the Tsar."

"I refuse to sing."

"At least you can read the words." Æreboe gives me an encouraging smile. "I'll write the words down, and then I'll teach you how to pronounce them."

"In Russian?"

"Yes, in Russian. And believe me, it's a beautiful language."

The strange *notarius* sets about writing down a sentence. There is something about him that I like. That may be because I don't know him. His eyes shine with childish joy. His quill pen scratches across the page.

I ponder what the Muscovites' tsar intends to do in Denmark, and whether it's true that he wants to help the king reclaim the territories of Scania. The Danes and the Muscovites are allies. They're preparing a raid on Sweden to undermine Karl XII, the warrior king. And I'm supposed to jump out of a cake. How unfair history can be.

"*Dobro poshalovalot! Vashe velichestvo, v prekrasnuyu datskuyu zemlyu...* Can you say that?"

I repeat the strange sentence: "*Dobro poshalovalot! Vashe velichestvo, v prekrasnuyu datskuyu zemlyu...*"

"Excellent. You have an ear for languages."

I nod. There's a special music to this language—something explosive that is provocative and so unlike Danish. I feel an urge to say the sentence again, but I can't remember the words.

The *notarius* smiles.

"*Dobro poshalovalot! Vashe velichestvo, v prekrasnuyu datskuyu zemlyu...*"

"What does *vashe* mean?"

"It doesn't matter."

I look at Rasmus Æreboe. A new strength has emerged on his face, as if he were deriving something from the language that he couldn't get from his native tongue. His gaze is firmer, his voice deeper. The more Russian he speaks, the more the sweat pours from his brow. His jaw gets wider, the movements of his lips look unfamiliar and grotesque.

With my dwarf vision I see the tsar's city before me. Not

Moscow but Petersburg. A city with canals and windblown palaces. A site surrounded by icy green islands and poisonous swamps, with beautiful bridges and yellow mansions.

"... *v prekrasnuyu datskuyu zemlyu* ... "

I watch the lips of the *notarius* and wait tensely for the new sounds they will produce.

In the meanwhile, time flies by. That's good. Almost too good to be true.

8.

THE TSAR HAS FINALLY ARRIVED IN DENMARK.

Not to Copenhagen, but to a town on the island of Falster. He has refused to spend the night in the city's castle. Instead, he has settled for fishcakes and a bed in a tavern.

All this I hear as I lower myself into the cake.

I have been drenched with perfume. My hair has been ludicrously curled by a French-speaking chatterbox. The shoes that they've put on my feet are made of tiger skin, the stockings are red like scarlet fever. I look like the world's smallest whore.

I'm even more nervous and irritable than usual. Dwarves have breasts; we are adults, not children. That's why the dress is too tight. But now I'm inside the cake, down in the sugary darkness where I'm supposed to stay until they knock on the wall.

They've built a staircase that I can climb. They've also bored a hole in the side so that I can breathe and look out of the cake. I'm sweating and trying not to crumple my speech. The Russian words are teasing me, vanishing from my head.

It's important that I arouse jubilation.

The tsar is known to be lacking in humor, but if he likes me, I'll be allowed to entertain him during his stay. Although no one knows what might please the tsar. No one knows what goes on inside a human being.

THEY PUT ON the lid, and the world disappears. I sit down on the bottom of the cake. There is very little space, even for a dwarf.

Soon my back is aching, and my legs start to fall asleep. I try to change position, but it's difficult, very difficult.

"You can breathe?"

The master of ceremonies is speaking. It's not really a question. It's a command.

The footmen lift up the monstrosity. Off in the distance I hear muted sounds: laughter, music, the baying of a dog.
The plan is for me to jump up when I hear a knock, but I'm afraid that I won't hear the signal.

We start climbing upstairs. The cake shakes violently. I hit my head on the side. I wonder once again how a cake like this is made. Are the onion cupolas edible? Isn't it blasphemy to devour a church? Perhaps the Muscovites will be offended to have God's house end up in their bellies. You never know with foreigners; it's not easy to understand them.

I stick my hand under the dress fabric to scratch myself. I keep on scratching, back and forth, while I worry about how ridiculous I look in this rigged-up garment. I hate the stomacher and the patterns. The dress has been sewn according to the newest fashions, but that doesn't make it any more comfortable to wear.

Outside the footmen come to a halt. I try peeking through the hole, but I see only the silk jacket of a footman.

"…delayed in there…"

"…the eighth toast to the tsar…"

It's Callenberg's voice, containing a fair amount of irritation—the sort of irritation that fills a human being when he can't control the world. At the same instant a cannonade is heard from the castle courtyard, followed by another. Then the doors to the hall are opened. The footmen march in with the cake. The orchestra starts playing a festive piece of music. I heard brass, flutes, and fiddles, and I feel a rare sense of peace in my soul. I have made a decision.

Finally the marzipan cake stops moving. The music ceases. The moment has arrived. Someone knocks three times on the wooden lid of the cake. The sounds fade away in the hall. Some-one knocks again, this time using his fists. Then the lid is lifted off the cake. A flood of light streams over me. Slowly I stand up, trying to shake some life into my legs and the rest of my body. Then I cautiously peer over the edge.

The hall is bathed in the light from thousands of candles. The tables are adorned with fresh branches and flowers from the orangerie. Everywhere are elaborate dishes and arrangements of fruit, along with sumptuous golden goblets. The fine folk are dressed in damask and magnificent robes. At the far end of the hall stands a pavilion where six musicians are seated, dressed in colorful garb.

Everyone is staring at me. Everyone is waiting.

I catch sight of the king. Frederik IV is sitting on a throne at the end of the table, wearing a dark green robe festooned with medals and orders and sashes. An enormous powdered wig makes his face look as if it's drowning in curls. Against my will, tears fill my eyes. I have never seen His Majesty before. I am touched, but astonished. Frederik looks anything but divine. He's small, almost dwarflike, with heavy eyelids, and his skin is pockmarked. He radiates both gentleness and rigidity at the same time.

His Majesty's eyes rest heavier on me than anyone else's. I have an urge to fly up the stairs and throw myself at his feet. At that moment I catch sight of Callenberg and the master of cere-monies. They are angrily gesturing for me to jump out of the cake and stop staring at the guests. The guests are supposed to be staring at me.

But I find the situation quite pleasant. I take pleasure in staring at the king of Denmark and Norway; at his gloved hand that is clenched on the table; at the impatient line of his lips dividing his face in two; at his eyelids that make him seem as melancholy as a dachshund.

I am enjoying this moment, even though I hadn't expected to enjoy it. And I hope that it will go on.

MY GAZE MOVES onward to the Queen of Denmark—to the dour, morose Queen Louise, who looks as mournful as I had expected. She has small, squinting eyes and a bitter mouth. She's looking down at the table as her hand plays nervously with a heavy string of pearls. But my eyes don't stop there. My gaze moves onward to the tallest man in the hall—to the only one who has cast aside his wig and who towers beneath a painting of a former king. The tall man is sitting two seats away from Frederik. Not for a moment do I doubt that this is the tsar of Moscow.

Peter Alexeyevich regards me with curiosity. He is a big man with a small head. His eyes are black, a big mole adorns his right cheek, and he sports a thin mustache. Peter's shoulders are narrow, but his chest is broad and manly. The Muscovite is not as elegantly dressed as the others. He's wearing a burgundy suit with ugly patches, but he's a handsome cavalier. And unlike the others in the hall, he is completely sober.

At that instant a chamberlain grabs me by the hair.

I snarl with fright, but all I can do is follow my hair up the stairs on the cake. A gasp passes through the crowd because I'm standing before the king, the queen, and the tsar without a stitch of clothing on.

My skin is wrinkled and pale. My breasts droop pitifully. Boils cover every inch of my small body. Entire families of crabs live in my pubic hair. My bowed legs are crooked and scarred from an old pox. I'm as unsightly as a dwarf can be—if someone is of the opinion that dwarves are unsightly.

The chamberlain lets go of my hair, and the master of ceremonies stares at me in shock. Utter silence in the hall.

I put my hands on my hips.

"*Dobro pozhalovat'. Vashe…vashe velichestvo…* "

I stop. The tsar stares. At that instant a Muscovite tosses a plum at me. The hall awakes from its torpor. Merriment spreads, and I stare at these dastardly wretches who have already made the vomit basins foam. The Muscovite is on his feet, and he keeps on throwing things at me. The flesh of one plum has landed on my left cheek and another on my right shoulder. At first I don't know what to do. The plums hurt. I jump down from the church roof and land on top of a regiment of marzipan soldiers. Soldiers, sleighs, and snowdrifts are crushed beneath my dwarf feet, squishing like cakes between my toes.

Silence falls over the hall.

Again.

Everyone turns to the tsar to see how he'll react. The tsar regards me with an inscrutable expression—an expression that no one can decipher.

Then I begin to dance. I stick my wrinkled buttocks in the air, as if they were silken cushions. I take a few fancy dance steps, back and forth, just like the fine folk do. Callenberg is giving the king a desperate look, but Frederik is just as difficult to read as the tsar. I keep on with my frivolous dance, spreading my legs, twirling around like a top, as I sing a bawdy drinking song.

Now a footman comes storming toward me. I jump down from the cake and run between the tables. Many of the guests start to cheer; others jump up onto their chairs to avoid the naked dwarf. I crawl my way past the knee-high stockings and the corsets, as fast as my crooked legs will carry me.

Three fierce footmen chase after me. I evade them by slipping between the legs of several countesses and crawl out on the other side of the table. But as I'm about to get to my feet, I'm picked up by unknown hands.

I kick and I bite. At that moment I discover that I'm looking into the eyes of the tsar of the Muscovites. For an instant my heart stands still, because Peter's eyes are the most peculiar eyes that I've ever seen. They are dark holes, compelling and inquiring, but not alarming. On the contrary. Everything can be seen in those eyes. Everything.

Peter holds me away from his face and stares at me, as if trying to read all my secrets. Then he tilts his head back and he laughs. The laughter makes his whole body shake—his narrow shoulders and his chest. To my astonishment, I discover that he has tears in his eyes.

"You are the most hideous dwarf I have ever seen," he says in German.

I blush. And then the tsar kisses me on the lips. After that he hands me to another Muscovite, who kisses me in the same fashion. I look down at my body, at the boils and the big scars, and I clench my teeth.

It's all over.

Some distance away I see the master of ceremonies approaching like a wolf, but Peter waves him off. Then he reaches for me again and swings me back and forth, as if I were his first-born child. And as if by magic, the musicians strike up a merry tune, and the footmen begin cutting into the huge cake.

"You are very naughty," the tsar says to me.

I nod sheepishly. I like the tsar's eyes. I like the way he smells of tar and salt water. The tsar is a man, and wenches like men.

At that moment a cannonade is heard from the castle courtyard.

The tsar continues to talk to me, this time in Russian. Then he tosses me up toward the ceiling and hands me to another Muscovite, who laughs just as raucously.

And in that manner I make my way around the table. People kiss me and stick their hands between my legs and pour aquavit down my throat from enormous goblets. For a long time I'm the focus of the entire hall.

When I'm no longer a novelty, the hands of footmen carry me out. I'm dizzy from the liquor. The only thing I want to do is throw up. We pass several paintings resplendent with opulent baskets of fruit. I shut my eyes as I sail past Flemish pears and heavy gilt frames.

At one point everything goes black, and I fall sound asleep in my own vomit. I have no idea where I am.

9.

WHEN YOU'RE A DWARF, THE WORLD IS IMMEASURABLY vast. It's like some cruel folktale, or a garbage dump for free-wheeling fantasies. The furniture is as tall as towering beacons, the doors are portals into gigantic spaces. Even a carpet is a sea that goes on forever. Maybe that's why people think that dwarves have the same view of the world as children, that we're endowed with the chaste minds of children, that we thrive on tomfoolery. But nothing could be further from the truth. Whereas children see the world as a long string of nonsensical events, midgets see it as a Coronation Charter, as a declaration of war from a sadistic Creator who spends His time devising new humiliations.

I was sold to a baron in North Jutland on my twelfth birthday.

I don't know how much money my father received, but I assume that he consulted Our Lord before setting the price. There was nothing dramatic about it. I left my childhood home in a wagon and was driven to Jutland along with chests of drawers, garden furniture, and a couple of old spinning wheels. After that I lived for five years at Count Rosenskjold's manor, where I worked as a servant and a taster. I became familiar with excellent wines and the exquisite art of portraiture from Venice—with everything in the world of the nobility. And I was allowed to spend time in the library when no one else was making use of it. I continued my reading of the Bible, I studied German, Latin, and French. I learned as much as I could, because I knew that my mind would be my only salvation in a world that tramples small creatures like thistles.

It was actually the intention of my lord that I should function as a court jester, but he quickly discovered that I was too testy and not the least bit amusing. I didn't smile as often as he liked. I frightened the children and the guests. I wasn't house-broken enough to be among all those people of refinement. At most I could be allowed to crawl across the chairs and pour wine for those who had newly arrived. But they soon tired of me after I'd spilled the wine enough times.

In actuality, my lord didn't have need for a court jester; he performed that role himself. He spent all his time putting on airs and expanding his manor in one way or another, seeking to make it a center for folk of *quality*. He created an orangerie for rare plants, he built a hall of mirrors in the French style, he hired an Italian composer who filled the halls with miserable cater-wauling. The refined arts may have come to Jutland, but outdoors it still stank of cow dung.

That's one of the things I don't understand about humans: their need to put on airs. Do they really believe that their identity lies in a fancy garden? Does a person become more powerful in the eyes of others if he imports highbrow culture from principalities whose names he can't even pronounce? That sort of extravagance displays a hollowness of the soul, a depressing emptiness. And that emptiness was quite obvious in my lord. Count Rosenskjold had only one wish: that the king would stay at his estate during one of his visits to Jutland. He lived for the day when His Majesty would arrive with his entourage, when he would dine at the sycamore table in the green hall. But the king never came. He chose to stay in Boller, at Skanderborg Castle, and never with my lord. A sensible person would have accepted this with peace in his soul, but fine folk are seldom sensible.

When pietism won a foothold in Denmark, my lord had something new to which he could devote himself. He began holding prayer meetings in the chapel, which had been deco-rated by a Flemish artist.

Because I was so well-read, I was allowed to participate.

It was an insufferable experience.

The pietists were marked by an incomprehensible love for their brethren. There was a great deal of repenting, as usual; there was sobbing and handwringing, done with an infernal zealotry. And the false doctrines were jammed down everyone's throat with gospels and books of chronicles.

When we were done with confessing our sins, we would meet in the library. That gave my lord the chance to show off his Chinese curios and his collection of clocks from Bohemia. In the library the lights were kept dim, the voices were fervent. The fire crackled briskly in the fireplace, though not at full blaze, so that no one would mistake the warmth of the library with Whitsunday in Hell. The conversation was of Our Savior Jesus Christ, but also of his long-suffering disciples, with whom we were supposed to have a close relationship. The disciples were supposed to live inside of us, or so it was said. They ought to find their way into our prayers, they were supposed to be embraced, even loved, like Jesus himself.

On one particular evening in the library, the intention was for each of us to choose our favorite disciple and speak of the specific qualities he possessed. We were supposed to describe the light that emanated from the disciple and that had become engraved on each of our sins.

"And who have you chosen, Sørine?"

My lord placed a gracious hand on my shoulder and gave me a loving look—something he did only with the Bible on the table and a bottle of aquavit stashed in his inside pocket.

"I have chosen Judas," I said.

My lord's eyes turned glassy. He leaned back. His big hands lay dead on his knees. And during my speech he looked only at his guests, never at me.

I spoke with great sincerity about Judas—why I was fond of him; how I felt that he had been cowed and misunderstood. Judas was not a criminal; he had merely allowed himself to doubt. Judas had asked questions of the Savior—questions that the Savior could not answer. He had been critical instead of howling along with the wolves who were his companions. And it was there that the greatness of Judas resided: He saw through the duplicity around him. He was not a hypocrite, and that made him dangerous in the eyes of the Christians.

Judas also seemed the most intelligent of the disciples.

He was not filled with hatred like Paul; he was not a coward like Simon Peter. He loved Jesus with all his heart, but he had seen through the hollowness of the rebellion, because Judas was a thinker, not a fanatic. But did this lack of fanaticism make him a demon? Did he take the silver talents because he was greedy and avaricious? No, Judas took the money because he was weak, just as all of us are weak at one time or another. It had nothing to do with a lack of nobility of soul. Judas was simply something that was not often found in the Bible. He was a human being!

After my little speech there was silence in the library.

No one looked at me. The participants looked away or down. The silence was deep, almost mournful—as if they had all been witness to a soul's fall from the heights.

My lord looked at me for a long time.

"Woe is you, Sørine, for you are treading in the footsteps of Cain."

I met his glance, but there was no more to discuss. There was never anything else to discuss in the world of human beings. I was blasphemous, sacrilegious, inflammatory. And there was no place for someone like me in Jesus. Or in the absolute monarchy of Denmark.

RASMUS ÆREBOE IS once again the person who comes to see me in my cell.

I have no idea how long I've been sitting here. Time never has any meaning in the dark; maybe it has no meaning at all.

I've slept off and on, been awake for a while and played with a couple of gluttonous rats. I've named them, pampered them, and let them sleep in my lap, as rats should.

As a child I collected grass snakes. I found them down at the marsh and took them home to the parsonage, but my father killed them with a shovel. Then there was a period when I collected toads and shrews. My father turned them loose in a vain attempt to educate me. On the other hand, he was fond of horses, so I was supposed to be fond of them too. A horse, he said, was a "good" animal, an animal that ought to be enjoyed. Not merely as a utilitarian beast, but as a "holy" and poetic animal whose beauty was apparent to everyone who had eyes to see. Yet horses are anything but beautiful. And even for an animal they're obtuse. I have observed them for years, and horses have a slavish temperament and a submissiveness that I find disgusting to a high degree. Add to that the fact that they can be tamed. If an animal can be tamed, I have no interest in it.

I have no interest in Rasmus Æreboe either.

He's now standing here, holding a tallow candle and wanting my praise in order to rescue me. But I don't want to be rescued. I'm done with running the gauntlet between tsars and Pharisees. Rather a public whipping at Torvet than the esteem of fools.

"Come with me, Sørine," he says in his melodic voice.

I stay where I am, seated in my cell. Why does the human being think that his world is so attractive? Isn't it possible that I feel better in the silence? Last night Terje visited me. He put his arm around me and called me his good wench, even though I had helped him on his way into the next world. Terje would never make an appearance in the Light. But in the Dark he came to me, bringing solace and relief. In the Dark he could slip away from God and whisper what he hadn't been able to say when he was a scoundrel here on earth.

"We have a new dress for you." Rasmus Æreboe smiles. "You're going to have a splendid visitor."

He turns around, expecting me to follow him.

Dwarves are always supposed to be grateful. We're supposed to be grateful for every crumb we receive—for every flatbed cart that does not run us over; for every axe that does not chop off our heads. Dwarves are supposed to be grateful to live in a world where seven-year-olds outgrow us!

"What's going to happen?" I ask.

The cavalier beams mysteriously but doesn't answer. His eyes are a lighter blue than I remember. In spite of the scar on

his forehead there is something virginal about his face. Against
my will I wonder whether Rasmus Æreboe is married; whether
he has children and a wife; whether his home is an earthly paradise with wig stands, a Bible, and chamber pots made of
faience—whether Rasmus Æreboe is a puppet, a human being,
or something else.

10.

THERE ARE LAVISH PAINTINGS OF VENUS IN THE KING'S
audience chamber, paintings of mountainous landscapes in
Italy with green silken rivers, of trumpet-blowing angels with
light blonde curls lapping around their cheeks and throats.

I've often seen these paintings of Paradise—of angels com-
forting the saved with lyres and peaches. The angels are always
looking up toward Heaven, even though they are in Heaven. Their
eyes are light-blue like holy water, their arms are chubby, their
penises so tiny that they could disappear in the beak of a blue
titmouse.

But the pudgy angels are not the worst part. Even worse
is their devotion to the Lord—a devotion that reminds me
of certain Schnauzers. Why waste devotion on something so
obscure? If you ask me, Our Lord should not be received
with open arms, but with a hailstorm of questions. Paradise is
and continues to be a form of bait—a heavenly hostelry with
corpulent angels who deserve a good taste of the truncheon.

Paradise is boring.

Even God can't stand the harmony. Maybe that's why He
feels the need to create chaos on earth, so that human beings
can appreciate Paradise when all hope is gone.

A chamberlain opens the French doors and motions us
inside to see the king.

Rasmus Æreboe tries to take my hand, but I swat his away.
My heart is pounding hard as we step inside a large room where
eight courtiers are sitting at a long table. I catch sight of the king,

the tsar, and several gentlemen I don't recognize. They are bending over a map. When they see me, they stop talking.

Frederik summons me over.

"So here we have little Sørine," he says in German.

Against my will I blush.

The king pats me on the head.

"Her Majesty the Queen still hasn't recovered from your dance number, Sørine Bentsdatter."

The tsar laughs heartily as he fixes his eyes on me. I'm struck once again by what a giant he is. Peter is three heads taller than anyone else in the room. Today he's dressed like a lieutenant in a soiled uniform with a truncheon in his belt. His pants are bound just below the knees with gaiters made of leather. His stockings are shabby, his gloves filthy. In his right hand he is holding a Dutch clay pipe, and he radiates a strange blend of joviality and restlessness.

And then there are his eyes—those black eyes that absorb the whole room.

For the first time the tsar turns to face Rasmus Æreboe.

"Isn't this my old friend Eerenbom?"

Rasmus Æreboe blushes.

"At your service, Your Tsarist Majesty."

"I remember you quite well. We met in Petersburg and in Moscow."

"Thank you, Your Tsarist Majesty."

Frederik IV smiles.

"Our *notarius publicus* is at your disposal during your stay in Copenhagen, dear brother. He will be your interpreter and show you around in our beautiful capitol."

"I am certain that Eerenbom will be of great use to me."

The tsar smiles. His eyes are searching and mocking. Æreboe lowers his eyes.

I look at the tsar and decide once again that he's an inoffensive man. His round head is good-natured, his enormous hands restless. The brown skin of his forearms is covered with cuts and scratches, as if he has been in a fight. And he probably has.

The king turns to his guest.

"By the way, are you content with the living quarters that we have found for you, dear brother?"

"Not in the least."

The king's smile vanishes.

"The rooms are too big and too bright. Since I haven't come to Denmark to dance, I have no wish to live in a ballroom."

"We will have our men find you another place at once."

The king snaps his fingers. A footman steps forward.

"Bring Callenberg, our Lord Steward."

The footman bows and leaves the room like a well-dressed bird of prey.

The tsar looks at me again. Once more it occurs to me how strange the Muscovites are. All of them, except for the tsar, are well-dressed, but the clothing looks wrong on them—as if they had been forced into the attire. Their manners are rough. They cough and spit on the expensive carpets. Many of them fart without inhibition and without apology—something that is seldom encountered among the fine folk in Denmark.

"The reason that we have granted Sørine an audience is that we wish to give you a modest gift, dear brother…" The king looks at the tsar. "A gift for your collection."

Frederik places his hand on my shoulder.

"We wish to give you Sørine Bentsdatter, the most splendid dwarf in the Kingdom of Denmark and Norway."

I stare at His Majesty in astonishment.

"We are certain that it will give you pleasure. Aside from the talents that it displayed at the banquet table, we understand that it can sing and perform. Isn't that right?"

The king casts an inquisitive glance at Æreboe, who hastens to nod. The tsar regards me with sudden coolness. Then he bows.

"I accept your gift."

I start to object. "But your Royal Majesty—"

Rasmus Æreboe stops me with a sharp look. The king turns his attention back to the map. The audience is over. I cast another glance at Æreboe, but he now evades my eyes. A chamberlain is ready to escort us out of the room, but as we turn to leave I hear the tsar's voice say, "Let the dwarf stay!"

I turn around.

Peter adds, "With your permission, that is, my dear brother."

The king nods graciously. Æreboe continues toward the door. I remain standing in the middle of the room, not knowing what I'm supposed to do. I'm sweating heavily, wishing I were back home in my cellar.

"May I ask you, dear brother, how many dwarves you have in your kingdom?" says the tsar.

The king gives his guest a look of surprise. "We ... have no idea."

"In my country," says the tsar, "we often succumb to the most peculiar sentimentality. That's why we treat our dwarves as if they were human beings. We dress them in colorful garb; we arrange lavish feasts at which they are allowed to participate. We frequently even allow them to live in elegant homes built in the European manner. And when they are ready, we allow them to breed with other dwarves so that we'll have an even larger crop."

The color leaves my cheeks.

"Many of these dwarves are hideous. But the more hideous the better. The good Lord has created us all, and a dwarf puts a person in marvelous spirits with regard to his own figure and appearance. I want you to know that your dwarf will be appreciated in my realm."

The tsar turns to me with a smile. "What is your name, my dear?"

"Sørine, Your Grace."

"Sørine? No one will be able to pronounce such a name. You shall be called Surinka."

The tsar studies me. Again I have the feeling that he is peering into every nook and cranny—and even deeper.

"Your voice isn't shrill like the voices of other dwarves. Why is that?"

"Because I'm not like other dwarves, Your Grace."

The tsar gives me a cold look and turns back to the map. A moment later I am escorted out, and as I walk along the winding corridor, I feel a longing for my cellar on Vintapperstræde. I miss my larder and my chest containing the henbane and the soothing mustard plasters. I miss the rats and the Scoundrel. I miss everything.

11.

I MURDERED TERJE.

The Scoundrel could have recovered from his illness, but I decided that he should die. I don't know why. Maybe I was tired of being a victim. Maybe I had a desire to feel guilty.

Death is irrevocable; that's why it's so beautiful. Death is the thin frost on the beech trees on Sunday morning. Death is the metallic sound of the church bells above a green lake in the forest. We love death because it promises us so much after we have received so little.

The Scoundrel still appears to me in the night.

Not every night, but often. He likes to comment on what is happening. At the moment he's gleeful about my fate. He thinks it's priceless that I have been given to the tsar as a present. He says that I will find Russia abominable—a country that is much more terrible than Denmark, even more terrible than Hell itself. The Scoundrel claims that I'll be there for ten years, that he can see my whole life from the place where he now finds himself. He says that my life is spread before him, written in a rough hand, not fine calligraphy.

For a few brief moments I miss him.

We used to walk around at the harbor, laughing at all the folly in the world, at the newly minted nobles with their yolk-

colored silk stockings, at the gypsy women begging from morning to night. It was a life filled with satire. No one was spared;
everyone was scorned and denigrated. We hated both the rich
and the poor. We saw no reason not to, since they all hated *us*:
the executioner's assistant and the dwarf, the craziest pair in the
king's city. But gradually I grew weary of my life. I grew weary
of the eternal taunts and of the smell of blood enveloping Terje.
The blood of the executed seeped into his skin; it sat in the
corners of his mouth, under his fingernails, even in his navel.
Maybe that was why I murdered Terje. Because I couldn't stand
it any longer. Because deep down inside I am evil.

The first time I fornicated with the Scoundrel, he told me
something strange. He said, "You have saucy little feet."

That was the only kind thing he ever said to me in six years.
You have saucy little feet! Since then I can't remember him ever
praising or appreciating me. I was merely a sewer into which he
could empty his seed.

Yet the victim can still miss the executioner.

But the roles are often reversed in life.

That may be the only form of justice that exists—the fact
that we take turns playing the victim. The fact that evil is not
permanent. It comes and goes like the tide.

12.

I'VE BEEN LIFTED UP FROM MY STOOL AND SET ON TOP
of the table. My small legs dangle helplessly, my hands are
pressed flat on the oak surface, and I'm trying to understand the
man in front of me. His name is Vasily Dolgoruky. He is the tsar's
envoy at the court of Frederik IV, and he is inordinately drunk.

"Danish is a homespun language not suited to silken
tongues!"

Dolgoruky looks at me through glazed eyes. He has poured
more vodka into my goblet. I consider declining, but I've
learned that it's futile when in the company of Muscovites.

"Whereas Russian..." Dolgoruky smiles blissfully, "is like

a plaintive breeze... a poem that rolls around in the mouth like the most delicious Rhine wine."

The Russian envoy is a man with red eyes and a malicious mouth. He has long since cast off his Western wig, and his voice has grown hoarser as the evening has progressed.

"Russian sounds like a beautiful language," I say diplomatically.

I have been given lodgings at Merchant Edinger's house along with Peter's envoys, but I haven't seen the tsar since coming here. It's rumored that he is not pleased with the king. The Danish troops are not ready to occupy Scania. And the summer is on the wane. It's now or never, if the Swedish king is to be defeated.

At that moment Dolgoruky stands up. He stares straight ahead. He reaches out for his goblet.

"We must drink a toast to the tsar!"

"But with your permission, we have already—"

The envoy grabs hold of me and lifts me up in front of his face. It's clear that he thinks he can frighten me, but I've seen uglier faces than his.

Dolgoruky puts me back down on the table. I land on my tailbone and feel an urge to scream. The liquor numbs me nearly as much as Dolgoruky's breath.

I catch sight of another Russian lying under the tile-topped table. His white singlet is hanging out of his trousers, one arm is hugging a crumpled sofa cushion. The knowledge that I'm not the first to fall gives me renewed strength.

"*Prost!*"

We drink from the Bohemian goblets. I have a hard time swallowing the vodka. It gets stuck in my throat and comes up again. I notice that I can no longer feel my knees.

I set down the goblet with a grimace. If I'm to follow the rules of etiquette, then it's my turn to propose a toast to His Majesty Frederik IV, but I just can't do it. I look down at Dolgoruky's leather boots, pondering what's in store for me, and when I might see the tsar. Will he take me to Russia and give me away, handing me over to someone else at random?

At that moment Æreboe comes staggering toward us. His chin is glistening with vodka, and his wig is askew on his head. He seems extremely drunk; his eyes are vacant and veiled. Today the *notarius* has come here to negotiate with Vasily Dolgoruky. I have no idea how the negotiations have gone. I know only that the Russians have been complaining about one thing after another: about the fact that they are called Muscovites, even though the tsar's court is in Petersburg; about the fact that the delegation receives only eight jugs of liquor a day, when it has a need for fourteen; and most importantly, about the fact that the tsar's one hundred titles were not declaimed at the official banquet at the castle. Instead they were abbreviated to forty-two. The Muscovites are suffering from a perpetual need to complain.

Dolgoruky looks at Æreboe, his eyes swimming.

"Have you got yourself anything to drink, Eerenbom?"

Æreboe nods and sits down. His lips are cracked. I've never seen him look so wretched. If I had any maternal feelings in my body, I would have tried to comfort him.

"I'm about to drink your dwarf under the table, Eerenbom."

"Is that so?"

"I am not impressed by its capacity. The Russian dwarves are much hardier than the Danish."

Æreboe stares at the envoy, then at me, as if he doesn't understand what we're talking about.

"A toast to your king," says Dolgoruky.

"We've already toasted Frederik IV eleven times tonight!"

Dolgoruky laughs boisterously. "That's eleven times too few!"

"With all respect, Your Grace, things are done differently in the Kingdom of Denmark and Norway…"

"The Kingdom of Denmark and Norway!" Dolgoruky

squints his eyes. "Who cares about the Kingdom of Denmark and Norway? You Danes are so arrogant that it turns my stomach! The only thing you think about is getting Scania back. Negotiating with you is like negotiating with mules."

I glance at Rasmus Æreboe and scuttle away.

"...Prussia and Saxony-Poland are proper allies. The tsar has respect for them. It's even possible to respect the Swedes, because at least they can fight, but the Kingdom of Denmark and Norway..." Dolgoruky leers. "The tsar has *no* faith in the Danish army. You lose every war you get into. When was the last time you won on the battlefield—the time of the Vikings?"

Æreboe snarls something in Russian. Dolgoruky replies. For several minutes the discussion surges back and forth between the two men. I sit a short distance away and watch those hotheads; how they vie with each other, how they argue in a way that women would never argue. Why are men so proud? Is it something that's part of their cocks? Or has God merely blessed them with a smaller-sized brain?

"You should have seen His Majesty the Tsar when he read that book your kings hate. What's it called?"

Æreboe flinches. "I have no idea what you are referring to."

"*An Account of Denmark As It Was in the Year of Our Lord 1692*...a splendid piece of writing." Dolgoruky nods spitefully. "The tsar doesn't usually read books, but he found the German translation profusely entertaining."

Æreboe's cheeks grow hot. "With all due respect, Count Dolgoruky, I have no desire to listen to your foolishness. You know quite well that Molesworth's book is a scandalous text, insulting to Denmark and the Danish monarchy—"

"But Molesworth is *right!*" Dolgoruky laughs. "Copenhagen Castle is a rats' nest. Danish cheese is the lousiest in the world, but your mutton is even worse! There are epileptics on every street corner, your capital is a provincial backwater overflowing with shit, and your taxes are the highest in Europe."

"I'm warning you..."

"You have no proper artists, no proper artisans. You can't even produce any proper idiots! Everyone is equally mediocre in spirit. No one takes the initiative for anything. Is there anything at all that you Danes have mastered?"

Æreboe stands up, looking furious. His face has swollen, and he fumbles for his sword.

"You Danes simply have to learn that you're nothing but pimples on the face of Europe!"

The *notarius* is still trying to pull out his sword, but he's too sloshed to find it. I scuttle down to the floor. At that moment everything starts to move: the carved door frames and the painting of Cupid with the apple cheeks.

Rasmus Æreboe has finally gotten hold of his sword, but at the same instant Dolgoruky's head falls backwards. He dangles from his chair and then slides down to the floor, where he sprawls in an awkward position. A stream of vomit seeps out over his double chins, just like some sort of Italian fountain.

I look at Dolgoruky and Æreboe. Then I wipe the sweat from my brow.

It has been yet another interesting evening with the Muscovites.

13.

A DWARF HAS NO TOLERANCE FOR ALCOHOL. WE ARE more delicate, more sensitive, and we quickly become intoxicated. Our bodies wither from wine; we can't compete with a human being who wants to drink us under the table. Even holding onto the large goblets is an impossible task with our dwarf hands. But no one takes such things into consideration— because drunken dwarves are considered priceless. Dwarves that walk right into chairs are enchanting; dwarves that trip over thresholds are charming. We will always be a curiosity at the feasts of Bacchus, and many of us die from the drinking that takes place at court.

The history of our race is even more dismal.

As a child I heard about the dwarves in the mountains. According to old legends, the dwarves were created from maggots that lived in the remains of Ymer's body. Ymer was a primordial giant, and the dwarves were present at the creation of the world. Back then we lived in underground caves. We were experts at forging weapons, especially spears and chains. If the sun shone on us, we exploded into bits that turned to stone. It was also the dwarves who carried the heavenly vault on our shoulders. And we were known to be evil. As we still are today. Evil.

I have actually thought a great deal about evil; about what evil is and where it comes from. Is evil the desire to do harm, or is it merely emptiness? Is someone evil because he doesn't believe in Jesus? Or if he refuses to surrender to the outward piety that characterizes this country? Maybe goodness is a luxury reserved for the rich. Maybe leisure time is required in order to be good. Maybe goodness demands a full stomach. And time.

The one who has time is good.

ANOTHER DETAIL FROM our history: the ones called trolls are also dwarves. The same is true of black fairies, pixies, and gnomes, who hide outdoors in nature. We are all known to be evil. We have been labeled and condemned as creatures that can't stand the sun.

Deep down it makes no difference what they call us. Because we do exist, and that fact alone is bad enough.

RASMUS ÆREBOE CALLS for Dolgoruky's servant.

One of the Muscovites gets up from the floor and looks around in alarm. Then he catches sight of the dead-drunk envoy and carefully gathers him up. The heels of Dolgoruky's boots scrape along the terracotta floor, and I glimpse a pile of sable furs in the corner.

The grandfather clock strikes without mercy. It's almost dawn, and I try to focus on what's in the room all around me. As usual, it has been turned upside down. Several of the beautifully carved door frames have been torn off and used for firewood. Two elegant chairs with broken backs have been tossed into a corner. The whole place reeks of malt and vomit.

A servant helps Æreboe on with his coat. He nearly loses his balance but manages to stay on his feet. Then he fixes his blue eyes on me.

"Come with me!"

The *notarius* stretches out his hand.

"Come where?"

"You're going home with me so you can sleep in civilized surroundings."

I ignore his outstretched hand but waddle after him, moving slowly. We step outside the house and find ourselves in the chill of a summer night. A couple of roosters are crowing somewhere nearby.

Æreboe's coach appears, and the *notarius* tosses me onto the seat inside. There is something savage about him that I haven't noticed before. The coach starts up with a lurch. I study Æreboe—those gentle features and the prudish mouth that looks more sneering the drunker he gets. It's impossible to tell what goes on inside of a human being.

I lean back and let the swaying of the coach rock me to sleep. I feel dizzy and confused. The world is made of splintered glass.

IT'S DANGEROUS TO drive through Copenhagen before dawn. The city's gates are closed; the goodfolk are sleeping the slumber of the righteous. Only churls are awake, and the sound of a coach makes the assailants sharpen their knives. But maybe the *notarius* is blessed. Maybe God protects him against all dangers. Or maybe it's the Devil who looks after his own. Without interruption. Day and night.

Not long ago Æreboe entertained me by telling me about all the perils he has survived in his eventful life. He has compiled a list of the dangers, assigning each a number on his meticulous list. A list that starts off with a drowning accident when he was just a little tyke; then a fall through the ice outside Svendborg when he was a youth; and a bloody battle in Novgorod, when he was confronted by twenty Russians but fought his way free with his hunting knife. It was one miracle after another. Twenty-three times when Rasmus Æreboe should have been dead, if it hadn't been for a merciful God up above.

But is God merciful?

I find Him utterly cold-blooded, a humorless lord who punishes His children, as if He were the most specious of castigators. The longer I live, the harder it is for me to see the difference between the Lord and the Devil. They use the same means; they fight for the same souls. They're both little more than peddlers of fancy goods, making overblown promises of sex or salvation. Which would it be better to cling to? And does it really make any difference? God and the Devil are cut from the same cloth, twins who have been joined at the hip. That's why I have a hard time with all these lunatic prayers of thanksgiving.

But Æreboe loves them. Every day he thanks the Trinity for the mercy he so little deserves. He even gives thanks for an accident he has suffered—for every stillborn child that his wife "blesses" him with. How can anyone be so eternally empty-headed? It's one thing to be grateful for the good things. But is it also necessary to be grateful for the bad?

I wish that I had such faith. Gratitude is a wondrous gift— at least for a simpleton.

"A dreadful book, Sørine. Utterly dreadful."

I glance up.

Rasmus Æreboe is talking to me, but his words don't reach me. I have no wish to listen. I want only to sleep.

"...there's no doubt that Robert Molesworth's book has damaged Denmark's prestige in the most appalling manner."

I nod.

"Have you heard of the book?"

I shake my head.

"All of Europe has heard of it. In the German district of Moscow, all the foreigners have read that loathsome text."

Æreboe suddenly begins to hiccup.

"But you'll hear all about it when you get there."

I nod despondently. The coach shudders and then slows down. I look out and discover that a cow is blocking the way. Several of the street's copper lamps have gone out, but the silhouettes of teeming rats are clearly visible.

Æreboe's servant jumps out to chase away the cow, but it doesn't want to cooperate. At that moment the stink of rotting kale fills my nostrils. The smell makes my stomach turn over.

Light is starting to appear on the horizon. A narrow fissure is pushing back the night. The first stars are fading in the pale sky.

The coach turns down Størstræde, heading for Holmen's Canal. Under the arch of the High Bridge the outline of a barge can be seen. Soon the farmers from the island of Amager will stream into the city with grains and peas.

We stop in front of a house facing the canal. There is a sense of peace over the area; only the barking of a dog breaks the silence. Æreboe's servant holds open the coach door, and the *notarius* attempts to lift me out. I lash out at him and end up landing in some horse droppings. The *notarius* laughs loudly at my stubbornness.

By the time we finally go inside, little streaks of dawn have cast an amber glow over the canal, Størstræde, and the city.

14.

THE *NOTARIUS* HAS HIS OWN STEWARD—AN OLDER MAN, bleary with sleep who comes to greet us holding a lamp. Æreboe tears off his wig and goes into his office. Delicate light seeps in through the small windows, and the steward lights the lamps in the wall brackets. He looks half-asleep in his nightshirt, but he is wise enough not to laugh at my size.

"Does my lord wish for a serving of soup?"

"No, nothing. We just want to...sit."

The steward nods and slips out of the office like a shadow. Æreboe throws himself into a chair, and for a moment it seems as if he has fallen asleep. Then he stares down at the leather pad covering his desk and turns to give me a hazy look.

"The Russians aren't so bad," he says.

"No."

"And remember that they're called Russians, not Muscovites. Russians are very proud and take offense easily."

I nod.

Æreboe smiles. "You'll do just fine over there."

"What do you think will happen to me?"

"You'll be very popular, there's no doubt about that."

"At the tsar's palace?"

"At the tsar's palace or living with one of his ministers. You'll have a good time with your fellow little people."

"What fellow little people?"

"The other dwarves."

"I can't stand dwarves."

Æreboe looks at me in astonishment. "Why not?"

"I can't stand anyone."

Æreboe collapses into convulsive laughter.

"You're priceless, Sørine. I wish you could stay here with me."

"I'll tell you one thing: I refuse to share a roof with a bunch of slobbering dwarves with hunchbacks and pitiful castrato voices."

"You must take things as they come. And you must for all the world do as the tsar commands. Watch out for Peter Alexeyevich. He is a powerful prince with a genius for many things, but the tsar is not like our beloved Frederik. He is brutal and merciless—and nothing, absolutely nothing escapes his notice."

I nod again and study the *notarius* in the flickering light from the lamps in the wall brackets.

"Even when the tsar is drunk, it's as if there is another tsar sitting behind him—a tsar who watches everyone around him and takes note of who can be used and who cannot be used. The tsar is a skilled craftsman, and everyone is a tool in his toolbox."

Æreboe almost tips over the desk as he stands up.

"If you're interested, I can lend you my diaries from my years over there. They will give you an idea of what to expect. Russia is a marvelous kingdom, filled with beauty and melancholy... but it's also a land of unrivaled cruelty. I can't explain it any better than that, but you'll understand once you're there."

I fix my eyes on Rasmus Æreboe as he goes over to the cabinet. He fumbles with a key, opens the door, and then places several books in front of me.

A moment later he staggers out. I'm alone in the office with the scissors chairs, the writing desk, and the exquisite copper engravings.

IN FRONT OF me are five brown leather volumes embellished with gilt.

These are the *notarius*'s diaries: *The Russian Years, 1709 to 1714*. Next to them is a cardboard folder tied with black ribbons. I don't know where to start, so I decide to read them from the beginning, which is October 1709.

To my surprise there is nothing frail about Æreboe's handwriting. It's bold and angular. The letters press up against each other, breaking away and then sticking together like hard candy.

I start reading about Rasmus Æreboe's first journey to Russia.

The *notarius* arrived in Moscow at the end of 1709 as private secretary to Just Juel, the *envoyé extraordinaire*. He had been hired because of his knowledge of Latin. The journey over had been awful, first by ship to Danzig, then along the coast to Königsberg, east to Novgorod, and by sleigh to Moscow. They stayed along the way at the tsar's mail-coach inns. They heard wolves howling in the distance and saw a populace so impoverished that it defied all description.

I keep reading. Outside Copenhagen is awaking. The

sounds stream in from the fish markets, but I'm no longer in this city. I'm traveling with Rasmus Æreboe to Moscow—a city so filled with highwaymen that every morning citizens are found dead in the snowdrifts. I'm in Petersburg, which is one huge construction site, rampant with epidemics and a cold that seeps into your bones. The *notarius* describes the beautiful churches with their gleaming gold icons. He is disgusted by the spiced head cheese and the chicken stomachs stuffed with ginger. He isn't used to being in the company of people of high rank, and he's indignant at the immorality surrounding the tsar, at the lack of respect for life in the mighty realm.

I grow more and more uneasy as I read.

That's when I catch sight of the picture.

It's in the third volume of the diaries: a copperplate engraving showing a number of people wearing peculiar attire. At first I think the picture seems straightforward enough, but when I study it more closely, I see that it shows two dancing dwarves. They're both dressed in elaborate garb, surrounded by people wearing powdered wigs. But something is wrong, terribly wrong.

I look closer, studying the faces of the two dwarves. They seem to be laughing. They're swinging around to the music. Their bodies are relaxed, but their eyes are vacant and empty.

I turn the page in the diary. The next pages are stuck together. Carefully I pull them apart. Another copperplate engraving is inside the book. It's much bigger, but done on thinner parchment. It has been folded scrupulously in half, and I open it with trembling hands.

The copperplate engraving shows a room adorned with tapestries and high windows. A number of fine gentlemen are eating as they sit with their backs to the wall. In the middle of the room are eight tables where a large number of dwarves are seated. I try to count them. There are at least fifty. All of them are eating from little plates, using little knives and forks. Their chairs are dwarf height, their goblets tiny. I have the impression that the dwarves are part of a performance, and that the fine gentlemen are their audience.

My eye is caught by a detail on the left side of the copper-plate engraving. Two chamberlains are bending over a female dwarf. At first I can't tell what they're doing, but then I discover that one of them is holding a hunting knife, the other a bludgeon.

I reach for Æreboe's spectacles on the table. Then I study the details. One of the chamberlains is laughing; the other is gawking. But there is absolutely no doubt: they are beating the woman. Below the picture it reads "Dwarf Wedding." And underneath that: "In the Year of Our Lord 1710."

I slam the book shut and stand up. The floor is alive, the furniture as big as altars. I close my eyes. I have never felt such a rush of fury before.

At that moment the door opens, and the *notarius*'s steward is staring at me without blinking. I walk past him over to the front door and try to reach the handle.

The steward looks at me.

Then he laughs.

15.

THE SCOUNDREL IS RESTING AMONG THE STARS. HE IS not in Paradise or in Hell. Sometimes he's in the sunset; other times he's a blackbird. But there is nothing frightening about him. Terje wants only the best for me. Terje has decided that now that he's dead, he's going to live.

Every time I close my eyes, he's standing right in front of me. There is something officious about him. The blood has left his face, and he is utterly sober. Terje says that he's not my guardian spirit. He hasn't been given any assignment. He's merely a nomad in the starry skies, a phantom passing through. If I wish, I can talk to him. Terje is with me, and he says that he wants to make everything good again. He regrets the boozing and his lack of interest in my life. Terje in his heaven wants to be forgiven, but I'm in no mood to forgive. Forgiveness requires an obtuse temperament; I'm not sufficiently obtuse.

I write every day, sitting at my dwarf desk.

It was specially made for me, and I have an excellent view of the street. At that desk I am ridding myself of my old life and making preparations for the new. But even in the words the Scoundrel tries to reach me. He's in every letter that I shape, every word that I write. He pushes ideas through the ink, he forces his way into my thoughts, telling me what I should write. Sometimes the pen moves all on its own, as if a demonic power were at work between my fingers.

I've told the Scoundrel that I don't want anything to do with the dead. Nothing will be allowed to live inside of me without my permission. I am not a mail-coach inn where he can deliver his letters. All thoughts must come from myself, otherwise they're of no interest to me.

Yet there are times when I grow curious to hear about the Creation, when I hope that the Scoundrel may have answers to life's big questions, when I have an urge to question him about the fifth commandment, which pleases me less than the others. There is so much that I would like to know about life on the other side. But the Scoundrel shakes his head and says that he knows nothing. No one has spoken to him, not even the Devil.

"What about Our Lord?" I ask. "Have you met your Creator?"

The Scoundrel looks at me, as if he doesn't understand the question. The Creator is not a term that is used in Heaven. The Creator is Heaven! The Creator is the light that burns in our bodies. The Devil is the wind that blows.

But what is it that the Scoundrel wants to make good again? And why even try? My life with him is past. We were drawn to each other for lack of anyone better. I thought I could rely on a man, but it can't be done. I was stupid and simple-minded. I'm wiser now.

16.

I HAVEN'T SEEN THE TSAR SINCE I WAS GIVEN TO HIM by the king.

Peter Alexeyevich is restlessness personified. When the negotiations lost steam, he set off on an expedition to find some Swedes. He headed out on a frigate with a handful of men, as if he were an impetuous youth. But the Swedes didn't take the bait; their ships stayed anchored in the harbor. And now the tsar is back. Angry, restless, and irritable. Annoyed at the slow progress dogging the negotiations between the allies.

The fine rogues can't agree who should command the navy. Frederik wants Gyldenløve, the English insist on Admiral Norris, and the tsar wants only the tsar. They fight like street urchins, interrupted only by equestrian displays and swan hunts in the king's gondolas. That's what I heard from a man named Ismailov.

Ismailov's father used to be an envoy in Copenhagen. Now he works under Vasily Dolgoruky, the unpleasant Russian who insulted the *notarius* on that drunken evening at Edinger's house. Ismailov is a tall, lanky man with morose eyes and eyebrows that meet in the middle. He has an oval face the shape of an egg. His hair is sparse. A big abscess protrudes from his right cheek. He's not what might be called a handsome man.

"The tsar often takes dwarves to his meetings," Ismailov tells me. "Maybe you'll be brought along to the political negotiations."

"In what capacity?"

"As an advisor on Danish affairs."

"I don't know a thing about Danish affairs."

"Maybe not, but it's important that you find a role for yourself so that the tsar feels he can make use of you."

I give my new friend a weary look.

"All right then. Tell me more about the war."

Ismailov lowers his voice and moves closer.

"The latest rumors say that His Majesty the Tsar is considering entering into a alliance with Sweden."

"But I thought that Sweden was our mutual enemy."

"It is today, but maybe not tomorrow."

"And what does Frederik say to that?"

"Your king is afraid that Russia will become the new great power in the North. But as Dolgoruky says, 'That's what we Russians are already. You Danes just haven't discovered it yet.'"

I nod and think over the situation.

"Do you think the king will get Scania back?"

"If that's what he desires."

"Why wouldn't he desire it?"

"It's what he says he wants, but maybe he's afraid that it will present too many problems in the long run."

"With whom?"

"With us Russians. With the other great powers."

"But you're all allies. You're the ones who are helping us to get Scania back."

"We're helping you only so that we can crush Sweden."

I look at Ismailov in despair.

"I don't understand a word of this."

"It's a game. It's always a game."

"And you find it amusing?"

"That's my job."

Ismailov pours himself a dram. I look at him with annoyance. In a moment I go back to reading the Russian grammar that Æreboe has loaned me. I want to learn the language. Only in that way can I prepare myself for my future in Russia. Maybe as the court jester, as an advisor, or maybe as something else.

OVER THE NEXT few days Ismailov explains the Russian situation to me: how the tsar has undermined the rule of the clergy, how he has taken away the power of the former elite. But also how much opposition there is to his reforms and his countless trips to the ungodly West.

We talk again about the war. I give Ismailov a nervous look.

"Do you think I'll be taken along to the front?"

Ismailov shakes his head. "We're most likely going to Holland when the war is over, but the tsar changes plans all the time, and it's wise not to ask him about things."

"Why does the tsar want to go to Holland?"

"To make purchases."

"What does he want to purchase?"

"No one knows."

I put my grammar book away.

I'm looking forward to seeing Peter Alexeyevich again. The tsar builds ships with his own hands, he drinks the Russian soldiers under the table, downing anise-flavored vodka. He's a man you can talk to. He's not snobbish like King Frederik, who flounces around in his silk robes. Yet I love Frederik all the same. Everyone in Denmark loves the angelic-minded sovereign.

On the other hand, no one loves Frederik's mistress.

No. No one loves Anna Sophie Reventlow, who is young, enchanting, and impossibly obtuse.

17.

SEVERAL MONTHS AGO I WAS SENT ON LOAN TO FREDerik's "queen of the left hand"—as the king calls her. Anna Sophie lives in Storm Manor next to the castle, where she spends her days and nights in constant boredom. I was driven over there in a magnificent coach. They set me on top of some silk cushions and put a bow around my neck. When Anna Sophie saw me, she gave a loud shriek. She picked me up and kissed me on the forehead with fierce little smacks.

"The two of us are going to be the best of friends," she said, carrying me into the parlor, past Chinese vases, polished bureaus, and gilded console tables. Everything in her mansion was extraordinarily hideous. Everything was green, and the pictures on the walls were mawkish. On the sofas sat three ladies-in-waiting drinking tea from the East Indies.

"What's your name, poppet?"

"Sørine Bentsdatter, my lady."

"You may call me Anna Sophie."

The king's mistress was around twenty. She was tall and stately, with lovely fair hair that had been bleached according to the latest fashion. Her eyes were dark and gave the impression that she was in an eternal state of infatuation. Her neck was long, her lips red and shapely. Anna Sophie was perfect, as long as she didn't open her mouth—she had abominable teeth. Why the king didn't demand that they all be removed, I have no idea. The royal barber could have done it in no time.

After that I was required to visit the mistress every day. I was introduced to Anna Sophie's empty world. I was placed under the wine-red canopy of her bed, and she lay next to me, telling me about all the sorrows of her heart.

Anna Sophie was wild about her king. But she was also wild about a corporal from the Guards. She was oh so *delighted*, as she told me in Swedish, by a Swedish envoy who visited her on Tuesdays. She was fascinated by a Frisian duke who visited her on Wednesdays. But, most important of all, she was unhappy that Frederik visited the queen's ladies-in-waiting.

"I'm afraid he's growing tired of me," she wept, showing me a clumsy letter written by the king. I read it with fascination. Frederik called her Angel Heart. He alternated between bad German and bad Danish. The king held absolute power, but he had no future as a poet.

"Do you think he'll leave me?" asked Anna Sophie, looking at me with her big eyes.

"I have no idea, my lady."

"But I thought that you dwarves had special powers."

"For what?"

"To see into the future."

"As you wish, my lady."

"So do you think that Frederik will leave me?"

"There's no doubt about it," I said.

After that she collapsed onto her silken sheets. Where else would she collapse?

IT WASN'T VERY kind of me to be so truthful, but that's an ancient prerogative belonging to us dwarves. People expect a certain malice from us, and I'm proud to have saved up a bucketful. It's said that the malice resides in the dwarves' hunchbacks. But since I don't have one, my malice is distributed through my whole body. It works its way up from my intestines, into my throat, onto my tongue, and then strikes whoever deserves the poison.

Anna Sophie Reventlow deserved it because she was so lovely. She deserved it because her body was so shapely. She deserved it first and foremost because I've been enlisted as a confidante to the amoral ways of her life. A dwarf is not a wall against which the fine folk can toss a ball. Why should I listen to tales about love in the boudoir? Why should I be forced to read sonnets from Swedish envoys? Love is a luxury for the fine folk. They have time for sorrows of the heart. They can lie around wallowing in deep-felt emotions while the rest of us bury our children in the cemetery for victims of the plague.

"…and now Frederik thinks only of war and those stupid territories in Scania. He used to visit me every evening. Now he visits me only a couple of times a week…"

I yawned but tried to show an interest in all her banalities. It was difficult to hate Anna Sophie, but I gave it my best effort.

IT WAS A summer day in September when I visited the king's mistress for the last time. She was wearing a rose-colored embroidered gown. Her hair was pinned up, and she was utterly enchanting as long as she didn't show her teeth.

We went for a walk in her magnificent garden with the box-wood hedges, the pavilions, and an exquisite orangerie. The sunlight was mild and gentle. For once Anna Sophie wasn't boring me. She was telling me about my new lord, the tsar.

"I haven't promised to meet His Majesty the Tsar this time. But I met Peter in Slesvig after I was married to Frederik... 'to his left hand,' as the court calls it."

She went on, "We dined in Husum in the light of two thousand burning torches, and both the tsar and Frederik were in a splendid mood. I was seated next to Peter Alexeyevich, and I found him amusing and charming. In a strange way I felt at home in his company—maybe because he has no use for formalities. I'm not very familiar with the customs at court... I don't always know what one should or shouldn't do. So it felt almost as if there were some sort of understanding between us—an understanding that made Frederik a bit jealous."

Anna Sophie giggled.

"I was the first to dance with the tsar, and it was a festive experience. The tsar held me so tight that it gave me bruises. I think he was afraid I might slip out of his hands. But he was jovial, sweet... eccentric. The tsar whirled me around with no regard for anyone else, and he growled to himself when he couldn't remember the steps."

The king's mistress smiled at her memories.

"It would be wrong to say he was a cavalier. I don't think the Muscovites use perfume... if you know what I mean. They're always quite direct in their behavior... like bears. At one point the tsar showed me his blisters. He had a couple of them on his hands, and when I didn't know what to say, he asked me to touch them. At first I refused, but I found him irresistible, and so I touched his blisters. 'I got them from crafting a gift for your king,' he told me. I caressed the yellow surfaces, hoping that Frederik would see me. The tsar looked at me intently, but to my disappointment there was no passion in his eyes. He didn't want me. 'I love your king,' he said. 'I love King Frederik because he can be trusted; because with him I know that a word is a word, and that is seldom the case among princes.' I nodded and saw that the tsar meant what he had said. He had tears in his eyes but did not seem intoxicated. The other Muscovites were drunk, but not Peter."

Anna Sophie straightened her dress.

"I must admit two things: the more I danced with the tsar, the more enchanted I became. His mood changed frequently. One moment he could be charming, the next he was vulgar and boorish. At one point the musicians played a piece that the tsar didn't like, and he rushed over to the fiddle players and threatened them with a beating unless they obeyed his commands."

She laughed.

"We ended up dancing together for most of the evening. If it had been up to His Majesty the Tsar, we would have continued until the early hours of dawn. That was how much energy he had. Afterwards, when I lay in bed next to Frederik, I could tell that the king was pleased with how the evening had gone. But he was also a little bit jealous. That made me happy. I like it when men get angry... in bed, that is."

Anna Sophie blushed. For a brief moment she stopped to look at her geraniums. Then she changed the subject.

"So now you're going over to great Russia to live. You're a lucky poppet, Sørine."

I gave the mistress a look of annoyance.

"I'm not so sure about that."

"The tsar is an exciting man, and you will undoubtedly be called upon to serve him in all manner of ways."

"That's exactly what I'm afraid of," I replied tersely.

"I think it must be exciting to be a dwarf. To see everything from below. To be like a child again."

I looked up at the king's mistress with all the contempt I could muster.

"I mean it, Sørine. Everyone is always so happy when they see you. You make people laugh and smile just by coming into a room. How lovely that is. And you've studied the great arts and the great sciences. I think you're an exciting poppet. I'd love to snatch you away from the tsar, if I could."

I looked away.

"I hope I haven't offended you." Anna Sophie gave me a solemn look. "I just don't know what I'm supposed to call a creature like you: dwarf, poppet, midget. I don't think gnome sounds very nice. No, I don't!"

She sat down on a stone bench. I didn't move from where I was standing, looking out across the garden. Off in the distance stood two of Anna Sophie's ladies-in-waiting. They reminded me of cats: cuddly one moment, malicious the next.

"They all say the same thing; they say that I'm stupid…" The eyes of the king's mistress flashed. "That's what all the men surrounding the king have decided, but it's not true. If I were truly stupid, they wouldn't need to be afraid of me… now would they?"

She gave me an enchanting smile. I looked at the geraniums and the prying ladies-in-waiting. The next instant she began to cry—at first gently, then so hard that it was heart-breaking. I tore myself away from my own thoughts and looked up. Anna Sophie's face was dissolved in tears. She did everything she could to evade my eyes.

Off in the distance the sun slipped behind the clouds. The light was a pastel blue. Two magpies were pecking at an apple. I climbed up onto the stone bench and put my arm around Anna Sophie. She took my hand and pressed it against her cheek.

We sat like that for a long time.

Much too long.

18.

THE TSAR WAS GROWING MORE AND MORE ANGRY WITH his allies.

There's too much bickering and mistrust—that's what Ismailov explains to me one evening at Merchant Edinger's house. That's where the tsar stays, if he stays anywhere at all. But I see only his shadow. The tsar has no use for a dwarf, or at least not yet.

One day something is up. Peter Alexeyevich goes down to

the harbor to meet his tsarina. Her name is Catherine, and she has arrived onboard a frigate. I'm eager to meet her. I'm not sure why.

Ismailov comes up to my room with a new child's dress that he wants me to try on. I obey at once. He looks away as I crawl into it. That's not what men usually do. And I'm disappointed.

After that we sit down to wait for the tsar. We wait for a long time. It's possible to spend an entire lifetime waiting for Peter Alexeyevich.

Ismailov continues to inform me about matters of state. We've become friends—as good friends as a dwarf can be with a human being. I've been given language lessons, and I've learned about the position of the church and about Russian history. I've heard about the boyars, who are a type of nobleman, and about the *streltsy*, who rebelled against Peter and were strung up on every street corner. The history of Russia is bloody, but also impressive in its cruelty.

Ismailov is a serious man, especially when he talks of his native land.

"The problem, Surinka, is that everyone underestimates us Russians."

I nod.

"The worst sort of things are laid at our doorstep. We're told that we are poorly educated, that we're lazy and ill-mannered. His Majesty the tsar does all that he can to educate ordinary Russians. Our nation is just as modern as yours. There is no cause for you to feel superior."

Ismailov regards me with his melancholy eyes. He lived in Copenhagen until he was eighteen. His father was frequently invited to Copenhagen Castle. But even in childhood Ismailov felt the coldness of the Danes toward foreigners. That's why he gets annoyed whenever he hears that the Russians have arrived from the steppes.

"Is there no one who speaks German in Russia?" I ask.

"Only the diplomats and the richest of the merchants."

"Are there many foreigners living there?"

"Only in Petersburg."

"And what is the Russian attitude toward foreigners?"

"They are suspicious of them."

"That doesn't sound good."

"They are deeply suspicious."

Ismailov smiles, but there is no humor in it. At that moment we hear several coaches rumbling through the street. We run over to the little garret window that is covered with pigeon shit. Ismailov lifts me up. We hear commands shouted in the courtyard below, followed by the enormous thunder of cannons.

"Have you ever met the tsarina, Ismailov?"

He nods.

"What do you think of her?"

Down in the courtyard three coaches have arrived along with a number of soldiers. Two horses rear up at all the clamor. The Danish soldiers salute.

"Catherine is quite ordinary," he says.

"Ordinary?"

"Yes, she comes from poor circumstances. Her family were apparently all peasants."

"How did she meet the tsar?"

"She was Menshekov's lover. And Menshekov was the tsar's best friend. At some point Peter took her over."

"Is she as stupid as snot?"

Ismailov shakes his head. "No, on the contrary."

"Tell me more."

"There's not much more to tell."

I try to catch the eye of the tsarina from the rooftop window, but I can see only several big banners. A company of soldiers salutes again. Thick smoke from the cannons fills the air and makes me cough.

The tsar and tsarina walk across the courtyard, followed by a number of Russians and Danes carrying swords and wearing hats with plumes. Their faces are rigid and watchful, as if they know that they're part of a dramatic performance in which they will soon be unmasked.

Something is wrong. Why do I sense that something is wrong?

DURING THE NEXT few days I keep hoping to run into Catherine, but I never see her. Neither the tsar or the tsarina has any use for a dwarf. At one point I'm chased up to my room by an angry Russian. He locks the door from the outside; I have no idea why.

There is thunder in the air.

Ismailov is gone. Everyone is gone.

I try to write in my diary, but put it aside because of the Scoundrel. Then I go back to reading my Russian grammar. I have nothing to occupy my time, but a dwarf is never lonely. I am second to none, so why should I be bored with my own company?

Down in the courtyard the Danish and Russian soldiers are squabbling. Everyone is bored with this idleness. Everyone wants the war to begin. If only the Swedes would come out of hiding.

ACCORDING TO RUMOR, Karl XII's men have begun setting fire to Scania.

They have no intention of fighting. They're going to flee north, burning everything along the way. The Russians and the Danes will pursue them until winter puts a halt to their advance. But when King Winter is at his height, the Swedes will strike. Then Karl XII will turn the weakened foe into kindling. That is his plan, and Peter Alexeyevich is the only one who sees through it.

In mid-September the tsar calls off the invasion. The allies should have attacked the Swedes in June or July. Now it's too late. The Battle of Scania is lost before it even began.

The tsar's decision hits the king like a bomb. Frederik IV summons the tsar to a meeting to argue his case. More than 50,000 soldiers are standing ready. The English, the Prussians, and the Dutch have all sent ships. The attack has been planned down to the last detail. But there is nothing to be done.

Three months of preparations have been wasted. The prospect of getting Scania back fades before his eyes.

That night Frederik IV weeps. I see him plod over to Storm Manor. His footsteps drag, his head is bowed. His Majesty has aged over the course of the summer. His complexion is gray, there are wrinkles around his eyes.

Now he goes to Anna Sophie to seek solace in her arms. A chamberlain assists him with his powdered wig. A footman removes his silk robe. Anna Sophie helps him get an erection.

The couple nurtures their love in the light from three hundred candles, but Frederik is in another world. His thoughts are on the lush provinces in Sweden, on the dreams of his ancestors about the lost land. And as he lies under the wine-red canopy of the bed, he has to listen to the reproaches of Christian V. He has to lend an ear to the laments of Frederik III. He has to quarrel with the worst rogue of them all: Christian IV, who lost half the kingdom. Oh yes, all the Danish kings are present above his bed. They hover like a cloud bank of impotence that should have been replaced with a triumphal procession through the Danish towns of Lund, Landskrona, and Helsingborg.

Oh yes, the slumber of Frederik IV is filled with torments— that's something that a dwarf can sense.

Maybe we notice it because we have better ears than human beings. We can hear the whispering of the gods, we can hear voices that rise up from the swamp: Scania will never be Danish. The Kingdom of Denmark and Norway will never be a force to reckon with in the North. We Danes are condemned to be a pillow on which the great powers can rest their heads.

19.

I RECEIVE WORD ON AN OCTOBER MORNING WITH PEARL-gray clouds. It would please the tsar to make use of his Danish dwarf. The Danish dwarf is to be brought to the foot of the Round

Tower, where Peter will have one last meeting with King Frederik before he leaves for the Continent.

I'm more excited than I want to admit.

For once I offer no resistance when they tidy me up. A female dresser delouses me, a lady's maid covers me in amber, and my graying hair is trimmed with the tsar's gold knife. This time I won't need to jump out of a cake.

My journey to the Round Tower is not nearly as memorable as the preparations. I'm placed on a flatbed wagon and driven to Købmagergade as if I were a sack of coal. Accompanied only by the stench of boar. And Ismailov. We get out at the entrance, and there we await the tsar. The place is swarming with people. Rumors of the arrival of the two sovereigns have spread through the city. Thirty soldiers are blocking the tower from the populace.

The king is impatient. He is sitting in his gold-encrusted portchaise, waiting for the tsar. The plan is for the two princes to be carried to the top of the tower, but Peter Alexeyevich has not yet appeared. The tsar is always late.

I hope that Catherine comes with him.

I hope that Catherine is fond of dwarves.

For some reason I sense that it's important for her to like me. I want to curry favor with this woman whom I've never met.

THERE IS ONE word that continues to fascinate me. It looks inconsequential on the parchment. It is easily swallowed. The word is "power." Where does power come from? Is it something that a human being is born with? Or is it a quality that develops as the person makes his way on this earth?

For some people, power is an integral part of their bodies. They don't need to flaunt it; they don't even need to raise their voice. They expect to be obeyed. Frederik IV is such a person.

The tsar is different. In a way he is more powerful than the king. The tsar empties every room of air. But he doesn't take his power for granted. When he gives commands, he doesn't necessarily expect them to be obeyed. Part of him is already preparing a punishment for the culprit if his commands are not carried out. The tsar is not merely tsar; he is also the mentor of his countrymen—and the instruction takes place with a cudgel. Frederik, on the other hand, is gentler; maybe because he was born without opposition. He is God's will dressed in a powdered wig and silk robes.

Ismailov lifts me up, and now I can see the tsar in the distance.

Peter Alexeyevich is approaching on foot, walking along Købmagergade. Only a single servant accompanies him. He sweeps through the crowds, shoving people aside, swatting at them with his hunting knife. The tsar has a peculiar gait. His long arms swing like pendulums. His legs stride across the cobblestones. He has on a black coat with threadbare hems. Under it he wears a simple linen tunic with white-thread buttons and embroidery the color of lead.

Ismailov lifts me up even higher. When the tsar sees me, he laughs his hearty laugh.

"You've grown taller since we last met, Surinka."

He snaps his fingers, and a servant appears with a horse. Ismailov lowers me down to the street; the world disappears among oiled boots and cow pies. The tsar grabs the reins and swings himself up onto the horse. To my surprise he enters the tower on horseback. Ismailov and I follow behind. The king is sitting in his elegant sedan chair. He looks annoyed but gives the tsar a polite nod.

The two monarchs exchange pleasantries in German.

For a moment there is silence. Then Peter Alexeyevich starts riding up the spiral ramp of the tower. The king follows in his stately *porte-chaise*. Then comes Vasily Dolgoruky and a procession of the fine folk and those in elaborate attire. Catherine is nowhere to be seen.

I'm forced to walk between Ismailov and the footmen. Even though the Russian carries me part of the way, it takes an eternity to reach the top. But everything takes an eternity in my world. The only difference is that today I'm not complaining. Today is a day for celebration.

FROM THE ROUND Tower you can see the Copenhagen of your dreams. You can see the lakes outside the city ramparts. You can catch a glimpse of the splendid gardens of Blågård where the nobles stroll with their lacquered walking sticks. You can stare out across the Øresund and catch a glimpse of Scania, the territory that has been lost. The tsar's troops are clearly visible outside of Nørreport and Østerport, near Svanemøllen, and west of the city. They're stationed in tents down by the swamp. The soldiers are marching like ants in the evergreen forests.

But we are the ones who live here.

The Danes say their prayers in this land. The Danes slave for the German-speaking squires and sell Valby chickens at the market for a pittance. That's how things are in Copenhagen, that's how things are in Denmark. My world goes no farther.

If the truth be told, I can't see anything at all.

Once again I'm standing between the legs of servants and footmen. My nose is at the same height as forty-one assholes. Smells that I would prefer to avoid find their way into my nostrils. But then I catch sight of the king's silk robes. I take pleasure in the spots of dirt on the tsar's linen trousers. I am bathing in the presence of power—the power that fascinates me because it's what I want for myself.

Frederik and Peter are conversing.

Rasmus Æreboe is standing at their side, should any language difficulties arise. He hasn't noticed me. No one has noticed me. And I wonder why I've been invited.

It's clear that the king and the tsar are at odds. It has been a summer marked by misfortune, distrust, and insults.

It all began with such promise when the tsar first arrived.

I wasn't present on that July day, but I can envision the whole scene: Peter's frigate rocking near Copenhagen Wharf.

The turquoise morning with the swallow-tailed flags snapping in the wind. The king standing in his Venetian gondola, which was adorned with tapestries and the colors of the house of Oldenburg. A livery-clad footman holding onto the king's hat so that it wouldn't end up in the waves. The seagulls hovering in the air like grayish-white shadows.

Frederik drew alongside the tsar's frigate. The rope ladder creaked under his high-heeled shoes; his silk wig tickled his cheek. As the king set foot on deck, a deafening cannonade resounded. The two sovereigns embraced. The cannonades continued to thunder, breaking windows in the homes of citizens and in all the brew-houses.

With my dwarf vision I followed the coach as it drove down Norgesgade, saw it rumbling over the newly-laid cobblestones, saw the monarchs seated side by side. From the ceiling hung their goldsmiths' work. Frederik's monogram adorned the windows; the gilded fringe of damask curtains gleamed like suns.

The tsar was too tall to sit erect. He had to hunch over as the coach continued through the festively decorated gates, past the newly-painted mansions, through the whole history of Denmark.

At the castle a sumptuous fireworks display was launched.

The pale summer sky was torn apart by rockets. The rain of fire exploded over the citizens and the canal's dilapidated boats. As the coach approached the High Bridge, it was surrounded by dancers. The women all wore the national costumes of Livonia, the Caucasus, and Little Russia. The tsar watched the dancers with tears in his eyes. He reached for the king's hand and clasped it in his own until the carriage entered the courtyard of the castle. "Dear brother, I have never experienced anything like this," he said. "Never."

That was how it was, on that July day.

And the day had ended as it should: with a lavish banquet with thirty-eight courses and a naked dwarf who popped out of a cake. That summer day had been filled with the sweetest promise, but Our Lord had other plans. Our Lord always has other plans. He is the One with the power.

FREDERIK AND PETER gaze out across the Øresund from their position atop the Round Tower.

The sun glides over the city, forming golden borders around the woods in Dyrehaven, covering the island of Hven with pale yellow stripes. Scania is still Swedish, but the tsar promises that the attack will take place the following spring. It's merely a question of a delay—a delay that will strengthen the unbreakable friendship between His Highborn Majesty Peter Alexeyevich and the absolute monarch of the Kingdom of Denmark and Norway.

I look at Frederik. The more he looks at Scania, the more the king wilts under his tunic.

"I promise you, on all that I hold sacred, that you will have your beloved land back." The tsar places his hand on the king's shoulder.

Frederik looks out over the rope works, across New Copenhagen and the grayish ramparts. For a brief moment his gaze shifts to Storm Mansion where Anna Sophie is waiting.

Peter's head is shaking with his eagerness to please, but the tsar is not the sort to be humble. The tsar does everything to suit *himself*. When the court sends a coach, the tsar chooses to walk. When the king invites him to a gala performance, the tsar goes to visit a local craftsman. The tsar has sabotaged every effort made by his hosts. He is a shameless and insolent guest. Is this a different tsar standing on the Round Tower? How many tsars can be found inside the tsar?

Ismailov has told me that His Majesty the tsar is a great acteur, and it's when he assumes one of his roles that he is the most dangerous.

Right now Peter wants to move on. Peter wants out of the confines of his Danish cell. He wants to travel through Europe and make new alliances. This is evident in the nervous twitches, in his hands that can't stop moving. But the tsar still has use for Frederik; that's why he is stooping a bit, as if wanting to say: "I am no taller than you. It only seems that way, but it is in no way true."

Frederik and Peter continue their stroll around the platform as the wind buffets their hats.

The rest of us follow, like pleasant-smelling ghosts. Everyone in the entourage is trying to listen to what is being said, but their words disappear with the breeze.

The Muscovites are not to be trusted.

Peter is not to be trusted.

THEY CONTINUE THEIR solitary walk. The tsar in his wine-red caftan with the long sleeves that swing like pendulums. Frederik in his beige silk robes with the sash full of medals, a scarf around his neck, and all his parched gestures.

The king has made every attempt to safeguard himself.

Before the tsar's arrival he gathered as much information as he could—from his envoy in Russia, from countless foreigners in Hanover, Saxony, and Poland.

I see the report with my dwarf vision:

> *His Highborn Sovereign is an eminent military Commander; a moody Conjuror; a talented and brutal Chameleon; a clever Craftsman; a superb Astronomer; a capable Barber; an energetic Fireman; a blood-thirsty Executioner with a genius for the cat-o'-nine-tails and the axe; a fearless Fireworks-artist who is fond of Chinese gunpowder; a formidable Toper; a Sea-Captain eager to learn in the Baltic waters… The greatest weakness of His Highborn Sovereign is a rustic restlessness… He cannot abide the stare of goodfolk.*

That was what it said.

And Frederik had made plans for everything: sumptuous banquets at Copenhagen Castle, hunting in the Royal Deer Park, and gondola rides in the moat at Rosenborg Palace. But nothing had gone as planned. Nothing.

Suddenly the tsar stops and embraces the king.

Frederik's head is clutched to Peter's midriff and rubbed against the brass buttons. His plumed hat falls off but is rescued by a footman. Frederik tears himself away. His gaze wanders to the horizon. The sky is dark with smoke, the Øresund is foaming with angry waves. The Danish frigates are putting in at Landskrona. The troops are overrunning the enemy in bold maneuvers; the Øresund is stained red with the blood of his archenemy. The Dannebrog flag waves over the villages that have been held by the Swedes. Scania is again Danish. God has drawn a line in the sand, and that line belongs to Frederik.

The king tears himself away from that vision.

The tsar smiles and kisses his ally.

AT THAT MOMENT Peter Alexeyevich turns around. His gaze sweeps over his ministers and secretaries, who all stand ready to obey him. Then he catches sight of me.

"Come here," he says.

Ismailov picks me up and carries me over to the tsar. Peter Alexeyevich takes me in his arms. I smile with pleasure. The tsar smells of tar and salt water; there is a mocking look in his eyes. He stares at me for several minutes. Then he kisses me on the lips and holds me over the railing. I close my eyes. Far below us are the rooftops of Kiøbmagergade, the dark blue lakes, and the student lodgings at Regensen. I sway back and forth. The tsar is swinging me over to Slotsholmen, out over the Øresund, up between the rose-colored clouds. My hat blows off and disappears into the great forests, among the foxes, the ferns, and the maple trees. Now I can see even farther. I can see into the homes of peasants where the mothers are sitting at their spinning wheels. I can stare into workshops where embroiderers are counting their needles. I see Denmark in all its lushness: the fjords of Jutland cutting through the heath; the old rune stones surrounded by fields the color of butter. I can see the vault of the sky with its stars and galaxies. And the tsar keeps on swinging me back and forth as the city disappears into a raspberry-colored twilight, into a fire that burns everything to ashes. For a moment we find ourselves in the most vulgar of infernos: in the city among the destroyed hospitals; among the burning churches, with carillons that cease to ring; amid the blazing heat that makes the spires melt.

"*Dania.*" The tsar laughs with pleasure. "*Prekrasnaya, pre-krasnaya Dania.*"

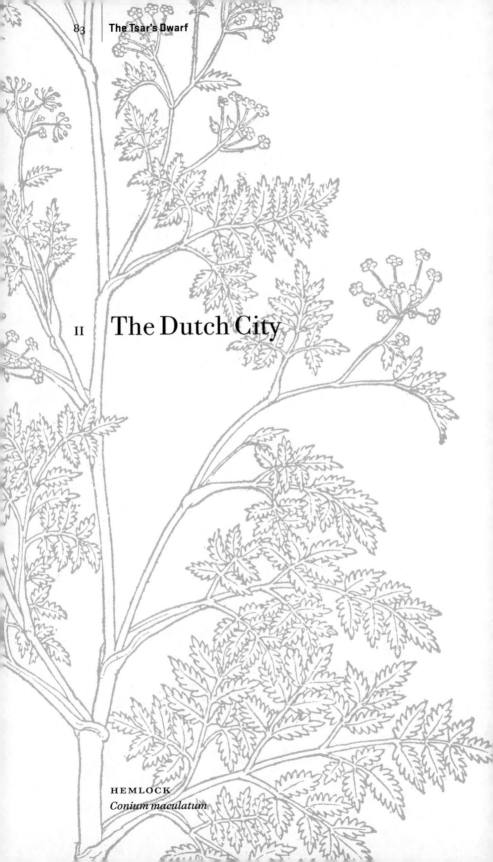

II The Dutch City

HEMLOCK
Conium maculatum

20.

THE SCOUNDREL FOLLOWS ME TO HOLLAND. I SEE HIM in the peasant cart that travels with the tsar's retinue. I see him above the ruined fields where war has raged. The Scoundrel has met his God. It took a while before Terje found his way up there, but now that he has, he insists on obtaining my forgiveness. He won't go away until he has it.

There are eight of us in the last cart in the entourage: two female dressers, a royal barber, three footmen, Ismailov, and me. I've learned some broken Russian. I've gotten better at drinking. It's all going to turn out just fine.

Each night the tsar's retinue stops at German and Dutch inns, with rats in the beams and chickens in the chambers. There are sixty-four of us in the entourage. We never pay for a thing. The Russians never do. In Denmark they left behind an enormous debt at all the inns and taverns—not to mention everything they had destroyed. Merchant Edinger's house was stripped bare. The tsar's men tore the paintings off the walls, they used the doorframes as firewood, they smashed all the windows. Svanemøllen was laid waste by the soldiers' vandalism. On the last day the tsar tried to steal a mummy from the king's Curiosity Cabinet, but his plan was foiled. So he attempted to buy the mummy instead. But Frederik refused to part with his treasure. On the other hand, he did want to part with the 27,000 Russian soldiers who were depleting the Danish treasury. He

wanted to part with the problems, conflicts, and misunderstand-
ings that had plagued the alliance during those long summer
months.

I don't share my king's opinion; I like the Russians.

They weep as if they've been whipped, they kiss on the lips,
and they're as bold as a butcher's dog. Life is meant to be lived.
Everything is black and white inside the soul of a Russian. There
is no middle ground, no room for compromise. Russians are
always right. It's impossible to discuss anything with them; you'll
just get a knife in the back.

WE ARRIVE IN Amsterdam on a cold and raw afternoon. The
Dutch city is filled with foul-smelling canals and houses painted
in a multitude of colors. It reminds me of Christianshavn across
the harbor from Copenhagen, but cleaner and more violent. The
people speak as if they have boils in their mouths, but the tsar
is enthusiastic. He lived in Holland during his youth. He learned
to build ships in a city called Zaandam. He speaks the language
the way the tsar speaks every language, in a comical and clumsy
fashion. Every day he goes to a tavern to smoke a clay pipe with
the local citizenry. The tsar is once again himself, after retreating
from Frederik IV.

In the evening I write in my diary. There is only a single
candle in the garret room. I sit on my bed, which consists of a
thin layer of straw and a rough blanket. Above my head is a little
window that lets in a terrible draft.

The Scoundrel is back in my writing. Whenever I start to
write, he guides my hand across the page; he forces me to com-
pose sentences that seem senseless. But slowly the letters form
messages. Terje is melancholy up there in his heaven. It feels
as though he's living inside of me; as though he's pressing from
the inside, quietly and cautiously. I'm a dark windowpane,
and sometimes you can see him through the glass. My features
become his features, my mouth explodes with rotting teeth, and
stubble from his beard pushes through my skin. I start to use

words that aren't mine. My hands become the hands of an executioner, covered with the dried blood from hundreds of executions. The Scoundrel and I are together once again, but this time inside my body.

I put down my pen and say a prayer. I have no idea who I'm praying to. I'm always in doubt about where I should direct my lack of faith. Terje is still inside me. He's in possession of my arms, and he's working his way up into my throat. I've become a ventriloquist for his anger. Why won't he leave me alone? What is it he wants?

I try to sleep, but the Scoundrel breaks into my dreams. When I walk along the canals of the city, he's inside the seagulls and the eyes of the local citizens. I have an urge to scream, but I don't. Because it will be the Scoundrel's scream. Maybe I've become him. Maybe I've never even existed as myself.

THE TSAR TAKES ill in Amsterdam. No one knows what ails him. He has gone to bed with a fever. His *medicus* has given him a powder and forbidden him to drink. Ismailov says that the tsar is often bedridden, but that he always recovers and is then stronger than ever. His men carry on the negotiations with France. Rumor has it that we're going to visit the boy king in Paris when the winter is over.

One evening I'm summoned to the tsar's bed to entertain him. It's dark in the bedchamber. Peter Alexeyevich is lying on his camp bed with a wool blanket wrapped around him. He has five pillows propped up behind him. His eyes are glassy, his skin is yellowish. Five wax candles have been stuck on the wall in the Russian manner.

Next to him sits the tsarina. This is my first encounter with her. Catherine is a reserved woman with a coarse face and little round eyes that look at me with an expression that is both guileless and mistrustful. She is elegantly dressed in a light-brown gown adorned with reliquaries and images of saints. Every time she moves, her idols clatter. It's a horribly annoying sound.

I attempt a drinking song that Ismailov has taught me, but after a few minutes the tsar throws a pillow at me. I pick up the pillow and put it back on the bed. The tsar shouts something that I don't understand. And Ismailov and I go back to our own room. I have a headache and I feel depressed. Why can't I find my proper place among these foreigners?

Ismailov consoles me over a drink. It's important for me to build up a repertoire, a number of amusements that will please the tsar. I must never present the same amusements in the same order, because the joy of recognition is not something in which Peter takes pleasure.

"But I don't know any amusements," I say.

"Can't you play an instrument?"

I shake my head. I don't play the fiddle, and it's impossible for me to play a wind instrument. Dwarves don't have the lungs for trumpets. We are delicate creatures with bodies that are more sensitive than human bodies. And as I sit there talking with Ismailov, I wish that I could perform, I wish that I were enchanting, gentle, even lovable.

"Lukas is good at clowning and playacting."

"Who's Lukas?"

"He's the tsar's favorite dwarf."

"Where is he now?"

"Back home in Petersburg. The tsar didn't bring him to Europe because he was unwell."

I scowl at Ismailov.

"Surely you didn't think that you were the only midget in the world, did you, Surinka?"

I ignore him.

"Why is Lukas the tsar's favorite?" I ask.

"I don't know. Someone has to be the favorite."

"Yes, but there must be a reason!"

"Maybe it's because he's so impertinent. The tsar loves it when his midgets are impertinent—up until the moment when his mood changes."

I give Ismailov a resigned look.

"I'm probably much better at being an advisor."

"But then you have to show that you have some insight, that you understand the political situation abroad. At the same time you need to contradict the tsar, but without letting him notice. Can you read fortunes from cards?"

"Of course not."

"Many dwarves do."

"There are also lots of dwarves who have hunchbacks. But I don't have one." I sigh with annoyance and lie down on my bed.

"Don't take offense," says Ismailov, smiling mournfully.

I look at my friend. Ismailov has taken good care of me ever since I met him. He reminds me of a morose Rasmus Æreboe. Ismailov can sit for hours just staring at the wall. There are days when he doesn't say a word. But then he cheers up, gives his egg-shaped head a good shake—and tells me about his childhood years in Denmark, about the time he spent in the German district of Moscow where the foreign envoys live, and where the tsar came to visit, carousing until the early morning hours.

"How many dwarves does Peter actually own?" I ask.

"I have no idea."

"But he has feasts for them, doesn't he? I once saw a strange copperplate engraving that showed a wedding for dwarves."

"The tsar does many peculiar things, but you mustn't misunderstand him. He's not an ordinary prankster by any means."

"I know that."

"Peter Alexeyevich has revolutionized Russian society. He broke the intolerable domination of the priests in Moscow. He built up the navy from nothing. He defeated the Swedes and the infidel Turks so that we now have access to the sea. He instituted a new alphabet and a new calendar. He has written edifying books for Russian youths, introduced a theater in the German style, put down the rebellion of the *streltsy* forces, and fought against corruption among the boyars. He has hired the best foreigners within all the art forms. He has transformed Petersburg from a swamp to a capital that is more beautiful than any other city in the world. He has built frigates with his own hands, invented water pumps to fight fires, crafted gifts for kings and princes. Peter Alexeyevich is utterly indefatigable. I don't think God has ever created a human being with more energy than His Majesty, our Tsar."

At that moment the door opens, and Vasily Dolgoruky comes in.

I don't like Dolgoruky. I haven't liked him since the time he tried to drink me under the table back in Copenhagen. There is something dishonest about his ruddy face and those squinty eyes of his. They're always on the lookout for the weaknesses of others.

Ismailov jumps up from his chair.

"The tsarina wishes to see the Danish dwarf in her chamber."

Dolgoruky gives me a scornful look and leaves. I straighten my back and smooth out my dress with my hand. Then Ismailov pats me on the head and follows me up the stairs to the tsarina's chamber.

21.

"I UNDERSTAND THAT YOU SPEAK RUSSIAN, IS THAT RIGHT?"

Catherine is studying me. She has a round peasant's face, but I only have to look into her eyes to realize that the tsarina is no goose. She is a monument of calm, with her rough hands and horse-like laugh that flays the silk right off the walls.

"I don't really care for dwarves," she says.

"No, my lady."

"But Peter loves all sorts of deformed creatures. He has just ordered a Sami for your king. What he wants with such a thing, I can't imagine."

I nod and bow.

Catherine tilts her head to one side.

"That wasn't a particularly amusing song you sang for the tsar."

"No, my lady."

"So now we know what you can't do." She smiles warmly. "Do you have any special talents?"

"I'm good with herbs."

"Anything else?"

"Good at sulking."

Catherine stares at me. Then she laughs loudly.

"And what do you have to sulk about, you strange little creature?"

"The fact that I am a strange little creature."

"But there's nothing you can do about that."

"No, my lady."

"Since we must assume that you're not going to get bigger anytime in the future, what could you imagine yourself doing for the tsar and for me while we sit here, bored to tears, in this God-forsaken Holland?"

"I could teach you Danish."

Catherine laughs again and then audibly farts.

"You are amusing, you little mite. I'm sure that we'll find you entertaining when the tsar is back on his feet. Are you well-read?"

"Very."

"Then see about improving your Russian. Otherwise many of my countrymen won't understand a word that you say."

"As you wish."

"If you don't have the books that you need, come to me. I might also be able to find you a castigator to teach you Russian."

I bow once again.

"What is your name, you little monster?"

"Surinka."

Catherine rings a metal bell, then she farts again. A lady-in-waiting shows me out and pats me on the head. Outside it's snowing. The canals look like white sheets. Amsterdam is deadly dull. I want to go to Russia as soon as possible.

ONE EVENING ISMAILOV tells me about the tsar's illness.

It's not just a physical ailment; it's spiritual. The tsar has problems with his son, Alexey. The tsarevich is a weakling who lacks respect for his father. At no time has he ever shown an interest in Peter's reforms. Whereas the tsar wishes to modernize Russia, Alexey wants to take the country back to its roots. Whereas the tsar is a workhorse, Alexey is a thinker. The father loves Petersburg, the son loves Moscow. Not even the art of war can bring them together. Alexey has said that he will give the Swedes their land back when he becomes tsar. The father and son are like fire and water.

And now Alexey has fled.

Instead of meeting his father in Denmark, he has gone to Vienna. No one knows what his intentions are. Is he planning a coup? Or has Alexey acknowledged that he is unsuited to succeed the tsar—and that Peter would have beaten him until he obeyed his every command?

Ismailov takes me into town.

The walls have ears, and he refuses to talk about Alexey when other Russians are present. We find some peace and quiet in a little tavern on a snow-covered alleyway. It's dark inside with a long wooden table set with heavy pewter mugs. We light our clay pipes, ignoring the laughter all around us. Then my Russian friend continues his story.

"There's no doubt that Alexey has committed treason. He has asked for protection from the Austrian Emperor, going behind the tsar's back. But I don't think he's doing this deliberately to harm Peter. He's simply terrified. Alexey is better suited to holding a rosary in his hand than a pistol, and he feels that no matter what he does, it will never be good enough to satisfy his father. The Tsarevich is actually quite capable. He just isn't a man of action."

Ismailov stares into space and shakes his egg-shaped head.

"But there's another problem ... something that the tsar has a hard time forgiving. The people love Alexey, whereas Peter himself is hated. Extremely hated."

We take a drink from our beer mugs. Behind us two seamen start fighting. They roll around in the sawdust, kicking each other until blood flows. But I pay them no attention. I'm thinking about the tsar and his son: Peter bending over Alexey. Alexey, who both loves and hates his father. Alexey who flees to Austria to find peace for his soul.

But his days are numbered.

Why do I have a feeling that his days are numbered?

AS WE WALK home through the snow, I think about why people have children. Is it a pragmatic arrangement, or do human beings have a need for a distortion of themselves? Parents never have children out of love but only because they wish to cheat God. They wish to stretch out a hand into the future—to survive through their offspring. Only when their own bodies wither do they develop an interest in their progeny. And by then it's too late.

I turn to my Russian friend.

"Do you have children, Ismailov?"

"I had a son, but he died at childbirth."

"What about a wife?"

"I do have one of those."

I nod as I try not to slip in the snow. We arrive back at the inn, where the tsar is staying incognito. He's lying in his room and waiting for spring—and for Alexey, who has fled and disappeared.

Several days later we receive an order. Ismailov and I are going to accompany Catherine and her entourage back to the homeland. To the Russian spring, which will arrive in a few months' time. To the tsar's kingdom and the frozen melancholy of Petersburg.

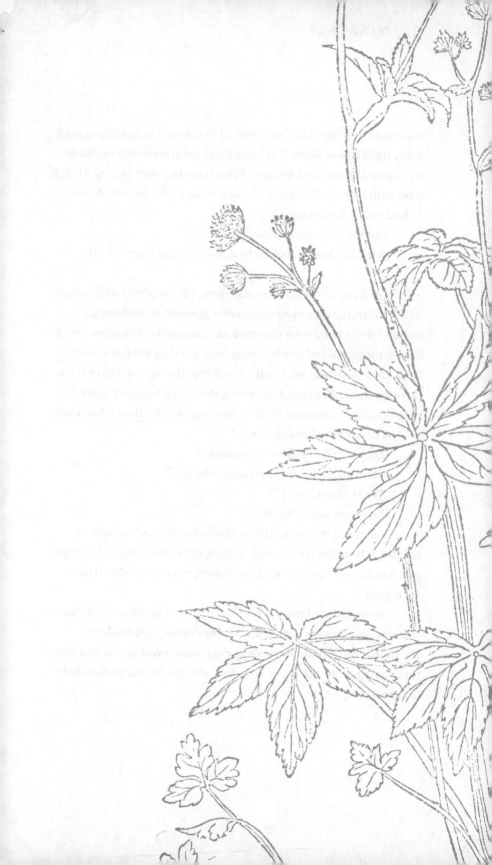

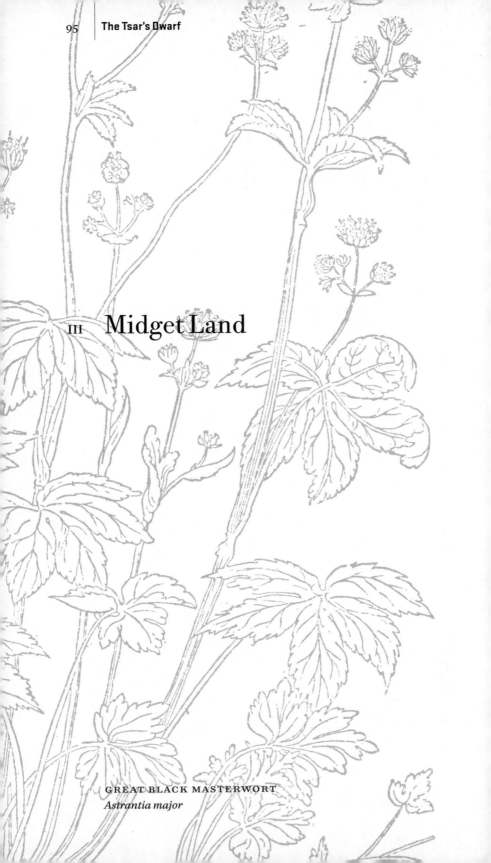

III Midget Land

GREAT BLACK MASTERWORT
Astrantia major

22.

THE LONG SLEIGH GLIDES THROUGH THE WHITE LAND-
scape like a ship. I stretch out in the foot end of it, reach for a
pillow, and try to sleep. The sleigh creaks. There is a rank smell
in the closed compartment. Ismailov is still in the arms of Mor-
pheus. He snores melodically; he's been doing that all morning.

I stand up and try to look out the little window. There are
big frost flowers on the pane. Cautiously I scrape off the rime.
The morning is clear and frosty, with a blanket of ice-cold stars.
The sleigh's pine torches burn holes into the black sky, which
seems endless and vast.

I'm inside the third sleigh in the convoy from Riga to Novgorod. We've been under way for weeks, with numerous nights
spent at the tsar's mail-coach inns. Catherine and her retinue
have eaten their fill of pancakes and borscht. We've heard wolves
howling outside the drafty windows. But now we've reached the
outskirts of Petersburg. We're driving along white streets with
small stone houses and bluish-gray smoke rising from the chim-
neys. Slowly a pale lavender streak comes into view. The night
unravels at the seams, fades away, disappears.

Ismailov wakes up. The abscess in his left cheek has grown
as big as a ball. He leans on his elbows and gapes at me, as if
trying to remember who I am. Then he gives me a sleepy smile
and runs a hand through his tousled hair.

Over the course of the next hour a new world appears

through the rime: onion-shaped cupolas bathed in the morning's icy sunshine, soldiers with sabers and fur hats, and peasants selling icons and bast fiber.

The traffic is intense. Hordes of sleds and sleighs make their way through the snow. Most of them are primitive and falling apart; some are shaped like swans, some are gilded and have pine torches. I keep looking around with big eyes. I'm enchanted by the architecture, by a wooden house built of enormous timbers, and by the emaciated horses adorned with foxtails standing in the street.

Finally the caravan comes to a halt in front of a house. Ismailov opens the sleigh's hatch door and steps out into the deep snowdrift. He is blue with cold, his fingers and ears are numb, and he shivers in the brutally icy weather. I bury myself in my fur jacket. My teeth are chattering, but I'm happy to have finally arrived in the great land of Mother Russia.

CATHERINE IGNORED ME on the frenzied journey from Holland. Only now, after we've arrived, does she speak to me. I have an audience with her in her traveling sleigh. As usual, her reliquaries clatter every time she moves.

"How is your Russian coming along, Surinka?"

"Good, my lady."

"Can people understand what you say?"

"I should think so."

Catherine smiles kindly and pats me on the head. One of her ladies-in-waiting gives me a look of disgust. The tsarina's kindness vanishes at once.

"You can stay with Lukas. I'll send word when I want you to entertain me."

She nods graciously, and I jump out into the cold, where Ismailov is waiting. The little caravan sets off, and I turn to look at the house in front of me.

It's a lovely wood-timbered building with three wings and a view of the frozen canal. Two linden trees stand on the property along with a fountain dripping with icicles. Ismailov and I go over to the brilliantly painted door. Ismailov knocks. No one answers. After a while we grow impatient and step inside.

"It's warm in here," I say with pleasure, looking around at the splendid surroundings. The deserted room is furnished in a wondrous blend of Russian and European styles. On the wall hang Persian brass plates, lamp brackets with mirrors, and Flemish portraits of gloomy-looking princes. The doors are made of lovely birch, the banisters along the stairs are beautifully carved.

"Am I going to live here?" I ask.

"Upstairs."

Ismailov leads the way up the steps that are made just the right height for a dwarf. He knocks and opens a small door. A rank odor billows out toward me. I peer inside but close my eyes in horror.

THERE ARE CERTAIN rooms that I have no desire to describe. There are certain rooms that are so odious that no words can put them on a page; they defy depiction in even the most miserable poetry. Such a place is that dwarf apartment with the little door handles, the blue-painted stools, and the diminutive windows, which allow the light to crawl in on all fours.

But worst of all is the dwarf sitting at the table—the way his face lights up when he sees me, his eager manner when he gets to his feet.

"*Zdrastvuy.*"

The dwarf waddles over to greet us. He's dressed in a costly caftan trimmed with fur. Around his neck is a rough scarf, but it's his face that fills me with loathing. There is no expression; it's perfectly smooth and lacking any distinction.

"Are you going to live here?" he asks.

I nod.

"Welcome," he says.

Before I can even react, he kisses me on the lips. Behind

me Ismailov has knelt down in order to fit inside the room. The dwarf apartment is furnished like some sort of malevolent museum. It's not meant to make things easier for those who live here; it's meant to mock them.

I set down my baggage. A carpetbag containing two tattered dresses, a pair of wool socks that I bought from the Jews in Copenhagen, and my father's Bible with the grease marks in the Gospel according to John. And my herbs. If they've survived the cold, that is.

"I hope that you will be happy here," says Ismailov, placing a heavy hand on my shoulder.

I watch him as he crawls out of the apartment.

Ismailov closes the door. The dwarf and I are alone.

Terribly alone.

THERE'S NOT A sound in the apartment except for our breathing. I study the Russian dwarf: the smooth face with the dark eyes, the tiny nose that could only belong to a doll. Some might call him handsome, but I see only the clumsy ears and the enormous back of his head, which make him look like what he is: a fool.

"My name is Lukas," he says.

I nod.

"What's your name?"

"Surinka."

"Where are you from?"

"*Dania.*"

Lukas nods like a man who has never heard of *Dania*. He lets his eyes slide down my body and stop at my bowed legs. For some reason he seems to like what he sees.

"There are six of us dwarves living here, but the others are on loan to Prince Menshikov."

"And who is Prince Menshikov?"

"A fine gentleman who treats us well."

Lukas continues to study me with annoying boldness. I

don't care for him. He spits when he talks. Not a lot, but enough
to be irritating.

"Would you like a drink of vodka?"

"No, thank you."

"It's important that you learn to drink. I'll get you a goblet
and we can drink a toast to each other's health."

Lukas waddles out, moving as hastily as he can. I sit down
on a stool. It has been a rough journey because of the jolting
sleigh and the old nags pulling it. Every muscle in my body aches,
and I feel as if the floor is still moving beneath me.

I pluck at my blouse with the slashed sleeves. I find a hole
that I hadn't noticed before.

Lukas comes back in no time. He's carrying two goblets,
each on its own salver. He hands one to me. It's dark blue, decorated with lovely designs.

The wine tastes awful, even worse than in Denmark.

Lukas stares into space as he empties his goblet. Then he
sets it down with a bang. I try to look away, but I can't take my
eyes off him.

He smiles.

"Do you like me?"

I give him an indignant look.

"Not in the least."

"You will."

I look around the apartment. The walls are adorned with
gilded leather. There are Dutch paintings on the walls; there
is a dining table covered with a cloth and set with earthenware
dishes. But the most dominant piece of furniture is the stove
and a diminutive *prie-dieu*. It's underneath an icon of Saint Nicholas, the miracle worker.

"Tell me, what do you dwarves do when you're loaned out?"
I ask.

"We clown around and entertain. Sometimes we jump out
of pies. We also have a six-man orchestra. I play flute and drums."

Lukas looks at me as if inviting my praise.

"How many dwarves does the tsar own?"

"I don't know, but the most important ones live here."

"And you're the tsar's favorite?"

"There's no doubt about that."

"And why are you the favorite, if I might ask?"

"Because I'm always in a good mood."

"How can you be in a good mood when you're running around with a pudding head like that?"

Lukas looks at me with astonishment.

"But I'm so handsome. Don't you think I'm handsome?"

I place my hand on his shoulder and smile. Lukas is the first Russian dwarf I've ever met. I pray to God that he's the last.

LUKAS CONTINUES TO show me around the dwarf apartment, leading me in and out of the small garret rooms, through ice-cold parlors with little porcelain stoves, walking across reddish-brown carpets made from fox skins. Everywhere are low chairs and worn furniture that must have come from some miserable nursery rooms. In the corners are stacks of splendid dwarf clothing, shoes in diminutive sizes, and fur blankets that aren't big enough to cover even a ladybug. On the walls are Russian copperplate engravings. The whole place smells of mold and cold stone.

The bedchamber is the largest room in the apartment. It's dark and dank, with the usual icons. One of the beds has a green canopy, the others are ordinary beds. I count eight beds, all in dwarf size.

"I sleep in the bed with the canopy," says Lukas.

I go over to the bed farthest from his. My back is aching. I still haven't warmed up after that terrible journey by sleigh. On the bed are a rough blanket and a pillow. I set down my baggage.

"Why are there eight beds instead of six?"

"Because there used to be eight of us."

"What happened to the last two?"

"I'll tell you some other time."

Lukas pushes back a strand of hair from his forehead and lets his pale hand fall to his side. For a moment he looks like a boy.

"It's possible that we could become friends," I say graciously.

Lukas's face lights up. "I think we can too. Are you a good cook? Natasha, who usually lives here, is a very good cook. She's the best in the world when it comes to cabbage and cranberries. Her bean soup isn't bad either."

I look at the frost flowers on the windowpane. Lukas continues his monologue about a woman's duties. I let my hand slide down my spine. Then I throw myself onto the bed, fighting to hold back the tears. A moment later I fall into a heavy, dreamless sleep.

23.

WHEN I WAS ABOUT TEN YEARS OLD, I GOT TO KNOW the elves. They lived out in the forest and showed themselves to me as often as they could. There was nothing mysterious about them. The elves take care of their kingdoms; they protect the trees, the shrubs, and the flowers. They are tiny and transparent. Elves can change shape and color whenever they like, they can speak any language, and they're always happy.

The first few times that I went to the forest, I wasn't able to see them. I merely sensed a power that was gentle and sunny. But eventually they began to show themselves to me. First as an outline in the air, then as pale bodies with the contours of arms and legs. The elves followed me to the marsh. They protected me at the river, under the hazel bushes, on my walks along the forest floor. But when I left the marsh, they disappeared. I could sense how they stopped at the edge of the woods, how they waved goodbye in the dusk. The elves were my invisible playmates who helped me to find the snakes and shrews that my father killed whenever I brought them into the house.

My father was not a bad person. He simply thought that the forest had an unfortunate influence on my spiritual life. It kept me from my Bible reading and my duties at the parsonage.

One day I was stupid enough to tell him about my encounters with the elves. My father gave me a long, mournful look. Then he took my hands, placing his own on top of mine, and told me about Satan's cauldrons; about the souls that were roasted over the low fire; about the witches that were pierced through with sharp instruments. And then he taught me to cross myself, the way people did in the old days. He told me to seek protection from the evil that can assume any shape: a tree or a shy little elf guarding its birch grove.

But what my father asked of me was that I should close my eyes.

I was supposed to practice walking through the woods under God's protection. I was supposed to constrict my world to what I could actually see; to what was in the Bible. I was supposed to keep away from nature, from the elves, from everything that was heathen and blasphemous.

But why is the ability to see considered blasphemous? Why should every creature that is not human be made into the spawn of Satan? I will always defend the elves, the trolls, and the fairies. I will defend specters and phantoms. Those who are holy have their own apparition, which they call the Holy Ghost. The Holy Ghost is received with prayers and gratitude. No one wishes to drive him away with iron tongs or some sort of emetic.

I was ten years old when I was accepted into the realm of the elves. I felt at home in their company. Their world lifted my spirits. It was a world that gave me a belief in gods that had been rejected by human beings; a world of unending beauty, of invisible waterfalls in nature—a sense of divine love, of eternal protection. I thought that their world would always be with me, but one day it vanished. One day there were no more elves in the forest. Either I had lost the ability to see them, or else it was the words of God that remained—the words of God and the temptations of the Devil.

But there was one thing they couldn't take away from me: the herbs.

And the herbs became my salvation.

ISMAILOV TAKES ME out to see Petersburg.

The abscess on his tooth has grown, but he seems happy to be back in his home country. I stare with awe at the cathedrals and all the red walls. I follow the fur-clad boyars and visit the Persian market, where you can buy silks, boots made of Moroccan leather, and spices. The Russians look at us with suspicion, and they count Ismailov's money five times before they hand over whatever he has purchased. Even though I've gotten quite good at speaking Russian, I understand only half of what everyone says.

On a street corner I catch sight of several murdered merchants. They're lying on a bloody snowdrift. Their mouths are open, their eyes rolled up. No one pays any attention to them. Everyone minds their own business, praying that God will protect them better than He has those victims.

At the city gates people are lined up to leave Petersburg. A crowd of Cossacks is waiting patiently, but two soldiers have grabbed hold of an old man. At first I can't tell what's happening, but then I realize that they're in the process of cutting off his beard.

I give Ismailov an inquiring look.

"The peasant hasn't paid the beard tax," he explains.

"What's a beard tax?"

"Many years ago the tsar decided to abolish old Russian customs. That's why he instituted a tax on beards. Those who pay are given a receipt affixed to the beard as a lead seal. Only priests are exempt."

We watch the curious scene.

"Even though it's an old law, there are still many people in the smallest villages who have never heard of it. So when they come to Petersburg, an ugly surprise is in store for them."

I stare at the old man. He has closed his eyes as he murmurs several prayers. There is something strangely resigned about his appearance, as if he knows that it would be futile to fight against the tsar's decrees.

We continue walking along the street, past merchants' sleighs loaded down with pelts; past small chapels with icons and oil lamps; past leather sleighs parked in front of majestic limestone walls. We pause on a bridge to look out across the frozen bay. Hundreds of goodfolk are skating out there. They slip in and out of the sunlight. Suddenly three naked women come running out of a wooden hut. They plunge shrieking into a hole in the ice and then storm back to their bathhouse. Several Russian soldiers look as if they'd like to follow suit.

On our way home, snow comes drifting down. It makes a delicate frosting on the church cupolas and on the rotting posts sticking out of the riverbed. Then the twilight slides in, silent and dark.

24.

LUKAS IS EATING KASHA, WHICH IS BUCKWHEAT PORridge with milk.

He eats quickly, making vulgar slurping sounds. His stubby little fingers move swiftly from the mush to the bread. His expression is solemn, his brow is furrowed. The food seems to bring something else to his face besides the eternal smile—a voraciousness along with something bestial that suits the little man.

We drink a toast with vodka. It's pleasant spending time with Lukas. Not because he's especially intelligent, but because he's ingratiating. And also because he takes each of my insults without flinching, which almost makes me respect him.

Last night he tried to get into my bed, but he quickly climbed out again. I have no idea what he sees in me.

Now I go to get the herbs from my carpetbag.

I unpack them and place them all on the table. Most of them are as hard as stone after the journey from Holland. Only the swallowwort looks as if it has retained its power. The hemlock wouldn't kill even a sparrow.

Lukas watches with curiosity. He asks me whether I'm a witch.

"All women are witches."

"Can you cure lung fever?"

"I can't cure anything at all."

"Then what do you use the herbs for?"

"Plenty of things."

I let the hemlock rest in my hand as I look at Lukas. His eyes are big and round, his chin is as white as the milk on his buckwheat porridge.

"You're a strange woman, Surinka."

"Thank you."

"Is everybody in your country as crazy as you are?"

I ignore him. If I know Lukas, he'll soon be forcing himself on me, with his disgusting kissing lips.

A moment later he shoves his bowl aside and smiles his self-satisfied smile.

"We could find you some clothes, if you're interested. We have plenty of German dresses that would fit you perfectly."

"No, thanks."

"The tsar wants us to look presentable, Surinka."

"When the tsar comes to visit, I promise to deck myself out like a whore!"

Lukas stretches and preens. He is once again beaming like the sun. It's an excruciating sight.

OVER THE NEXT few days I speculate over why Lukas is always so cheerful. Why does he insist on seeing the bright side of life, when there is no bright side? Is he somehow possessed, or is it merely a form of obtuseness? If you look at someone's smile, you'll see that it's often phony, that the person is using it for a specific intent. A serious demeanor is the most natural state for an intelligent person. A single burst of laughter might benefit the digestion, but there's no reason to go overboard.

"Lukas, where are you from? Are you from Petersburg?"

He shakes his head.

"No one is from Petersburg. I come from a town called Preobrazhenskaya."

"Where is your family?"

"I have no family."

"You must have had a mother and a father at one time."

Lukas nods and wipes off the porridge with the back of his hand. It takes a few minutes before I realize that he doesn't intend to reply.

"And?"

"Well, of course I did. But today the tsar is my father. He's the one I can thank for everything."

"Why?"

"Because he saw me at the fair and took me along to his *dacha*. From the very first he treated me kindly. He gave me warm clothes and a place to live. I've traveled with him throughout our land, all the way up to Arkhangelsk and as far south as the Turkish frontier, where I entertained him every night in his tent. I love Peter Alexeyevich, and Peter Alexeyevich loves me."

"What about your parents? Were they dwarves or human beings?"

"They were both."

I stand up. Lukas watches me as I move around the dwarf apartment. He has suddenly turned quiet and introspective.

It's a hard thing for me to admit, but I'm actually enjoying my home.

I don't have to climb ladders to reach pots and goblets. I can fly around like a fairy. I can reach more than I've ever been able to reach before. And when I curse the world and tell it to go to Hell, I do it with far less conviction. The only thing that annoys me is Lukas, but he's not as bad as he could be.

"Surinka?"

"Yes?"

"Surinka, may I ask you something?"

I nod.

"If dwarves aren't human beings, then what are we?"

25.

THERE IS A PLACE IN COPENHAGEN WHERE MOTHERS take their infants. It's behind Holmen Church, at the end of a narrow alleyway. The mothers hurry through the twilight, past the outbuildings, carrying their bundles in their arms. On the way they hide in doorways as they work their way down toward the harbor and the ships. When they reach the right spot, they stop and look in both directions. Some of them murmur a prayer; others want to get it over with as fast as possible. They let go of their bundle and watch as it hits the black water. Then they gather their wits about them and rush back to where they came from, as the bundle sinks toward the murky bottom. Sometimes the blanket slips off the infants and they fall naked to their fate. At other times they whimper as their chubby arms push aside the seaweed and mud. Finally they reach the bottom—the bottom that is an endless mountain of God's tiny children, of enchanting faces that have found peace in Paradise. They sleep sweetly, these tiny ones, with their crystal-clear eyes and delicately wrinkled fingers that are clasped around some-thing invisible. They sleep sweetly until they're awakened by angels. They have been spared from the world; they belonged to it for just a few days, and now they're back where they came from. But they miss their mothers. They call to them from their Heaven, through pastel-blue clouds, through the heavy salt water that glitters like silver. But the mothers can't hear them. No one can hear them. There are more and more of them. Children lying on a soft carpet at the bottom of the sea, silent and sad. One of them is mine. A little boy that was too ugly for this world, with an enchanting harelip and a nose pressed flat. I see him often in my dreams. He has kept on growing. It was God that took him. Or the Devil. I merely laid him to rest in the water. With my frail voice I sang to him as he met death. Afterwards I went back through town like a ghost, going from tavern to tavern, until I couldn't remember anything more, and for a while everything grew dark.

LUKAS TAKES A book from his cupboard. It's big and bound in leather—one of the many books written by the tsar. In the book Peter describes how the modern citizen ought to live. For breakfast he should drink coffee and abstain from vodka; he should wash himself and brush his teeth. In the summer a cavalier should wear Saxon jackets and full-bottomed wigs. He should be freshly shaven, practice clean habits, and show consideration to his fellow men. In the winter: Hungarian garb with leather boots that creak on the snow. But above all, the Russian should learn manners: such as not to belch at the table unless he's alone; that it's forbidden to wipe his nose on his clothes; that taking a shit behind statues and curtains just isn't done. In the evening he should drink tea and read from edifying books—preferably others published by the tsar. For instance, books about the modern Russian theater, where depressing plays are not allowed and where singing and lewdness are banned.

Lukas reads aloud to me.

He looks rather sweet as he sits there wearing his steel-rimmed spectacles. If there's something that I don't understand, he repeats the words for me, as if I'm an idiot. Slowly, with his mouth open wide, so I can look down at his uvula, where the Russian words are fired off like cannons.

"The tsar has truly done his utmost to cultivate us Russians. But fortunately there is still a need for fools. And we can be as crude and boorish as we like."

I nod.

"Have you ever performed for His Majesty the Tsar, Surinka?"

"Twice."

"Did Peter like you?"

"In Copenhagen he loved me. I jumped out of a cake and danced for him. The second time didn't go as well. That was in Amsterdam, when he was ill."

"Maybe we should put together a show for His Majesty the Tsar."

"Maybe," I say.

Lukas smiles. When he reaches for my hand, I hasten to stand up. The little man has a pleading look in his eyes, but I refuse to see it. The only thing I choose to see is that he spits when he talks.

When I go to bed the Scoundrel's laughter rings in my ears.

I have to get rid of him.

I have to get rid of him, no matter what the cost.

26.

IT'S THE DREAMS THAT GIVE ME THE MOST TROUBLE. In the old days I always dreamed that I was a human being, that I woke up with a well-proportioned body and strong lungs that could contain the world, and with a spine that supported me without pain. I got up from silk sheets and went out to a sun-filled pleasure garden, where I peered over the heads of counts and over the boxwood hedges. In that world no one picked me up, no one mistook me for a doorstep, no one paused to have a good laugh. I was visible because I was invisible. The dreams were marvelous while they lasted, but cruel when I awoke.

The same thing happens this morning. Terje is with me.

I notice it at once when I wake up: a scrap of light, a denseness in the dark. The Scoundrel talks about God on high and about the meaning behind his demise. But he isn't satisfied with things. Paradise is not a place to build a nest. He gets impatient with all the clouds, with the threat of eternal salvation. The Scoundrel wants to bore his way inside of me from the seventh Heaven; he wants to be a devil like he usually is, a guardian spirit with a stiff cock. It's more amusing that way.

Lukas wakes up in the middle of our conversation. He sits up in bed, under his canopy.

"Who are you talking to, Surinka?"

The little man blinks his eyes, sensing Terje like a ceiling of reproaches. The Scoundrel blows into my face, lets his cock slide sullenly up the inside of my thigh. I push him away. The Scoundrel laughs raucously and tells me that he's been frequenting taverns and whores, that he fills his mouth with dried-up vaginas. But life is distancing itself from him. The earth will no longer be his playground. There is a battle going on for his immortal soul, but Terje doesn't know what is light or what is dark. They are merging with each other, offering short cuts that turn out to be detours. Terje is perplexed about being a ghost. He weeps. He has an arm around my neck, but there is no life in his breath. Everything is dying around him. Everything.

"Go away," I cry. "Why won't you go away?"

Lukas jumps down from his bed and comes to my rescue. He slides right through Terje, as if the Scoundrel were a cobweb. Outside the stars are fading, and the moon disappears from the sky. Terje is no longer here. He has vanished. Only his smell lingers in the room.

Icicles fall from the roof. More and more mud appears in the snow. The sun pushes its way into the outbuildings. It's spring, with birds singing and bare branches. The last frost settles on the banister.

Lukas puts his arms around me. I weep against his shoulder and let the tears fall without stopping them. I haven't wept in a very long time, not since I was eight years old.

At that moment someone knocks on the door. Lukas waddles over to open it. Outside stands a soldier with a saber and beaver-skin cap. He hands Lukas a letter with a scornful gesture, as if it were beneath his dignity to deliver messages to little people.

Lukas spells his way through the missive, frowning and squinting his eyes. Then a smile spreads over his face. Catherine,

the Tsarina of Russia, requests that her dwarves should entertain her three days after Lent.

We look at each other.

Outside an icicle falls to the ground and shatters.

27.

CATHERINE IS NOT OF NOBLE BIRTH. SHE'S THE DAUGH-
ter of a peasant from Livonia, but she has climbed to the top of
the Russian cake. First she was the mistress of a Swedish officer
in Marienburg, then the lover of Peter's best friend, Prince
Menshikov, and finally mistress to the tsar, who found pleasure
in her round peasant face that was both maternal and coquet-
tish. She became the tsarina five years ago, and now has more
power than is good for her.

Lukas doesn't like her. He won't come right out and say as
much, but I can sense it when he talks about her. His voice gets
deeper and a bit sarcastic. Lukas doesn't care to see scum rising
to the top. Catherine is too common. And she talks incessantly.
The jaws of the first lady of the land are never still. She has something to say about everything, big and small. Granted, she always
speaks with a smile, but it's still annoying.

And now she has grown fat. She is short and stout, and she
walks about her mansion on her flat peasant feet.

"It's somehow sinful that a peasant's daughter should rise
so high," says Lukas. "But at least she's not a foreigner. That's
why she's so popular with the people."

"What's wrong with foreigners?"

"They're heretics."

"Well, then I'm a heretic too."

"At least you haven't brought your deviltry with you."

"What deviltry is that?"

Lukas doesn't reply.

We've been working on the tsarina's entertainment for
days. The little man is unbelievably limber. He can stand on
his head, leap through barrel hoops, and juggle several kittens

at a time. On the other hand, he's not especially quick-witted, so it's my role to introduce him, to act hot-tempered, and to insult the guests at random.

I sit down on a stool.

"I had an audience with Catherine when we were in Holland. She told me that she doesn't care for dwarves."

"I'll keep that in mind," says Lukas.

"So why does she want us to perform for her?"

"Because her women friends love midgets. And Catherine always howls along with whatever wolves happen to be her companions. She has no taste of her own, but if someone tells her that a performance is superb, then she loves it too. That's why she'll agree that we're good if the others in the party decide to praise us.

"Do you think she loves the tsar?"

Lukas shrugs. "The only thing for certain is that the tsar loves her. She has him caught in her net. And she's unbelievably strong. I once saw her lift a grown man."

We keep on practicing our performance. Lukas tries to get me to do a cartwheel, but my body refuses to obey. He can do it easily, with no effort at all. He dances and writhes like a snake, while he sings drinking songs. I understand only half the words.

At night, as I lie in my bed, I speculate about a rumor that I've heard. That the tsar is not of noble birth either, that one summer out in the country he was exchanged for the real Peter. The boy who had left Moscow was small and slender. The Peter who came back was a strapping fellow, taller and huskier than the tsar's son. Is that why he finds pleasure in a peasant's daughter? Could this explain why Peter is so pleased with primitive conditions? Or why he uses his hands like a simple carpenter's son?

I blow out the candle and feel the blanket being lifted aside. Lukas lies down next to me. His breath caresses my cheek. Then: a smooth dwarf hand touches my breasts. I feel his tender kisses on my neck. I try to remove his hands, but Lukas is excited.

"Surinka," he whispers. "Oh, Surinka."

I hear a sound that I don't want to hear, and at that instant I shove my knee up against his nuts.

Lukas falls out of the bed like a winged chicken.

"Good night, Lukas."

I turn onto my side while the little man gasps in pain. He starts crawling over to his own bed, slowly, painfully.

A moment later I fall asleep and dream peacefully about birds and clouds.

THE NEXT MORNING Lukas shows me his bruises in the glow of the candle. He takes stock of his noble parts right in front of me, as if that sort of thing would interest me.

I go out to the kitchen. Lukas follows me like a puppy. He's just as ingratiating as always. Right now he's hoping that I'll conjure up a meal, but I merely pour myself a tankard of vodka. Outside it's gray and overcast.

Lukas puffs out his chest.

"Today is an exciting day, Surinka."

"Is it really?"

"I want to introduce you to two of our fellow players."

"What do you mean?"

"For our little performance."

"I don't want any fellow players. You're quite enough."

"But you're going to love them. They're waiting outside. Come with me."

Lukas motions me to follow. There's a mischievous look in his eye that I don't care for.

We leave the dwarf apartment and walk down the low steps with the carved banisters to Menshikov's empty rooms. Lukas leads me out the door to a filthy yard in the back. A rank odor envelops us. I give him a puzzled look. The little man keeps going until he reaches a ramshackle shed. He opens the half-rotten door.

"Here."

I'm staring at two huge boars. One of them is waving its disgusting tail, the other has its snout buried in a pile of garbage. Both have red eyes that ignore us with lofty indifference.

I turn to look at Lukas. At the same moment he bends down to the biggest of the boars and kisses it right on the snout. Then he looks up at me, as if hoping that I'll love him, admire him, and laugh at his foolishness.

I give him a smile that is almost affectionate and go back inside where it's warm.

28.

CATHERINE'S MANSION IS BATHED IN SPRINGTIME sunlight. The mud is gone from the roads, the puddles of water have dried up. The first flowers cautiously peek out and then close up again. The world is cruel, they say. Is there anyone who can explain to us what we're doing here in the cold?

Only women have been invited to Catherine's festivities.

They have painted their teeth black in the old Russian fashion. Many of them have freshened up their faces using beets. When the tsar is abroad, a childish mood of insubordination spreads over the tsarina's parties. It's as if the women are thinking: We are Russians first and foremost; after that we're subjects of the tsar.

Lukas and I are serving in one of the elegant drawing rooms. We crawl up onto the chairs like silk-clad monkeys. We pour wine into the goblets from our little pitchers. We are kissed and pawed by the Russian ladies. The worst part is when they tickle us under the arms so we drop the pitchers on the floor. But the only thing we're allowed to say is: "Thank you, my lady" or "You must forgive me, my lady."

"Who is that new dwarf who speaks so strangely?" asks a woman with gray hair. She's swatting holes in the air with a fan decorated with scenes from the Bible.

"That's Surinka. A present from King Frederik of Denmark. Frightful, don't you agree?"

"It's a female, isn't it?"

The woman peers at me, her eyebrow raised.

Catherine laughs and pats me on the head. She is always smiling. I follow her with my eyes as she continues making her way among the guests. Once again it occurs to me how unattractive the tsarina looks when she walks. But her laughter is infectious. The guests are fond of Catherine. They don't act in an affected manner, like they do when the tsar is present.

I crawl up onto yet another chair arm to pour some more vodka. At that moment Lukas comes over to me. He's wearing a brilliantly colored costume with a vest and a fool's hat. His eyebrows are black and he smells of Hungarian cologne.

"Come with me," he says with a nod.

I put down the pitcher and follow Lukas out to the servants' corridor. I'm sweating and I feel ill. We keep going along the narrow passageway with the gray walls. Then Lukas opens a door to a dimly lit room. My eyes try hard to adjust to the lack of light, and finally I catch sight of a woman. She's sitting with her feet propped up on a table, holding a wooden flute between her toes. Just as I'm about to say something she puts the flute to her lips and starts to play. Only now do I see that she has no arms.

Behind her stands a blackamoor, leaning against a pair of stilts. He's wearing a golden headdress, and he has a little spear stuck through his nose.

Lukas takes my hand and squeezes it.

I close my eyes and smile bravely.

At the same instant the woman stops playing. She removes the flute with her foot and gives me a plaintive look. As if it's my fault that she's suffering, as if I were the one who had created the world in six days and have now decided to rest without even a trace of regret.

LUKAS AND I sit astride the pink boars, entering the hall with the distinguished guests, the whipped-cream desserts, and the icons. I see the table laden with food and the straw that has been strewn all over the floor. Lukas lashes his boar with a golden whip as he sings a bawdy song. I'm trying to keep from sliding off the boar's back. The animal stops to look around, and I slowly slip down to the floor, which is crawling with vermin. The boar grunts; its jaws are open. And when I try to climb back on to its back, the boar kicks at me, as if I were an annoying insect. I tumble into the straw and land in front of a countess, who shrieks in terror. I feel dizzy. The glittering chandeliers are glowing like planets. Behind me Lukas is bellowing. He's sitting astride his boar like a little king, while Catherine's guests laugh themselves silly. Some collapse onto the table, others have stood up, pudgy and pleased. I get to my feet and welcome everyone, speaking in Russian. But no one is listening to me. Everyone's eyes are on Lukas—Lukas with the beaming face, the red and yellow jester's hat, the voice that goes right through bone and marrow. Now he's saying something to Catherine. It sounds like a declaration or a bombastic poem. The guests laugh, and Lukas starts to sing. I don't understand a word, but I can tell that the song is bawdy and frivolous, that it moves below the belt and stays there. I'm still standing in the same spot in the straw, with my hands on my hips like an affronted female. Sweat is running down my fore-head. I fix my eyes on the boar. It trots over to the table and swipes a piece of head cheese. A servant takes a swat at it and then throws soggy cakes after the animal. Lukas isn't paying attention to anything. He's sitting on his boar, striking it with a golden whip and bellowing obscenities to the fine folk. His tiny eyes are lively and insolent. Suddenly the boar bucks and tosses him off. Lukas is flung into the straw. His eyes open wide in fear; he lands awkwardly and looks up like an endearing infant. His mouth is full of straw and vermin. I catch sight of a footman standing in the doorway. He's laughing so hard that tears are rolling down his cheeks. I glare at the kitchen maids who are peeking in at all the commotion. Lukas stands up, brushes off his back and hair, and gives the boar a reproachful look.

"What do you think you're doing, boar?"

The animal glares back at him with red eyes. For a moment
it looks as if the boar regrets what it did—then by God if it
doesn't launch itself at Lukas. Desperately, he flees around the
long table, fear painted on his face. The boar follows, grunting
through its flaring snout. Lukas jumps onto the lap of a princess
as he screams in terror and begs for mercy. At that instant the
boar comes to a halt next to a serving table, as if it has seen something in the hall that no one else can see: his Pig God. The Ten
Pig Commandments inscribed on pink tablets. Then it closes its
eyes and shits into the straw. Catherine is laughing hysterically.
Her face has dissolved from all the Rhine wine. She pounds her
fists on the table. Behind me I hear the sound of necklaces
hammering against the tabletops, and bottles of French liqueurs
sloshing over. Slowly I turn my head, oh so slowly. From where
I'm standing in the straw my gaze moves to the opposite end of
the hall, away from the cruel laughter, away from the shitting
pig with the rapt look in its eyes. And then I see him. He's about
six years old, a little boy with blond hair, green eyes, and a nose
pressed flat. The boy looks as if he has a harelip. Our eyes meet
for a brief moment, then he waves and vanishes into the wall, as
if he doesn't want to be seen. I try to go after him, but I can't
move. I stand there at a loss, while Lukas beats his boar with his
fool's hat, while Lukas dances around in the straw, as graceful
as an elf child. Lukas has never had it better. He's basking in the
admiration of a fresh audience of ladies. Lukas is the tsar's
favorite; it's only to be expected, at least for a while longer. And
then I peer inside the wall for my boy, but once again he has
vanished. He has disappeared. He's gone.

29.

LUKAS HAS BROKEN HIS ANKLE. WE DON'T DISCOVER IT
until we get back to the dwarf apartment. His ankle turns blue
and swells up beyond recognition. Lukas can't put any weight on
his leg. He is forced to lie in bed, watched over by Saint Nicholas
and various other saints who tend to broken bones.

"Do you know how it happened?" I ask.

"I never notice anything while I'm performing," he says, smiling bravely. "Didn't you think I was good?"

I take away the soup bowl without answering him. Then I shake out the comforter and carry the tray out to the kitchen. To my surprise I actually enjoy waiting on him. It reminds me of my days on Vintapperstræde—of those pleasant hours spent with the Scoundrel, back when he was healthy and boisterous.

Over the next few days I continue to nurse Lukas. I cook soup and bake pies made of fox meat. I sweep the courtyard and take care of the wash. I'm a good little dwarf woman: servile, industrious, and helpful. In the morning I go to the market to buy herbs. I mix up a concoction of aloe and angelica to give Lukas strength; I add some henbane and a teaspoonful of cumin. One evening I massage his leg under the flame of Saint Nicholas. I rub on salves, and slowly his ankle starts to mend. Once again the herbs have done their work.

A couple of days later Lukas is hobbling around on crutches.

He's like a child learning to walk. The color comes back to his cheeks. He hobbles down to the Neva River, enjoying the trilling of the birds in the larch trees. The more his ankle heals, the more he starts ordering me around. Something metallic has slipped into his voice; demands and expectations sprout out of his mouth like thorns. Then suddenly he changes course and is struck by the sweetest self-pity.

"No one loves Lukas," he tells me. "Absolutely no one." He gives me a gloomy look. "What about you, Surinka? Don't you feel lonely once in a while?"

I shake my head. "Never."

"Why not?"

"I don't know. Maybe because we dwarves don't crave company in the same way that human beings do."

"I wish you'd stop using that word, Surinka. I am not a dwarf."

"Then what are you?"

"I'm a *midget*."

"The balls of goodfolk still hang in your face whenever you step outside the door. So call yourself whatever you please."

"Stop being so vulgar. I don't like it when you're vulgar."

"Then find yourself a lovely *midget* who feels like humoring you."

I slam down the tray with the soup onto Lukas's lap. The little man gives me a startled look and meticulously wipes off the spots from the blanket. He tastes the soup, wrinkling his nose. A fair amount of time passes, with Lukas's slurping noises the only sound in the room. Then he pushes the soup bowl away and studies me pensively.

"You're a strong woman, Surinka."

"You're damn right I am."

"And to be honest, you actually scare me a bit."

"There's good reason for that."

"But you're not as tough as you make yourself out to be. You know that, don't you?"

I give Lukas a warm smile. He fixes his gaze on me as I move around the apartment. It's clear that he enjoys being bed-ridden—as all men do.

Then he clears his throat.

"May I ask you a question, Surinka?"

I nod.

"Is there anyone in *Dania* that you're still fond of?"

"No, no one."

"Are you sure?"

"Yes," I say with a laugh.

He tilts his head.

"And is there anyone you're fond of here in Russia?"

"Stop fishing for compliments, dear Lukas."

"Why?"

"Because compliments aren't worth a damn."

"They can make people happy."

Lukas mischievously reaches for my hand. I pull it away,

but before I even know what I'm doing, I give him a kiss on the forehead. We stare at each other. Then I turn around and slip out the door. Behind me Lukas is applauding as if he'd brought down a wild animal.

I walk down the narrow stairway, but my legs are shaking.

When I reach the street, I have a horrifying feeling that I've done something stupid, that something terrible awaits me, that there is something in my life over which I have no control.

AS TIME PASSES, Lukas grows more and more unbearable. He orders me around the dwarf apartment while he continues to boast that he's not a dwarf. Lukas once had his limbs measured by a Dutch scientist. Aside from the back of his head, his measurements are perfect. His legs are as long as legs ought to be when attached to such a small torso. And as if that weren't enough, one of the tsar's scholars once told Lukas that all dwarves should have proportions like his.

One morning I get tired of listening to his drivel, and I throw an earthenware pot at Saint Nicholas. If Lukas is the tsar's favorite dwarf, then the tsar's servants ought to be taking care of him. I have better things to do.

Lukas is filled with regret, as men often are. One day he comes in dressed in his finest attire and wearing an idiotic wig. He has dabbed on perfume, and he acts as charming as can be.

"I just want to thank you for your help, Surinka. You've been splendid to me, splendid!"

He hands me a bunch of dates. I give him a gracious nod.

"Yes, I would even go so far as to say that you're the best little wife a man could have." Lukas smiles. "Wouldn't you consider becoming my sweet little spouse?"

"Who in the world would want to be such a thing?" I ask in astonishment.

Lukas's voice becomes cloying.

"I realize that you're a foreigner, Surinka, but here in Russia a woman obeys her husband without question. We have an old adage that goes like this: a wife's light should never go out at night, and her hand should rest on the loom from early in the morning until late in the evening."

"Then you'd better find yourself someone else for your loom."

Lukas gives me a mischievous look. "But we Russians also say that a good wife is more precious than jewels."

He lets his hand slide over my backside. I give him a resounding slap.

Lukas drops a handful of dates on the floor. I turn around and head for the door. Just as I'm about to curse him up and down, I notice that he's standing there surrounded by twenty-two dates. They're scattered on the floor. They look like deer droppings.

An endearing smile flits across Lukas's face. Why can't I hate him? I would dearly love to hate him.

30.

THE SUMMER IS HOT AND HUMID. THE AIR STANDS STILL, burning like ash against the skin. Everyone seeks out the shade or goes swimming in the swamps of Petersburg. There are mosquitoes everywhere—mosquitoes in search of aging skin, mosquitoes sucking the blood from naked ankles. Summertime is hell. It settles like a damp quilt over the city, creeping into the armpits and out between the toes. Summertime is fiendish. It makes the Russians lecherous and physically indolent.

One hot afternoon I see Prince Menshikov through the window of the dwarf apartment. The tsar's right-hand man steps out of his golden carriage. He pauses at the fountain and lets the spray cool his face. Menshikov is fat and pear-shaped, but even from a distance it's possible to see that he was once handsome. He has teardrop-shaped eyes and delicate cheekbones that are like a shadow beneath his skin. Now his eyes are yellowish, his lips moist, as if they can't get enough of things.

Our house is Menshikov's love cottage. We heard the

sounds coming up through the floor. At first I think it's a woman laughing, but then I hear the lash of a whip followed by whimpering. With my dwarf vision I see a woman tied to a wooden timber. She is nude, and the gashes on her back are as long as the tributaries of a river.

"*Daaaaaaaaa*," she moans.

Menshikov is standing near her, stripped to the waist. He's sweating hard, but there is something routine about his lechery—as if to say today is Wednesday, so today we whip women.

Lukas and I have been strictly forbidden to go downstairs whenever the prince is in the house. We're imprisoned in the dwarf apartment while the women moan and the birch rod sings. Afterwards Menshikov comes upstairs to be with his *midgets*. He can't stand upright in our apartment, but he sits down in a chair that is much too small for him. The prince's fingers are heavy with rings, and he takes me on his lap like some sort of nice old uncle.

"Where are you from, little Surinka?"

His breath is surprisingly pleasant.

"I'm from Denmark, my lord."

"From Denmark? How did you come to Petersburg?"

"His Majesty King Frederik gave me to the tsar as a gift."

"I know your king. He's the most miserly monarch in all of Europe. He sits so heavily on his royal treasury that his rear end has been pressed flat."

Menshikov bellows with laughter and tosses five biscuits into his mouth. Then he continues to insult King Frederik, saying that the Danes are incompetent in the conduct of war. Saxony and Prussia aren't much better. Only the Russians are capable, especially Menshikov himself, and he has won many battles for Peter.

"But soon the tsar will return to his own country, and then we'll hold a great banquet, and you'll entertain us with your clowning."

Menshikov puts me down and picks up Lukas. He takes the wig off the dwarf's head and throws it into a corner.

"Would you like a treat?"

Lukas nods with enthusiasm. Menshikov tosses a hard candy onto the floor. Lukas runs after it like some sort of eager lap dog, and comes back with the candy in his mouth. He looks ridiculous, completely ridiculous.

When Menshikov is about to leave, he pats me on the head. I have an urge to bite his hand, but I don't. Down in the drive waits a golden coach with six steaming horses. Unlike Peter, Menshikov is fond of luxury. It's said that he has mansions all over Russia, and that he has just as many enemies as the tsar.

We stand at the window and watch the golden coach disappear.

Two dwarves, waving.

Two ass-kissers waving to their patron.

LUKAS TURNS TO me with flushed cheeks.

"So, what do you think of the prince, Surinka?" He looks at me expectantly.

"I didn't care for him," I say.

"Why not?"

"I didn't care for what he said about my king."

Lukas frowns, looking offended. "If the prince says something, then it has to be true."

"Why do you think that?"

"Because the prince is a great man. He used to be the tsar's stable boy, but Peter promoted him, and today he's a general and the tsar's foremost advisor."

"I thought you didn't like it when scum rises to the top."

"When it comes to his colleagues, Peter Alexeyevich never pays any attention to titles or family lineage. He's only interested in people who have a thorough understanding of their art."

"And what exactly is Menshikov's 'art,' if you don't mind my asking?"

"He's said to be a clever negotiator."

"And that's why you like him?"

"I like all human beings."

"Only lunatics in the madhouse like all human beings. That's why they've been locked up."

Lukas grimaces with annoyance. "You should show more respect, Surinka. If you keep talking that way, you're going to shrink a head shorter."

The little man goes over to the *prie-dieu* and the all-knowing Saint Nicholas. As Lukas falls to his knees, I wonder whether he's praying for my soul or whether I'm just as lost as all the other foreigners who have been swallowed up by primitive Russia.

I study Lukas with a growing feeling of tenderness.

Where does he think his prayers actually go? And who is listening to them? Maybe it's not the one that he thinks. Maybe it's never the one that you think. There are so many different gods, and they all seem to be hard of hearing.

Suddenly I have an urge to give Lukas a shove, or to haul him out of his sanctimoniousness, but I don't. Lukas should be allowed to act holy. He should be allowed to pray into the void, which is nothing more than an echoing vale. I think he's adorable all the same, with his head that's so big in back, and those small hands that are attempting to reach Saint Nicholas.

For a brief moment I consider making him declare his faith to me—to tell me about his Russian Savior and about the fervor that streams forth from his body.

I pour myself a tankard of vodka and feel myself filling with an ethereal warmth—a warmth that doesn't come from prayer.

It's good to be alive. Sometimes it's suddenly good to be alive.

31.

MENSHIKOV'S OFFICIAL MANSION IS THE MOST BEAUTIful building in all of Petersburg. It's huge, the color of egg yolk, and it's right next to the Neva River. One wing is covered with scaffolding, but the grand ballroom is in use. A fresco depicting the tsar adorns the hall. Chinese silks cover the walls, and there is an impressive banquet table. The floor is littered with a thick layer of straw, as is usually the case whenever there are festivities.

The most distinguished of the guests arrive in boats that pull up to the dock. Dukes, counts, and envoys from the foreign delegations stream into the mansion. Most of them have plumes in their hats. They wear diamond-studded stars, gold chains, and sashes full of medals that wrap around their sleeves and collars.

As usual, Lukas and I are serving. We crawl up onto the chair arms, scurry around between the legs of the dignitaries, and charm those who cannot be charmed.

But I have a hard time hiding my disappointment. The tsar has not returned. He won't arrive for a few more weeks. According to rumor, Peter has gone somewhere for his health, and he's dejected about his son's treachery. But now he has convinced the tsarevich to come home.

During the banquet, Lukas and I entertain everyone with a boar-free performance. We sing, we parody Menshikov and others among the fine guests. It's Lukas again who draws all the applause; I am completely superfluous.

When we get back to the servants' room, Lukas throws off his jester's hat. He gives me a fervent embrace and then vainly runs a hand through his hair.

"I love working with you, Surinka. We're a beautiful couple, don't you think?"

I would like to say something kind, but I can't. Lukas embraces me again, but it's too hot for caresses. Besides, I don't copulate with dwarves. I find the thought disgusting.

The door opens. A man dressed in a robe of German velvet gives me a searching look. Even though he's wearing a powdered wig, he looks like an errand boy.

"Are you Sørine Bentsdatter?"

To my surprise the man speaks Danish.

"Yes, I am."

"His Royal Majesty's *envoyé extraordinaire* wishes to speak with you at once."

Lukas gives me a puzzled look. I nod nervously and accompany the man back to the banquet hall. Several footmen are lugging in barrels of vodka. There is salted meat on the platters, head cheese, garlic sausages, and bliny, which are Russian pancakes.

The secretary leads me through the crowd, which is smoldering with fornication. Menshikov has two whores sitting on his lap. Many of the fine folk are dancing. Two hunting dogs are fighting over some chicken guts. I find myself in the depths of sin, but I'm no longer fond of sin.

We approach the banquet table, adorned with peacock feathers and elaborate culinary displays fashioned from plaster.

"*Envoyé extraordinaire*, this is Sørine Bentsdatter, the tsar's Danish dwarf."

I'm standing in front of a man with blue eyes and a wizened face. He has an open and honest appearance. He scratches his cheek and studies me for a long time.

"You are uncommonly ugly."

"Thank you, my lord."

"I have just arrived from Denmark. I bring you greetings from His Majesty's *notarius publicus*, Rasmus Æreboe. He has been thinking of your welfare."

My face lights up with a warm smile.

"Thank you," I say.

"He has written you a letter."

The envoy nods to his secretary, who takes out a letter and thrusts it into my hand. I want to open the letter, but I know that it would be rude to do so.

The Danish envoy looks around.

"What a barbaric place this is, this Russia. The food is heavily spiced and inedible. The wine corrodes the intestines, the people are baffling and conniving. Have you become accustomed to the conditions here?"

"More or less."

"And you don't miss your native country or your king?"

"At times I do," I say, feeling an urge to burst into tears.

"For some reason you have made an impression on His Majesty's *notarius publicus*."

"Thank you."

"Don't thank me, you little mite. I'm not the one who is being overindulgent." He laughs in a kind way and looks at me with lively eyes. "I've never met a dwarf before. Would you like to sit on my knee?"

I shake my head and think about Rasmus Æreboe. I had almost forgotten the *notarius*. Maybe he was too kind to me to have made an impression.

A tall chamberlain approaches the table. He's wearing a golden caftan. In his hand he holds a silver goblet of Hungarian wine. The servant has a round head with short brown hair and a birthmark on his cheek. His eyes are black and alert. Those are not the sort of eyes you expect to see in a servant.

"Here you are," he says kindly as he places the goblet in front of the Danish envoy.

The Dane shakes his head.

"A drink for you, my lord," says the servant.

"I don't care for any."

"Here."

The servant lifts the goblet to the envoy's lips. The Dane looks in surprise at the impudent man and shakes his head, this time more vigorously.

A strange silence has settled over the table. Spellbound, I stare at the tall servant. The envoy is bewildered. It's clear that he has no idea what to do.

At that instant I hear laughter from someone at the table. The laughter catches on. The Russians sitting closest laugh loud and hard. Now the tall servant grabs hold of the Dane and forces the goblet to his lips. The envoy struggles to resist as best he can, but the servant has a good grip on his head, and he forces the wine down the man's throat. The envoy is sweating, and his face gets greener with every swallow. He tries to spit out the wine as he flails his arms around. The next moment he vomits. The servant smiles, unperturbed, and keeps on pouring the contents of the goblet down the Dane's throat. The expression on the servant's face is as loving as a father admiring his child's first steps. The envoy's body goes limp. When the servant lets him go, he collapses and slides down onto the straw that's littered with food scraps, crumbs, and all sorts of excrement.

Peter Alexeyevich turns around and smiles at me from inside his servant's costume.

"Surinka."

"Wel... welcome back, Your Majesty the Tsar."

I bow. Behind him I see that the servants have begun to force all the guests to drink.

Peter Alexeyevich holds a goblet to my lips.

I know it will do no good to refuse. I taste the strong liquor. The last thing I notice is that the walls of the room are getting closer, that the tsar is leaning over his dwarf while laughter rolls around the banquet table, hovering over the silver platters and the Chinese silks.

WE'RE FORCED TO drink twenty-five punishment toasts. No one knows why, but it's a Russian tradition that no one is allowed to be sober when the tsar is present. Peter Alexeyevich wants to know what's going on in the minds of the foreigners, what alliances and agreements are brewing. No one can have any secrets from the Highborn Monarch, especially during these times.

The Danish envoy and I are lying on the floor, trying to gather our wits. At one point I try to make myself throw up, but I have no more inside of me. I'm feverish, my head is pounding, I've been scattered to all the winds. And then I'm out driving. A cool breeze strikes my face. I try to say something, but no one hears me. I'm inside a chest. The frost blasts through my lungs. A chandelier made of silver spreads out its arms like an octopus. They come in with censers and their barber's itch; the saints climb down from the church tower with vodka-eyes, bowing deeply, unctuously… The tsar is holding me affectionately, giving me little kisses on the lips and hair. There is an altar in front of me; someone has wrapped me in the singing of a choir. I know that I'm about to croak; it's just a matter of time. The pupils of my eyes melt, the metropolitan floats on a cloud of incense. It's all chiming bells and scarlet canopies dancing above my head…

The tsar offers me solicitous support. We're drinking companions now. He loves me above everything else on earth. "Surinka," he whispers. "*Moya lyubimaya karlitsa, moya prekrasnaya datskaya karlitsa…*"

I sob pitifully. I miss my father. When he was dying, he lay in bed at home in the parsonage, stretched out with Jesus overhead. I nursed him just as I later nursed the Scoundrel. I followed the illness with my dwarf vision. I saw how it ate away at his stomach, how he slipped into the darkness, or rather how the darkness slipped into him. I hated how my father slipped through my fingers—how everyone slips through our fingers— because God is a devil who wishes for death, sickness, and extinction. I don't understand Him. I refuse to understand Him. I just want to die.

32.

IT TAKES TEN DAYS FOR ME TO RECOVER.

Ten days of alcohol poisoning that nearly kills me.

This time it's Lukas's turn to nurse me—by spoonfeeding me, by administering herbs, and by applying wet cloths to my forehead. He sits next to my bed, tenaciously keeping vigil. He holds my hand. He's sweet. I have to admit that he's sweet.

I have no use for anyone who is sweet.

AUTUMN HAS ARRIVED. I tell Lukas that I'm worthless, that I'm hot-tempered and bitter. I have no heart, and I don't share his outlook on life. If I'd been given a different body, things would have been different. But that was not to be. I'm a bundle of wickedness, and that's how I will live out my life—with clenched jaws and blood that boils with hemlock. It's too late to save me. There is nothing to save.

Lukas bends over me, no doubt to stick his finger in my eye.

He kisses me. It's a long, tender kiss. Lukas tastes of head cheese. I can't stand head cheese. I'm just about to tell him as much when he kisses me again.

I study the dwarf, push back a lock of hair from his brow. Outside the night is black.

Lukas smiles. I let my hand slip under his shirt, over his hairless potbelly, up toward his chest. Lukas is frightened. He has beads of sweat at his temples; his small body is tense.

"Surinka…"

I shush him, open his pants, taste his world. We fornicate beautifully, silently. I sit on top of Lukas so I can study him, as if he were a human being. Lukas is naked. His small trousers lie crumpled on the bed. His shoes sit next to the tile stove, his socks look like rags under the window.

I am dressed, as dressed as anyone can be.

Later we fall asleep in each other's arms. We drink anise-flavored vodka and bite into garlic cloves the size of fists. Lukas tells me about the tsar, about how he used to put out fires in Moscow. Peter's servants had been given orders to find him whenever there was a fire. Peter Alexeyevich was bravery personified. He would go into the city and climb up on rooftops; from there he would direct the firemen. He rescued commoners from timbered houses and got burns on his arms and chest, but he spared no effort to help the citizens of his realm. He often let the homeless sleep in his *dacha* in the woods, or forced the rich boyars to open their mansions to the fire victims.

"Peter Alexeyevich will do anything for those he loves, Surinka. No one has a bigger heart than our Peter Alexeyevich…"

We fornicate again. I'm on top, riding Lukas, enjoying the view. He has no wrinkles on his face. Lukas is perfect, almost perfect.

I lean down and kiss him. Lukas's cock gets harder. I stroke his chest with loving dwarf hands, let myself go, disappear. The world wraps itself around me like velvet, a finger trickles down my spine. I open my eyes and look down at my lover. The black strands change; his hair grows lighter. His muscles are like ropes beneath his skin. The feminine dwarf face slowly vanishes, the beard stubble explodes, the nostrils widen. It's chillier in the room but I begin to sweat. Strong arms reach out from the dark…two blue eyes open cruelly. My eyes slide downward: the blood is pooling like a lake in his navel, a scar gleams on his hip. It's the Scoundrel. I recognize his smell; I recognize his mouth that's like a gash in the lower part of his face. "Where is my son?" he screams. "I want my son." I try to get up, but the Scoundrel puts his hands around my neck. I cough. My eyes congeal in their sockets. My pupils glaze over, the room vanishes before my eyes…first the bed, then the stove, the walls.

Beneath me someone is sobbing. Fists are pounding against my face. I weep and draw the air deep into my lungs. I don't dare look down. I don't dare look at the body underneath me. It disappears into the dark. I close my eyes for a long time, much too long a time.

33.

IT TAKES DAYS BEFORE I EMERGE FROM MY TORPOR. The snow is deep outside the windows, the sleighs are sailing through the street on silent runners. It's ice-cold in the dwarf apartment. Even the water basin is covered with ice.

Outside in the city the sun rises above thick columns of smoke. The trees are bowed with rime, the soldiers' halberds glitter in the winter sun. Peasants smeared with soot walk past, their fur coats turned inside out. A prophet collapses, frothing at the mouth and cursing the passers-by.

I try to remember the past few days, but I'm not myself. My strength has vanished. I feel hollow and empty.

One evening I find Æreboe's letter that was given to me by the Danish envoy.

I had completely forgotten its existence, just as I've forgotten everything else about Menshikov's banquet. There is frost on the envelope. The handwriting is angular. I open the letter with gratitude.

> *Dearest Sørine Bentsdatter,*
>
> *I hope that this letter will reach you at your residence in the tsar's Russia. I have given a good deal of thought to your health and well-being in that foreign land. It can be difficult to find your place in a society that is so utterly different from our own, but I am convinced that you will serve your king well by spreading the Lord's joy in the tsar's capital of Petersburg.*
>
> *When I found myself out there in Russia as a young man, I was naïve and inexperienced. I was teased because I smelled too much of schools and textbooks. So you must not despair if the same thing happens to you. Our Lord has filled you with purpose. He has given you a task, so that you, with God's help, will survive. Yet it is particularly important to avoid the immoderate boozing of the court. I often felt myself lost among the Russian barbarians, and there were times when my blood was so agitated that it refused to calm down. So, Sørine, beware of drunkenness or it will cost you your health.*
>
> *Here in the city of Copenhagen there is not a great deal to report. His Majesty Frederik IV has decided that the kingdom cannot afford another attack on the Swedes. The common citizens have drawn a sigh of relief, but the noblemen are dis-appointed. Many fear that Scania will never be Danish again. Perhaps that is all for the good, since it would mean more*

*mouths for the Crown to feed. And besides, the Scanian land
is said to be exhausted after so many wars. The Swedish occupation may mean that the Scanians would not be interested
in becoming Danish again, no matter how strange that may
sound.*

*In my own world, the Lord has seen fit to inflict upon my
dear wife and myself a sorely burdensome cross. It happened
during the second childbirth. My wife developed pains in
her breasts and thus developed many lacunae and lay in bed
for sixteen weeks, enduring excruciating pain and suffering,
while I spent each day in lamentation, sorrow, and trepidation.
Shortly thereafter the good Lord blessed us with a stillborn
son, whose body I have myself interred in the churchyard of
Holmen Church. I thank the Blessed Trinity with all the
humility of my heart. May His name be blessed for all eternity.
May He also lead you, Sørine, toward happy hours in Russia,
which I at times miss whenever my work at the stock exchange
feels monotonous and unmanageable.*

Your friend in Denmark

Rasmus Æreboe

I STOP READING and put the letter aside. Then I read the three
last lines again: *Shortly thereafter the good Lord blessed us with
a stillborn son, whose body I have myself interred in the churchyard
of Holmen Church ...*

I stare at the words.

How could anyone write that God had *blessed* him with a
stillborn son? Does the human being also have to thank his
Creator for the misfortunes in his life? Are there no limits to the
heavenly ass-kissing?

I get up. I'm glad to hear from Rasmus Æreboe, but also
annoyed. Sometimes his faith seems like an exalted form of
stupidity—a depressing simplemindedness reserved for

blithering idiots. Or am I merely envious that someone can love God with such zeal?

I look out the little window. Everything is covered in white. Under the snow I can glimpse the contours of a well. A cat is searching for food in a larch tree. I study its hunger and the desperation in its paws. Why is it that all creatures wish to survive? Is there something that I've failed to understand?

LUKAS COMES INTO the room. He studies me in the dim light. His shoulders are stooped; the little man is apology personified. In his hand he is holding a fur hat. It reeks of coal. He twists it around, as if he doesn't like what he's about to say.

"Surinka?"

I turn around.

"Yes?"

"I want to talk to you."

I put down the letter again and wait.

"I want to talk to you about what happened."

I get up, feeling sad.

"I don't understand it," says Lukas. "But I'd like to understand."

"Understand what?"

"The way you—"

I stretch out my hand to caress Lukas's cheek, but he moves away at once. He has several red marks on his neck that I haven't noticed before.

"Maybe it was a mistake," I say.

"What was?"

"What we did."

"I don't think so," he says quietly.

I lower my eyes as I pluck at my sleeve. Lukas comes closer. He takes only one step, he doesn't dare take any more.

"Maybe you ought to see a priest," he says.

I open my eyes wide.

"…a priest who could help you."

"Help me with what?"

"I've made the acquaintance of one. He knows Latin. He's also knowledgeable about the great sciences."

"I don't *need* any help!"

Lukas looks at me and then turns on his heel. His shoulders are covered with a fine layer of snow. He straightens his fur coat and walks over to the door, as if there is no more to be said.

I sit down on the chair.

The door slams.

Saint Nicholas and I are alone.

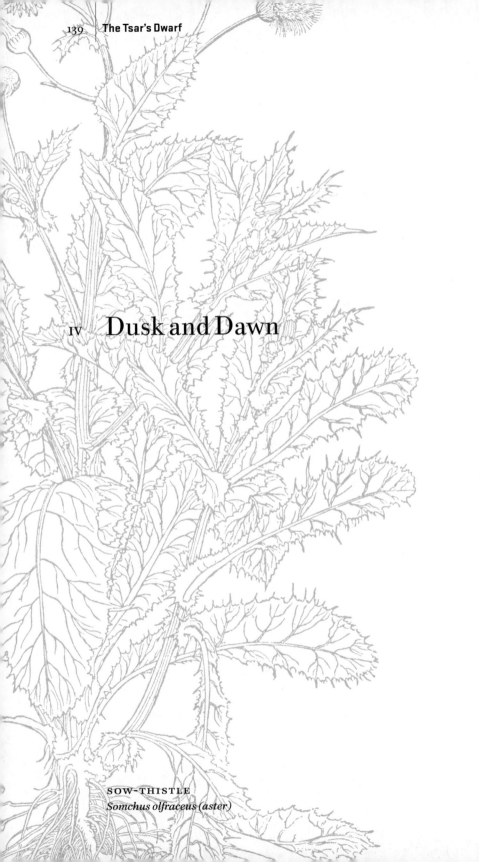

IV Dusk and Dawn

SOW-THISTLE
Somchus olfraceus (aster)

34.

IT SEEMS LIKE A LONG TIME AGO THAT I WENT TO TORVET, the marketplace square in Copenhagen, to sell my herbs. I had a wheelbarrow filled with curly mint, camphorwood, and sunflower seeds. I sold them to the townswomen and the fine folk. On rare occasions I would do a little laying on of hands, but I had to be careful with that sort of thing. Many a hag has ended up in the stocks and condemned to hard labor, accused of witchcraft.

One day I found myself pregnant. I didn't wish to have a child, but the Scoundrel was excited. He was convinced that the fetus would be a new Terje: a hard-drinking child without the features of a dwarf, a drinking companion who would be able to use his fists. I followed the miracle in my body, noting how heavy I was becoming, and how shapeless. I vomited time and again; I felt kicks inside my belly from an invisible army of one. How could we afford to feed yet another nuisance?

On a day in May when the anemones were blooming, I gave birth to my little boy. His face was wrinkled and adorable; his hair was red like a forest fire. Was he a dwarf or a human? I had no idea. Years would have to pass before I could be sure. But God had left His mark. The boy had a harelip. I stared in despair at the infant. He looked back at me, as if he were saying, "I won't be here for long. You will only have to suffer my presence for a quarter of a year."

Terje was excited. He called his son Mathias. But I refused

to give him a name. He was a soul who was not of this world. At night he was visited by spirits. "Life is too hard," they whispered to him. "Things will be better for you in the spirit world. Stay with us in the spirit world."

The Scoundrel celebrated the birth by going off on a binge for days. When he came home, he had no money. Things got so bad that I had to beg from the bag-snooping guards at Torvet. Terje was and would always be unreliable. He drowned his promises in Rostock beer. His money all went to drinking bouts at the tavern.

One day disaster struck. It was a dreary Thursday. The stink of whale oil hung in the air. "The plague is coming," we heard from our neighbor. "The plague is coming."

The dread disease spread quickly—first to the Nyboder district, where the sailors lived, then to the slums. Those who took ill had black spots that spread from their armpits across their chest and stomach. They babbled in delirium, they spied demons passing through, they developed boils. The contagion was carried in the air, on clothing, and on door handles. The city's *medicus* worked overtime, setting up hospitals for plague victims, where the goodfolk died like flies. Houses were quarantined, walls were painted with white crosses. Screams spread from the slums to the mansions on Norgesgade. The plague got greedier, paying no heed to priests or to bloodlettings. At dusk you could see the plague galloping through town on the backs of black angels. In the churchyard an evil stench hovered in the air; the coffins were covered with quicklime. Drying-rooms at the bleaching grounds were used as infirmaries, but the whole city was disintegrating. The king and his court fled to Kolding. They took along their royal wine and masquerade costumes, but they were terribly bored all the same.

Most of Vintapperstræde managed to escape. The sickness slipped under the skin of only one: my little boy. The first boils appeared in his armpit. The boy was sacrificed to the gods, and in the end there was nothing left of him. "Mathias is fine," bellowed the Scoundrel during his rare visits. "Cure him with your herbs." In despair I looked at the infant, seeing death's shadow creeping across his face. There was nothing I could concoct that would save him. I watched over the boy's death throes. I gave him herbal extracts, the bones of toads, and elixirs to combat the plague. The boy's cough grew looser, the little blue-tinged chest rose weakly. In a moment of desperation I prayed to God to save him. "He'll get over it," the Scoundrel roared drunkenly. "Mathias will be fine." I shook my head and looked at the tiny body that was clinging to life. Why wasn't it Terje or me who had taken ill? We'd already had a life, after all.

I tried to nurse my son, but he refused to drink my milk. His little eyes were blue and plaintive. Mathias grew into his name, he filled up my world even though I didn't want him to do that.

The Scoundrel wept. He lay in the straw and sobbed. Why did he always drink himself into such a state? What was so wonderful about being a rag doll with limbs that refused to obey him? "When I'm drunk I can't see the difference between light and dark," he said.

That's how Terje was.

That's how he lay in his own vomit on the straw pallet, demanding that I be the one to act.

One evening I wrapped the boy in a rag and walked through the ghost town. The stench from the corpses was unbearable. Every once in a while the infant sniffled. I did not look at him; I refused to look. On a side street I passed a night-soil man who was burning heaps of clothing and tossing fresh corpses onto a cart. The bodies were yellow with death. My son wept quietly inside the rag wrapped around him, but I did not hear him. I wandered along the border between Heaven and Hell, heading for the harbor, past hovels and sheds. "Sørine, he'll get better," shouted the Scoundrel. "Mathias will be fine."

I turned around but couldn't see Terje. Had he followed me? Was he inside of me? Darkness fell, the stars glittered in the

sky. They were neither happy nor sad—they simply were. When
I reached the wharf, I stopped. There was no one in sight for
miles around. I shut my eyes and let go. My boy dropped into
nothingness. I heard a loud splash. The rag remained floating on
the surface. As I stood there, I considered taking the same route
as the boy, but I lacked the courage. I had only the Scoundrel—
the Scoundrel and his sobbing, his freckled arms around my
stomach, his caresses, his curse.

His curse.

35.

ISMAILOV PAYS ME A VISIT AT THE DWARF APARTMENT.
It has been a long time since I last saw him. We drink tea
sitting next to the cast-iron stove, and we talk about one thing
after another. Ismailov tells me that Alexey, the tsar's son, is back
in Petersburg. Peter has forgiven him his treachery, but the tsarevich has had to renounce all claims to the throne.

"But make no mistake," Ismailov whispers. "Peter Alexeyevich is furious."

"Why?"

"I'll tell you another time."

Lukas is standing in the background, listening. He has an
odd expression on his face, an expression that I can't interpret.
Now he comes over and sits down. Ismailov has to hunch over to
drink his tea so as not to bump his head on the ceiling. He has a
linen scarf around his neck. He has big bags under his eyes.

"Are the two of you going to perform for the tsar soon?" he
asks.

Lukas shrugs. "When Peter Alexeyevich has use for his
clowns, he will summon us. We are his faithful servants."

"Surinka told me that you had great success when you…"

Lukas nods curtly, looking annoyed. His little face is
seething with surliness.

We finish our tea, but as Ismailov and I are about to leave,

Lukas takes me aside. He places an urgent hand on my shoulder and lowers his voice.

"Watch out, Surinka."

"Watch out for what?"

"For Ismailov."

"What do you mean?"

Lukas turns around and goes into the bedroom. I watch him go. His shoulders are slumped, and he looks offended.

Ismailov has crawled out of the dwarf apartment. I follow him down the stairs to Menshikov's love nest. It's a beautiful day. The sun is glinting on the snow. Several Cossacks wearing sheepskin coats ride past on the street.

"A few days ago the city gates were closed," Ismailov tells me. "And scores of people were arrested. The tsar wants to know who's behind the plot against his throne."

"What plot?"

"Peter Alexeyevich thinks that Alexey was the leader of a conspiracy to overthrow him."

"But he wasn't?"

"There are many things that go on inside the tsar's head that no one understands. I'm afraid that we're heading for bloody times."

I look at my friend. Ismailov is paler than usual. The abscess in his tooth has gone, and his cheeks have caved in.

We head for the tsar's winter palace as people point at us. Ismailov lifts me up and carries me over the snowdrifts. The closer we get to the palace, the more people fill the street. A moment later we understand why. The tsar and Alexey appear on the backs of light-gray horses. They have only three men accompanying them. Peter is tall and erect, as always. He stares straight ahead, looking fierce though he fixes his eyes on no one. Alexey is pale and stooped, at least a head shorter than his father. The tsarevich's gaze slides over the crowds and then settles on the snow. A moment later they disappear through the modest gate of the small winter palace.

With my dwarf vision I follow them into their chambers.

There are Dutch tiles on the walls and thick carpets from the Ottoman Empire. The tsar wears a reserved expression. Alexey's face is delicate. He's a handsome man, but without his father's radiance. His face is slightly bloated, as if he's had too much to drink.

The tsar and the tsarevich sit down in the room and smoke clay pipes. A servant bustles about as they settle into their hatred of each other. "I ask your forgiveness," says Alexey. "I am not worthy to be your son." The tsar questions him intently about the time he has spent in exile. What was he doing in Austria? Why did he flee to Naples? There must have been someone in Russia who gave him information that helped him to leave the country.

Alexey is submissive, but not submissive enough. He looks his father in the eye longer than he should. He apologizes for his offenses without seeming particularly apologetic. And even though Alexey is afraid, a nervous smile plays over his lips, as if he would like to say: "I'm scared but not that scared. I know what upsets you, Father. I can play you like a violin."

ISMAILOV AND I continue toward the mansion, through the snowdrifts, past the vendors' stalls and the workshops. We go inside a lovely church. A thick cloud of incense hovers over the room; the icons glitter in the somnolent light. As usual, I can't see anything at all, but when Ismailov picks me up I catch sight of the priests in their vestments. They're sitting along the wall, silent and menacing. A metropolitan is standing beneath a purple canopy, swinging a gold cross.

I look at the churchgoers. The Russians pray with greater intensity and more rapture than the Danes. Many of them kiss the metal crosses they wear around their necks. Others have dropped to their knees. Ismailov has closed his eyes. Tears are running down his face. Russians weep often. They are a people of melancholic temperament.

Ismailov explains to me the various church ceremonies, and I enjoy the whole thing, the way I might enjoy an opera: the singing, the deep voices that work their way up from the diaphragms of the metropolitans. I let my gaze slide over the silver chandeliers, the thick incense, and the tawdry saints.

The metropolitan carries the large gold cross over to an old man, who kisses it fervently. When the metropolitan starts to move away, the old man holds on tight to the cross.

"What's happening over there?" I whisper.

Ismailov doesn't answer. He's listening to the hymn, letting the music wash over him.

I close my eyes for longer than I would have wished. The deep voices slide through me. Something has burst. I remember a warm light that used to stream through me, a warmth from the dawn of time. For a brief moment I sense that I'm living in twilight, that I'm a soul of the dusk or the dawn. A sense of joy bubbles up inside me—a joy that I've never known before in my life.

We leave the church. When an elderly woman stumbles over me, Ismailov picks me up. His eyes are still filled with tears. I have an urge to tell him how grateful I am for his friendship, but Ismailov doesn't care for compliments. Like most Russians, he's more comfortable with the sting of the birch rod.

When I get back to the dwarf apartment, I take out Æreboe's letter again. I light a little candle and start reading:

Dearest Sørine Bentsdatter,

I hope that this letter will reach you at your residence in the tsar's Russia. I have given a good deal of thought to your health and well-being in that foreign land. It can be difficult to find your place in a society that is so utterly different from our own ... When I found myself out there in Russia as a young man, I was naïve and inexperienced. I was teased because I smelled too much of schools and textbooks. So you must not despair if the same thing happens to you. Our Lord has filled you with purpose. He has given you a task, so that you, with

God's help, will survive ... May He also lead you, Sørine,
toward happy hours ...

I put down the letter and stare into space.
The letter is filled with tenderness and warmth.
Why didn't I notice that the first time I read it?

36.

THE APARTMENT IS SWARMING WITH DWARVES. THERE
are five of them with little suitcases, little canes, and little hats.
They toss their wet clothes into the corners, warm their splayed
feet in front of the cast-iron stove, and speak in shrill, castrato
voices that pierce right through the shutters and mica windows.
Lukas is happy to see them. He thrusts out his chest as he regales
them with stories. Everyone laughs, grateful to be reunited.
Lukas introduces me as Surinka, the Danish dwarf. They greet me
kindly and kiss me on the lips. After that they buzz around like
horseflies, taking care of various tasks. They make the beds, bake
bread, and open their carpetbags that are filled with dried fish.
Several of the dwarves are deformed, with swollen bellies and ugly
hunchbacks. They speak in different dialects, describing their
experiences in distant cities and at a place they call the Dwarf
Museum. Then they hug each other and start swilling vodka as if
competing for the big gold medal. Their names are Igor, Natasha,
Petrushka, Marek, and Karina. Their names make me feel like
an outsider. I start to feel a longing for Denmark, for the dark cellar on Vintapperstræde, the good stockfish, and the sunrise over
the Øresund.

At some point Lukas comes over to stand next to me.
"His Majesty the Tsar has sent for us," he says.
"All of us?" I ask.
"Just you and me. This is a difficult time for Peter Alexeye-
vich. That's something I think you should know."
"Why?"
"Because he's still having problems with the tsarevich."

Lukas looks at me intently. "But you can always ask your friend Ismailov about that."

"What do you mean?"

"You can ask him, because he always sides with Alexey—like certain other people I could mention."

Lukas turns to Igor and starts talking to him, as if I don't exist. He tells more stories and takes little dance steps, as he enjoys the attention of the oldest of the dwarves. For a moment I'm not even sure that our conversation actually took place.

LATER LUKAS PUTS on felt boots, a shirt, and a silk vest. He has on eye makeup, and he has drenched himself with French perfume. I'm wearing my most beautiful dress with the lead-colored embroidery. The skirts have been stiffened with fishbone.

They come to get us in a simple leather sleigh, but to my surprise we're not taken to the palaces but instead to an ordinary stone house on the outskirts of the city. Outside a great crowd has assembled. One of the tsar's servants leads us through the throngs and inside the house. It smells of spoiled fish, and the walls are black with soot. Strangely enough there are no window-panes behind the heavy shutters.

The guests are crammed together like herring in a barrel.

I look around for the tsar. As usual, I can see nothing but everyone's asshole.

"What sort of place is this?" I asked Lukas.

"We're here for a funeral."

"A funeral? Why should we—"

"It would be best if you didn't ask so many questions, Surinka."

The guests turn around to stare at us. Many of them laugh. At that instant I catch sight of a woman lying on a bed with her hair spread out. In a circle around her stand six women, professional mourners who have been hired for the occasion. They are expertly wailing as they offer up their prayers to Our Lord. At first I think that it's the woman on the bed who has died, but

then I catch sight of another bed. There lies the deceased, clad
in the green uniform of a colonel. He has an annoyed expression
on his face. Four priests are saying mass over the body and
swinging their censers. The guests, weeping and moaning, bow
before the pictures of saints on the walls.

At that moment Peter Alexeyevich comes through the door.
He is dressed in black, with a brown scarf around his neck.
On his belt he wears a hunting knife. On his head he wears a cap
covered with green oilcloth.

The tsar greets several boyars. His arms are trembling, as
they always do. After a moment he goes over to the deceased
and kisses him on the lips. The rest of the guests follow suit, mur-
muring prayers and lamentations. Many of them are drunk. A
neighbor squats behind a bench against the wall.

The hired mourners howl.

An icy wind comes in the door, penetrating bone and
marrow.

Everyone gets ready for the funeral procession.

IT'S SLIPPERY ON the narrow road. The party sets off, passing
an inn where a ram's head hangs over the door. The guests crane
their necks, peering at Peter and pointing their gnarled fingers.

I'm happy to see the tsar, but he hasn't even noticed
Lukas or me. I try to press through the crowd to reach him, but
as usual I'm too small. I wonder what role we're supposed to
play. Are we meant to entertain the guests?

The snow is piled up in drifts along the road. Scores of
leather boots are creaking merrily. The funeral procession
makes a detour around a dead horse. More women who are professional mourners join the crowd.

The procession passes a lovely cloister with oil lamps.

Several beggars throw themselves at Peter's feet. The tsar
speaks kindly to one of them, his round face emanating benevo-
lence. A man in rags pushes his way forward, shoving the others
away with wild gestures. Peter Alexeyevich draws his knife and

brutally attacks the man. A moment later the beggar lies bleeding in the snow.

Word begins to circulate through the neighborhood that the tsar has come to visit.

After walking for a mile or two we reach the gravesite. The coffin is placed inside the crumbling mausoleum. The closest family members have brought along frozen meat and vodka for the deceased. An old woman spreads beautiful branches at the base of the coffin. A moment later everyone kisses the lips of the corpse for the last time.

I shiver in my fur-lined jacket. I'll never get used to the Russian customs or the terrible cold. On my way out I catch a glimpse of the priest, who slips the vodka belonging to the corpse under his coat.

OUTSIDE THE MAUSOLEUM the tsar is talking to a young woman. She is holding his gloved hand in hers. She falls to her knees and pleads with him about something. The tsar tells her to rise. Then he catches sight of me.

"Surinka."

My heart leaps with inexpressible joy.

"Your Majesty the Tsar—"

"I'm here too," Lukas interjects.

The tsar nods and pushes goodfolk aside to reach us. Then he lifts up Lukas and gives him a kiss on the lips. The tsar's eyes are black and amiable, but not the same as before.

"Let's raise a goblet to the memory of good Petrov. And you and Surinka will drink three pots of wine with me and my servants."

"As you wish, Your Majesty the Tsar."

Peter puts Lukas down. He smiles at me and runs his big hand over my hair. In the alleyway a post-rider is trying to get past the procession, but there isn't enough room.

At the next corner Peter's sleigh is waiting. It looks like a chamber on runners, with six seats, blue cushions, and beautiful sable furs. To my joy, the tsar orders us to join him in his sleigh. Someone is already sitting there in the dim light: a thickset woman wearing French attire. It takes a moment before I realize that the woman is Catherine.

Lukas and I bow obsequiously.

Peter Alexeyevich gets in and sits down. The sleigh sets off with a lurch, gliding through the snow of Petersburg. People bow. Beggars shout for bread and a dram to warm themselves. I have an urge to ask where we're headed, but I refrain.

The tsar doesn't say a word.

His expression has grown more solemn.

Catherine's gloved hand seeks Peter's. She smiles kindly, looking at ease. The tsar stares stone-faced out the little window, which is hoary with frost.

I enjoy the drive and the fine company.

Catherine smiles. Her head is rounder than I remember it. If she weren't the tsarina, I would never have remembered her gray eyes or her mousy brown hair that is visible under the fur hat.

We keep on driving.

The sounds around us vanish.

Suddenly Lukas laughs as he moves his little legs back and forth. Peter Alexeyevich glares at him. There's not a trace of humor in his eyes.

Again, silence.

I hear only the horses and the clumps of snow striking the sleigh.

We continue to glide through the white city. A few dogs bay desperately. It's not a baying to mark their territory; it's a baying for life or death.

I let one hand slide down to my lap while I wait.

A spasm passes over the left side of the tsar's face.

It appears with great violence, followed by another that closes his left eye. Peter groans and stares straight ahead with his good eye. The spasms increase. I send a terrified glance in Lukas's direction, but he seems unaffected and cheerful.

The tsar groans. The next spasm works its way down to his shoulders and left arm, like an army conquering land. A vein swells up on Peter's neck. Saliva seeps out of his mouth. The whole left side of his body is twitching and trembling.

Catherine moves calmly away. At that instant Peter gives a kick. It's a hard kick that makes the sleigh rock. The next kick is weaker, but hard enough to break off the door handle. The tsar starts making a rattling sound; it comes not from his throat but from his stomach. I try to catch Lukas's eye, but he's looking out at the snow, as if everything is normal, as if he hasn't noticed anything at all.

The tsar's cap falls off. His head bumps against the ceiling. One convulsion follows another. I have an urge to offer my help, but Catherine is staring down at her hands without reacting.

At that instant the tsar looks at me. His eyes are sharp and alert. Suddenly he smiles coldly, almost condescendingly. Slowly his shoulders drop back into place.

Peter Alexeyevich has been testing us. He just wanted to see how we would react. I smile with relief, but I don't know where I should look. I cast a glance at Lukas, but he's still stubbornly staring out the window.

At that moment the tsar's spasms return. Sweat springs from his brow, the pupils of his eyes roll up. A great twitching occurs in his shoulder and arm. He bellows loudly. It feels colder inside the sleigh, much colder.

I start to pray.

There is absolutely no doubt: I'm looking at a human being who has disappeared, who is no longer home.

CATHERINE PLACES A gloved hand on the tsar's thigh. She whispers something soothing as her hand wanders up to the back of his neck with the brown curls. The tsar makes a rattling sound; another convulsion shudders through his body. Catherine keeps on talking. There is something light and reassuring about her voice, but also something condescending—as if she is teasing him, as if the spasms have given her a role that she can exploit.

The sleigh comes to an abrupt halt, and the door with the broken handle flies open. Lukas jumps down from the seat. He pulls a flute out of his pocket and plays a tune. The music is surprisingly lovely and melancholy. Peter Alexeyevich has closed his eyes. His head is resting on Catherine's shoulder, his hair is lank and wet. Saliva is still gathered at the corner of his mouth, but the tsar is sleeping like a child. Calm and trusting.

I sit frozen to my seat, motionless.

A moment later Catherine turns toward me and winks.

37.

IT'S EVENING. THE DWARVES ARE BAKING BREAD AND making pancakes. The apartment is fragrant with cardamom and vanilla. Igor, Natasha, Karina, Petrushka, and Marek are all bustling about and hastily setting the table. I'm cooking soup and chopping onions as I try to understand what Marek says. Marek comes from Poland. His speech is incomprehensible, and he keeps wanting to touch me with his stubby fingers.

Lukas takes no part in the kitchen work.

"I'm sampling the vodka," he says as he charms Natasha, telling jokes left and right. Natasha is a beautiful midget. She has no warts, and she's as well-proportioned as a dancer. Lately she's been on loan to a prince in the Ural Mountains.

"Volkov helped the tsar to quash a rebellion, and so I was given to him as a present."

"Were you treated decently?" I ask.

"Yes, more or less."

Natasha blushes.

"Surinka is always so nosy," says Lukas, giving me a stern look.

He starts lighting the candles. The other dwarves come in carrying pots and buckets. Igor has managed to get some patriarch beer. Marek has brought frozen goat meat, and Karina has fruit preserves and pickles.

"Where have you been the past six months?" I ask Marek.

"At the Dwarf Museum."

"What's the Dwarf Museum?"

"That's just what we call it. The Dwarf Museum is the place where—"

Lukas silences him with a stern look. A strange mood spreads over the room. I want to ask more questions but I know it won't do any good. There's no way to force a Russian to do anything. That's something I've come to learn.

Lukas bows reverentially to the icons and laboriously says grace. Then he throws himself at the food. The others follow his example. No one talks at the dinner table the way we do in Denmark. Everyone concentrates on sating their appetite. The Scoundrel would have felt right at home in Russia.

I drink and carouse with the others.

Lukas smiles.

Lukas ruins everything with his smile.

IT'S IGOR WHO saves the evening. We've been drinking steadily, but the old man is more soused than the rest of us. I sit on his lap and tease him. Igor is the proud owner of a swollen belly, a bald pate with liver spots, and eyes that see the world through inflamed lids.

Igor is telling us about his life: how he was born in Moscow and found work in the German district—a district where the foreign heretics lived. It was there that bad habits flourished; it was there that people drank tea, carried swords, and spoke peculiar languages.

"I was an assistant to a Dutch nobleman," Igor tells us. "He was a remarkable man. Peter Alexeyevich often visited him. They would drink and play cards until late into the night. Oh yes, I have plenty of good stories I could tell you."

"Have you ever been married?" I ask.

"Twice." Igor nods. "My first wife died of dysentery fifty years ago; the second I would rather not talk about."

"Why not?" I tickle him under the chin.

Igor fends me off with a smile. "Oh, that was around 7218—what you Westerners call 1710. Believe me, I can remember it as if it were yesterday."

"Was it a festive wedding?"

I pour wine into Igor's goblet. Lukas is sulking. Karina is plucking at her sleeve.

"I don't know. All of us got married together, after all."

Petrushka gets up and tosses a chicken thigh into the corner.

"What do you mean?"

"All of us little people. We were married all at one time, on the orders of the tsar. Sixty or seventy of us. I don't recall exactly how many."

I snap out of my intoxicated state. "Are you talking about the dwarf wedding?"

"Yes. Have you heard about it in your country?"

"And all of you got married?"

Igor nods heartily. "Yes, every single dwarf in the land entered into holy matrimony on that day."

"How was it done?"

"Oh, it was a celebrated event, Surinka, highly celebrated. I hardly know where to begin. All the most distinguished citizens of Petersburg were invited. The tsar himself was the host. Oh yes, it's true. Quite true. The wedding festivities took place at Prince Menshikov's palace down by the Neva River, the one with the yellow walls and the red roof. Have you seen it? It looks like a cake. About seventy of us were married, dressed in our very finest."

"Are there seventy dwarves in Petersburg?"

"No, of course not. We belong to a noble race. There is very little fruit on our family tree. No, we were brought here from every corner of the land and handed over to the fine folk. There were dwarves who came all the way from Siberia—even from places no one had ever heard of. I was brought from the German district of Moscow and taken to one of the tsar's ministers, the venerable Peter Shapirov. There I was clothed in the most costly garments from heathen Europe. I wore red brocade, a gold-embroidered vest, and exquisite shoes that were too big for me. Then I was doused with the most terrible perfume. I stank like a woman. But I did look quite elegant. And I'm not bragging when I say that."

"Who were you supposed to marry?"

"Well, I had no idea that I was even going to a wedding. I had been told only that I was going to attend a banquet given by the fine folk. Princess Anna had been married the day before to a prince from Latvia, so I thought that I was going to take part in the festivities. But that very morning I overheard Shapirov talking about the massive dwarf wedding. Well, I wonder what's going to happen? old Igor thought to himself. Of course I was curious, but the fine folk don't like questions, so I had learned to keep my mouth shut. Besides, I thought: Igor, you're so ancient that your bride has to be younger than you. Make no mistake, that was a reassuring thought."

Igor empties his goblet.

"So, the day finally arrived, and I was driven over to the huge church in town. When we got there, the tsar decided who each of us should marry. I was supposed to get hitched to a young girl from the Black Sea. She was adorable. A little Tatar with long black hair. 'What's your name?' I asked her. 'That's none of your business,' she told me. Of course she refused to have me, so Peter's soldiers gave her a good beating. It was an ugly scene, but the tsar won't stand for disobedience. And my bride got quite hysterical, that she did. Well, then we were lined up two by two, and we went into the church. At the front was Jakov, the tsar's oldest dwarf, and the little midget who was to be his wife. Then came the tsar, Catherine, all the fine folk, and finally the rest of us dwarves. The grooms were blind old men who had to be supported by their brides. Many of them stumbled on their way inside, which prompted a great deal of merriment. The priest was also blind. And deaf. When he asked Jakov whether he would take his bride as his wife, Jakov said yes, loud and clear, whereas she mumbled her yes so that no one could hear it. Well, the ancient priest held the velvet caps over the heads of ten or twelve couples, but then he got tired, and the tsar took over the task. By the time I made my way up front with my young bride, the tsar had resumed his seat among the fine folk while the priest struggled with the caps and the other rituals. It was a long, drawn-out affair. I think the priest probably croaked from all the strain."

Igor laughs delightedly.

"Well, after the ceremony we were taken by boat over to Menshikov's palace. I remember the mood as the doors opened and we stepped inside the enormous hall. Everything glittered with gold. There were chrome-plated mirrors and strange paintings on the walls. Thousands of wax candles were lit. Along the sides of the rooms sat all the fine folk with their backs to the wall. They were dressed in their very best, with powdered wigs and jackets made of silk. That is to say, not all of them. Some of them wore costumes with animal heads and cat tails. The tsar and the tsarina were dressed as Frisian peasants— I have no idea where Frisia is, but it's no doubt somewhere in godless Europe. Well, we were hustled into the center of the hall, where we were supposed to eat. Around us stood waiters and soldiers holding trumpets. Every one of us was introduced by the master of ceremonies, who was a hundred years old. He had an enormous paunch and could hardly stand up straight. And like the priest, he was deaf in both ears. No one could understand a thing he said—that was why he had been chosen. The tsar loves burlesque performances. We dwarves know that better than anyone."

Igor is still thoroughly enjoying himself.

"The whole thing was a bit of a show, but old Igor is fond of shows. Among other things, there were two trained bears that plodded around among us dwarves. We were afraid of them, but the bears were good-natured enough. At one point Menshikov decided that they were too good-natured, so he got one of his men to poke them with his lance. And that made them bellow horribly, which prompted many of us to flee, but the soldiers kept hustling us back to our seats. Ha ha! Well, the only thing I *didn't* like were the epileptic brides. Every once in a while one of them would go into convulsions, and always at the most inappropriate moment. I remember a lovely young girl who lay on the floor, frothing at the mouth. Her eyes were rigid and frightened, but we weren't allowed to help her. The fine folk were supposed to have something to laugh at, and they laughed all night at everything that tickled their fancy. They laughed at the little cannons that had been brought into the hall; they laughed at the little tables on which everything was miniature, just the right size for a dwarf. In a sense, the fine folk had crawled inside a dollhouse where they could point their fingers at us *midgets*. Many of the dwarves sat at the tables and cried, but not old Igor. I was looking forward to the wedding night, even though my bride wasn't willing. 'Keep your old man's fingers to yourself,' she said. Later on she loosened up, and she allowed me to dance with her, but only once."

Igor smiles at his memories.

"Well, I'm babbling, just babbling on and on. But we've now come to the banquet. During the dinner we drank ourselves into quite a state again, of course. We sat at the tables that were much too low, with plates that were so tiny there was barely room for even a cracker. We were served roast swan with cranberries, turkey with a piquant sauce, sausages spiced with cardamom and aquavit. Even the little forks were something to behold. They were adorned with mother-of-pearl and tortoise-shell, and the wine was served in a royal taster's glass. Once in a while the tsar would come over and order punishment toasts if we weren't drinking enough. My young wife tried to slip away after dessert, but she was caught and soundly beaten. I can remember watching them over in the corner as they punched her. It wasn't the least bit pleasant hearing her scream. Afterwards she was not as beautiful as before. Well, there was nothing to be done about it. All in all, I have to say that it was a peculiar wedding. But the banquet was magnificent, and old Igor never says no to a good drinking bout."

A RESOUNDING SILENCE fills the room.

I turn to Lukas.

"Lukas, how about you? Were you married too?"

A short pause is followed by everyone laughing at his embarrassment.

"You were married to Natasha," says Igor with a laugh. "Isn't that true, Natasha?"

Natasha nods.

"The tsar himself was your best man. What's wrong with your memory, Lukashka?"

I look at Lukas. I look at Natasha.

Igor goes on with his drunken babbling—about Prince Menshikov's son, who died late in the evening, so the rest of the festivities had to be canceled; about the foreign envoys who had found the ceremony godless and blasphemous; about half of the dwarves who lay dead-drunk on the floor, dressed in their German attire and their Morocco leather boots.

"…but I enjoyed myself immensely," says Igor. "I've always been a great one for hoisting a goblet. I can drink even the most strapping fellows under the table. I can hold my liquor— isn't that right, Lukashka? Tell Surinka the truth: those shitbags couldn't bring Igor down. They think dwarves are playthings, they think they can treat us any way they like. They think they're sitting in Our Lord's inside pocket, but we're better than they are. May they all die in sin, every last one of them. May the fires of Hell consume them all!"

Igor pounds his fist on the table.

I look at Lukas with a smile on my face. Natasha gets up to clear the table. There is no more wine in the goblets.

38.

AFTER MIDNIGHT LUKAS AND I FORNICATE, LYING CLOSE to the cast-iron stove.

I'm on top, as usual. From that vantage point I have a view of Lukas's chest and his sweaty face. I close my eyes, thinking about everything and nothing. Outside the moon is glowing, the stars are shining through the shutters. A bird dog barks. Maybe it will soon be morning. Maybe it won't.

I think about the tsar, who is just as much an epileptic as the brides. I think about his spasms, about the tsarina who calmed him inside the sleigh. I think about the dwarf wedding, the deaf master of ceremonies, and the priest who was older than Methuselah.

And Natasha. I think about Natasha. Then I fall asleep on top of Lukas. An ungodly snoring washes over us from the bedroom. Natasha is sleeping off a drunken stupor along with Igor, Petrushka, Marek, and Karina.

Lukas doesn't move. He is very still, much too still.

I love him. But I don't know whether I care much for that particular feeling.

Later I try to catch Lukas's eye as he lies there underneath me. The stars have disappeared. Someone has closed the shutters so that the night can't reach us. I look down. Now I can see the outline of my lover: the hairless chest, the huge bulk of his head that makes it hard for him to lie on his back.

Lukas has deep scratches on his chest. His nose is bleeding. Or is that a shadow? I can't tell whether it's a shadow.

"Lukas?"

Lukas is weeping angrily. His little hands are clenched into fists. It's a sweet sight. Sweet, but pathetic.

"Lukas, what's the matter?"

I shake him. I whisper his name again. There's so much that

I want to say, but the walls would laugh if I did. Even I would laugh—it would be degrading and unbearable.

Lukas opens his eyes. I see how bloodshot the whites are around his pupils, and how black the rims are, looking like ditches. I tickle him under the arms, I pull on the tiny hairs until he screams. Lukas smells of seawater; he has always smelled of seawater.

I'm just about to say something sweet, but I restrain myself.

Lukas's eyes are filled with hatred. He tries to get up. I stroke my hand over his hair and kiss him gently on the forehead—the scratches on his forehead. Lukas again tries to get up, but he still can't get to his feet.

I stay like that for a long time, sitting on top of him. For a long time.

39.

EARLY ONE MORNING THEY COME TO GET ME IN A SWAN-shaped carriage. It sails through the snow, first along the river, and then along the wide boulevards. The snow is slowly melting. Petersburg is losing its white cloak and becoming a murky, muddy soup. The runners have been replaced by wheels. The first birds build their nests in the larch trees.

We drive for a long time, first through the city gate, then out to the country and into the woods, which are very quiet. Suddenly we can't even see our hands in front of our faces. The carriage has to stop in the slush and wait until the fog lifts. I shiver inside my bearskin robe. Then we go on, past little huts, past horses with bast mats and men wearing foxskin furs. Deeper into the forest.

After a while we arrive at a big stone building. It's wrapped in fog. A low, eight-sided tower comes into view. The driver tries to help me out of the carriage, but I jump down from the step and slip in the thawing snow. The driver laughs and escorts me to the entrance, where a man is waiting. He's wearing a black cowl. As if by magic, the door opens. I look inside what appears to be a cloister. We walk down several dark, damp passageways. Our footsteps echo. Plaster falls from the ceiling like snowflakes.

We make our way into the heart of the building, past a storeroom and a cell with a fireplace made from boulders. Two women stare at me and burst into paroxysms of laughter. Farther along the corridor a door opens. I'm shoved into a cell with a big wooden cross. A man stands up. He's wearing purple vestments. He has the longest full beard that I've ever seen in my life. It's yellow and gray and reaches almost to his knees. The man's eyes are light-blue. They're gleaming with joviality, which makes him seem even more forbidding.

When he sees me, he spreads out his arms like a falcon.

"My name is Ludwig Danilov. I've been waiting for you."

The man speaks Russian with an accent.

I start to sweat.

In the corner is a cot with chains and handcuffs. A wax candle is stuck to a worm-eaten book. The door shuts behind me. We're alone.

"IN THE OLD days they came from far and wide. People from all levels of society: peasants, boyars, and soldiers who had deserted. They were full of complaints about this life on earth. They came here seeking shelter from the storms in their mind. They washed the icons in holy water, they submitted to the required rituals. But often they found only one thing: doubt."

Danilov's voice is deep and resounding.

"Things are no longer the same. Today there is a hole in Heaven. Today the angels come down to this cloister. Only the chosen come here. And to them I say: 'The Antichrist is standing at the gate to the world. You must learn to hate the Antichrist with all your heart.'"

I interrupt Danilov.

"I have no idea why I'm here."

"You're here because God has willed it."

He picks me up with a swift motion. I strike out at him but miss. The man dumps me onto the wooden table.

"God has a plan for all creatures, even for you. The Devil blew into your mother's ears when you were conceived. He stood by at your birth and prevented you from growing. He filled you with poison and gave you ungodly thoughts that took up residence in your heart. Every time you invoked the Devil, he flew into your mouth. He took the form of elves and monsters. He instilled you with heathen thoughts from the black Bible of Luther. You were lost from the moment you were born. Your salvation is God's representative here on Earth: Peter Alexeyevich, who has taken you under his wing."

"Is he the one who has sent me here?"

"You're a doubter. That's why God allowed you to be born misshapen. But today is a joyful day. Soon your soul will burn for God. After you have been cleansed, the Devil's chalice will no longer seem desirable."

I stare at Danilov and count the bits of food in his beard.

"Who has sent me here?"

"Come," he says.

WE GO OUT to the corridor, walk farther into the cloister, past a kitchen that smells of freshly baked bread. Outside the wolves howl. We stop in front of a cell. A filthy curtain serves as the door. Danilov tears it aside, and I catch sight of a woman. She's sitting on the floor. Her right arm and leg are chained to the wall. She is pale, with sunken cheeks.

"This is Sanka. Sanka, say hello to Surinka from *Dania* ..."

Sanka doesn't move.

"Sanka is a whore from the local village. She is possessed by two spirits. The first is the spirit of indecency, which makes her lure men to their ruin. Sanka has fornicated with all the men in her village. She has turned their heads with her witchcraft, but now that's over. Isn't that right, Sanka?"

Danilov smiles and goes on.

"The second spirit that has possessed Sanka is the spirit of arrogance. Sanka is wiser than those with book learning—she says as much herself. She can read and write, and she's quick to boast about her skill. The brothers and I have worked with her round the clock, but Sanka is a little too pleased with her spirits. Isn't that right?"

The woman opens her eyes and looks at me. Her gaze becomes clearer. I stand there, bewitched. A brief moment passes. Then we both laugh at the very same time.

40.

THERE IS A MUSHROOM THAT GROWS ONLY IN THE WINTER. It grows as a parasite on dead trees. Contrary to what people believe, it's not poisonous. It was born at the wrong time—too late to be an autumn mushroom, too early to be part of the spring. From its place it hears the screams of the dying mushrooms. It hears their sorrows and lamentations.

If I were not a dwarf, I would be that sort of mushroom. I would be cold and slimy; I would renounce the sun. I would live on my tree trunk without distinguishing night from day. I would surrender myself to snails and insects. Death would never frighten me. I would reappear winter after winter, yellow as the sun, and with new gills.

They chain me to the cot.

I try to resist, but I'm too weak and too small. Above me hangs a bouquet of dried herbs. A black-garbed monk comes in. Several more follow. They look shabby and starved. The next moment they form a wall around me.

Danilov says something, but I'm not listening. I'm staring at the cross—at the air that is heavy with emptiness. When the knife cuts into my flesh, I set off flying: out of my body, out over the world. I glide into the sun and peer at the angels and demons. Some of them are dark with shiny surfaces; others are flames of light with black spots. They fight for power, get tangled up in each other, grow blurry against the golden clouds. It's a fight for life and death. It has been raging since the dawn of time. It will always rage on Earth and in Heaven. Swords flash, blood colors the clouds red and drips to the ground in fiery splashes.

"Do you renounce the Devil? Do you reject the Antichrist and his countless minions?"

I'm flying above the angels, above my life, which lies beneath me like a paintbox. I see the Scoundrel and my little boy... my father in Brønshøj bending over the Bible. I see the great fire that consumes the city, the golden flames, the churches that are transformed to ash... I see Rasmus Æreboe lying in bed with his back to his wife. His eyelids are moving; he is dreaming of Russia. I see my withered body surrounded by black-clad monks. Their voices resound, reach up to the roof. I am far away from my body and the world, where everyone dreams the dream that they call life.

"Do you choose the way of God or the way of the Devil?"

The monks stand around me like a wall of piety. Their eyes smolder. They whip me. They whip me lovingly on the back, the shoulders, the legs. The gashes open beneficently. Blood streams out and tickles me across my stomach.

"I don't think..."

Danilov bends toward me to hear what I'm saying.

"I don't think..."

Danilov nods.

"...that I can tell the difference."

For a brief moment I see the Scoundrel and the boy. They're standing in a meadow filled with flowers. The sun is shining gently. The sky is lavender with scarlet clouds. They're holding each other's hand, they wander away, into the forest. They're gone. The trees close gently around them. I fall into a dreamless sleep.

V *Karlitsa*

PIMPERNEL
Anagallis fœmina

41.

WE COME OUT OF OUR CELLS, THE MEN IN ONE GROUP, the women in another. I'm wearing a checked kerchief and a shroud that reaches to my ankles. My shoes are made of bast fiber and they creak. We enter the chapel as a monk strikes an iron plate that serves as a bell. Peasants arrive from the nearby villages. They cross themselves with two fingers, laboriously sink to their knees, and buy candles for a kopeck. The old icons are gilded and beautiful. More cloister servants come in, lining up along the walls to listen with lowered eyes to the priest. Outside the crimson dawn rises over the forest. Several ragged children are begging inside the chapel. Someone kicks them out, giving them a box on the ears for good measure.

I listen to the reading of the text and sink into the rituals. The members of the congregation bow their heads like whipped dogs. The atmosphere is beautiful and melancholy. Later we leave the chapel, the men in one group, the women in another. The residents of the cloister gather around the stove to eat bread that has been mixed with one-third flour and two-thirds bark. I catch sight of Sanka. She looks better, now that she's been released from the chains. We smile at each other, eat the meager bread, and go back to our cells and our prayers. That's how the days pass. Everything is repeated. Everything is repeated.

THEY SAY THAT Danilov fled from the temptations of the Antichrist when he was a young man, that previously he'd been a
privateer and a seaman on the tsar's ships. One day he went into
the forest, where he had a revelation. He saw a flaming pillar
of fire above the marsh. After that he built a hut on the site. He
plowed up a section of the earth, he dressed in buckskins, and he
started preaching to everyone, even the animals of the forest.
People from the nearby villages sought him out. He allowed them
to say confession in the wilderness, he offered them blueberries
as a sacrament. On Sundays he exorcised spirits. The spirits
could be heard as they vanished over the lake—as they repudi-
ated this world and took up residence in wolves. Danilov
acquired more and more disciples. They built a cloister, caught
fish, gathered mushrooms. The disciples were whipped by their
master, but with each broken rib their faith grew stronger.

Sometime after I arrived, the cloister was attacked by
outlaws. They came riding up in the twilight, wearing masks of
dried goatskin. They claimed that the tsar had sent them to
punish those who held onto the old beliefs. They demanded
cream and fish and eggs. When they decided that wasn't enough,
they beat the monks with clubs, they set fire to the nave, and
they disappeared into the night, taking along icons and silver.
They didn't touch me. I was too insignificant, too little.

Danilov railed against the outlaws, calling them the Devil's
spawn. And then he tended to the wounds caused by their clubs.
I saw him sitting near the hearth, his face smeared with blood.
His body emanated an unbelievable strength. As if he were
grateful for his sufferings. As if every wound brought him closer
to Paradise.

THE CLOISTER IS going to be expanded. The intention is to
have separate sections for the men and for the women.
We will no longer be allowed to share our sins. We are to follow
the dictates of the Orthodox Church.

Every morning we pound posts into the ground, we clear

away trees, we remove branches. There are twenty-two of us.
Danilov assigns the tasks. I insist on helping, but I'm not much
use for anything. I gather herbs, make soup, and generally
get in the way. To my surprise, this has become my life. The forest
here is much more beautiful than in Denmark. It's full of ever-
greens, hares, and exotic mushrooms. In the swamps there are
wading birds and ducks.

Danilov visits me in my cell every evening.

He puts salves on my cuts and prays for me under the
picture of the saint. I don't know why I used to be afraid of him.

Danilov is kind. At least the Danilov that I encounter one-
on-one. He is genuinely interested in my salvation. He takes
time to listen to my confessions, as if I were the only person in
existence.

"There is one thing that you must understand." Danilov
looks at me with his light-blue eyes. "The soul is a knife that slices
through the body. It opens the flesh and brings light. But at
the same time, it will kill you. Since you women have no soul, you
have no knowledge of the nature of suffering. You have no spiritual pain, no longing for the divine. You are like peaceful animals
grazing in a meadow. If you had a soul, you would feel that you
were wandering in the dark. You would feel removed from your
origins—you would understand that life on earth has no
meaning. But that's not how things are for creatures like you.
Since you've been released from the spirits, you've become
peaceful and carefree. You live in the present without worries
or reservations. In a sense we can say that you are fortunate. It's
easier to fill you with light. Or with darkness."

I object. "But if women have no soul, why do you receive
them here at the cloister?"

"To demonstrate mercy. God wishes to reach all creatures."

"Even me?"

"Even you, Surinka."

Danilov smiles. Today I feel quite fond of him. Maybe
because I feel lighter in my heart. Or because I'm a fool.

"Why do you think that God has created me as a midget?"

"Because you have a task to carry out."

"And what sort of task would that be?"

"That is what you will find in serenity. Through God and your suffering."

"I'm not especially interested in suffering."

"But perhaps suffering is interested in you."

Danilov towers over me. I stare at his beard to see what he has eaten today. Then I fold my hands and tilt my head to one side.

"Where is it that you actually come from, Father?"

"I come from God."

"But where did God put you when you were born on this earth?"

"My physical form is not important, Surinka."

"It's important to me."

Danilov smiles. His eyes are beautiful but sorrowful. Suddenly he takes off the bronze cross that he wears around his neck and presses it into my hand. I thank him with astonishment. Then he leaves my cell, wearing his purple cape.

Against my will tears rise to my eyes. I sit there for a long time, holding the cross, feeling its warmth, filled with happiness and joy. On the wall I catch sight of a beetle. It pauses under the peephole, rests for a moment, and then continues on its way toward the light.

42.

IT WAS DURING THE EXORCISM OF THE DEVIL THAT I discovered that the Scoundrel had a bird in his chest. It wasn't a real bird; it was a creature that filled him with darkness. The bird had restless wings. It was trapped inside him. It wanted out, it wanted to get away. Sometimes I could sense its desperation at having to live inside the chest of a man. It shrieked, it beat its wings, it refused to leave him in peace. The Scoundrel tried to escape the bird through drink, but the bird stayed there inside his chest. When he awoke in the morning, the bird was still there. When he vomited the bird whispered: "You can't drive me out. I'm still inside of you." But one day the bird flew away. I don't know how it got out of the Scoundrel's chest, but it rose up like a stork, it flew up toward the sky and disappeared into the clouds. At first the Scoundrel was relieved. He celebrated his freedom, he drank himself into a stupor, he awoke without hearing wings. In the beginning he thought that the pain was gone, but slowly he discovered that it wasn't. The Scoundrel began to miss the bird. How could it have gotten out? He thought that it was chained to his body. In some way the bird had kept him in check. Now there was nothing. Only dreary nights in the damp cellar, only the cloying smell of aquavit and candles, only the sense that he was alone, that no one lived inside of him, that nothing could grow.

That was what he tried to tell me whenever he drank until he was drunk.

About the bird inside of his chest. About how he had suffered when it was there. And how he suffered when it was gone.

THE NEXT DAY we gather in Sanka's cell.

Danilov has tied her to an enormous cross. He moistens her lips with a sponge and nods to two monks, who stand ready with whips. Then he opens the Bible, chooses a passage of scripture at random, and begins to read. His deep voice is warm and hypnotic. It fills the cell and all of us present.

I don't understand the words.

There are holes in Sanka's shroud. She has long welts on her thin legs; her arms are bony and fragile. It must hurt to be hanging there like the Savior, but at least she is tied and not nailed to the cross.

The monks start to whip her.

Sanka's screams echo through the cell. I look down at the floor and catch sight of a mouse. Several of the monks are praying loudly. I bite my lip and look up again. Sanka's eyes are open wide. She is bleeding terribly, and she gives me a pleading look. Tears run down her cheeks, her body shakes in delirium. She has huge wounds on her hips and legs. She looks at me again. A spasm slides across her face. Then she laughs heartily.

The monks whip her even harder.

I study her closely.

Sanka laughs again.

I leave the cell. Outdoors the snow has collected in deep drifts. I can see the tracks of wolves and deer. The forest seems dead, but it's a beautiful death: a petrified, frozen landscape that will awaken again when God blows on the snow.

A squirrel falls to the ground. The frost burns like knives. I'm alive.

43.

AT THE CLOISTER WE HAVE NOTHING TO EAT. God is testing us.

But I have found Him.

Or is it He who has found me?

44.

ONE MORNING MY CURTAIN IS PULLED ASIDE. An old monk comes into view. He is bald, with an intricate network of wrinkles on his face. At first I think that he's mute. He says nothing, just stares at me with amiable curiosity.

"*Karlitsa*, you have a visitor," he says.

I put on my shoes made of bast and follow the monk. We walk along the corridor, past the storerooms, the cells, and the sitting rooms. A sour smell hovers over everything, but I'm used to that smell. We continue on up several stairways. The steps are too high, but I scramble my way upward with my usual alacrity.

The monk shows me into a gloomy chamber. Two candles are burning in the dark. In front of me stands Lukas, holding in his hand a cap made of marten fur. He seems nervous, but he's well-dressed, as always. A German coat with brass buttons, a light-blue scarf, and new felt boots.

"Surinka."

Lukas kisses me on the lips. He smells of perfume.

We look at each other.

"How are you?" he asks.

"Fine."

We smile and sit down at the little table. Outside is the chicken yard. We can hear the cackling, we can see monks bringing in baskets filled with eggs. It's springtime. The snow has practically vanished.

"You look good, Surinka."

I nod.

We look out the window, glancing only rarely at each other. Lukas's hair is now gray at the temples. He seems smaller than I remember—runty, delicate, like a crystal glass that might shatter at any moment.

After a while our conversation finally gets going. Lukas tells me that he has put together new acts that have drawn him closer to the tsar. He has started using cards to tell fortunes. He has even stayed at the Winter Palace, where his advice was sought regarding "decisions of the greatest importance." Lukas has been granted privileges that no other dwarf has ever possessed.

"The tsar has decided to build me a house," he says proudly.

"Congratulations."

"A half-timbered house on Vasilevsky Island. I'm allowed to decide for myself how it should be furnished. And who will live there."

I let my hand slide over my shroud. I want to go back to my prayers. How long have I been in the cloister? An eternity? I don't know.

"The house is going to have two stories and a little orchard. I've told the tsar that I want to have pears for breakfast. And Spanish cherries. 'You're a spoiled midget,' the tsar said to me. 'I've created a monster, a parrot man who babbles worse than a wench.' That's what he said yesterday. And by the way, he asked me to give you his greetings."

I smile gratefully.

"Surinka, I'd like to show you the house when it's finished. There are so many things that have to be decided. Furniture, decorations, and the like…what sort of roof I should have. And there's going to be a kitchen and a chicken yard too…and maybe even a small bathhouse."

A caravan of ants is working its way under the table.

"You're not mad at me, are you?" Lukas gives me an anxious look.

I shake my head.

"Because I couldn't bear it if you were, Surinka. I couldn't bear it if you blamed me for what has happened…"

"For what?"

"For the fact that you were sent away."

I reach for his hand and squeeze it. Lukas stares at me as if he's trying to find something that doesn't exist.

"I could easily get you out of here. You know that, don't you? A word from me, and you'd be back in Petersburg. I know Ludwig Danilov. The tsar thinks very highly of him. Peter Alexeyevich visited the cloister several years ago, and he made a promise that none of Danilov's monks would be seized by soldiers."

I nod again.

Lukas's expression grows solemn. "Things are better for you now, aren't they?"

"Yes, Lukas. Of course."

"That's good to hear, Surinka. Very good."

A blessed silence sets in. But Lukas doesn't care for silence. He tells me about the dwarf apartment. About Igor, whose health is failing. About Petrushka and Karina, who have formed a new band. They perform at markets, and they're going to Moscow to play in the German district. Not once does he mention Natasha.

Lukas reaches for his marten-fur hat and his cane. We climb down from the tall chairs.

I accompany him to the door. Two monks are standing on

either side of the curtain. They laugh uproariously when they see us.

"These are uneasy times. The tsar has arrested Alexey and many of his supporters. But I suppose you've heard about that?"

I shake my head.

"One of them is Vasily Dolgoruky, and another is your friend Ismailov. They're both sitting in Peter & Paul Fortress, awaiting their fate."

"Ismailov? What has Ismailov done?"

"He put his faith in a crazy man."

"What do you mean?"

"I think you know quite well what I mean."

"No, I don't, Lukas."

"Alexey. He put his faith in Alexey."

Lukas kisses me on the lips. Outside an elegant carriage with four horses is waiting. Beggars flock around it. They laugh when they see Lukas. A man lifts him up and swings him around like a doll. When Lukas thinks he's about to be put down, he's tossed instead to a beggar, who drops him in fright.

Lukas gets up, looking dazed. He crawls into the carriage. His cane is left lying in the mud. A moment later he sets off back to the tsar, who loves him.

45.

SANKA AND I HAVE BEEN GIVEN PERMISSION TO TAKE a walk in the woods.

We carry big cudgels, in case we should be surprised by wolves, but the cudgels would be of little use. We can only hope that we're under God's protection—if such a thing even exists.

I love the pine forest that stretches on forever. I dream of gathering herbs, speaking to the animals, and studying mushrooms. Every once in a while Sanka and I see deer. We head farther into the woods, away from the cloister. We want to find a place where we can be alone, on the other side of the lake.

Sanka is emaciated and gaunt. Her long hair is pulled back

into a knot at her neck, her green eyes are filled with distrust. She laughs often and always at the wrong time.

We sit down on the grass, swatting at the insects. In front of us is a meadow with yellow flowers. From the lake we hear frogs and ducks. Birds of prey circle overhead. We're alone, yet not alone.

Sanka has promised to tell me about her life, but her life refuses to come out. It stays trapped in her throat like a nervous cough, at times like a fit of laughter. I can see that she was once beautiful. There is something refined about her, a delicacy buried in sores and bruises.

"I was once in love with a cavalier. He was tall, with broad shoulders. He had dimples as deep as marl pits. Ludovich came from an excellent family, and he wanted to marry me. My father was extremely happy with the dowry, and so there was nothing more to say about that. A couple of days before our wedding, Ludovich gave me a present. It was a whip. He intended to use it on me if I didn't obey. 'If you ever strike me with that whip, I'll leave on the back of a werewolf,' I told him. Ludovich laughed. He had no idea how stark raving mad I was—men never know."

Sanka picks some flowers and puts them in her hair.

"Well, of course I wasn't very old at the time. I didn't know that marriage is like a locked cupboard and that the key hangs around the man's neck. So I moved with Ludovich to Moscow, where he had business trading in whale oil and skins. We lived in an elegant house just a stone's throw from the Kremlin. Everything was so elegant that it made me want to scream. I was not allowed to leave the house. In Russia women are expected to stay indoors; we mustn't be seen on the street, we mustn't feel or think. But I can't live like that, so I fell in love with a peddler who taught me something important."

"What?"

"That men are more fun if they have a big cock."

I laugh loudly. At that moment the ducks all flee from the lake. The pine trees come alive with birds. Sanka lies down next to me and reaches for my hand. Suddenly she seems smaller than me. She gasps for air and starts to cry. At first I don't know what to do, but then I put my arms around her. Sanka is nothing but skin and bones, and as we lie there, I feel as if we're both part of the heath.

"What do you really think about Danilov?" I ask.

Sanka looks up at the sky. "Danilov?"

"Yes. Does he visit you in your cell?"

She shakes her head. "Never."

"Do the monks?"

"All the time."

"Do you let them lie with you?"

"If they're nice."

"But the monks are old and disgusting."

"That's not their fault."

"Tell me, how long have you actually been here?"

"Maybe forever."

"But you had a life before you came here, Sanka."

"I'm not so sure about that."

Sanka wipes the tears from her cheek.

"Surinka, why don't we run into the woods and find a few squirrels to eat? Let's run as far as we can go. Wouldn't it be fun if we disappeared, never to be found again?"

Sanka jumps up with all the eagerness of a little girl. I get to my feet with sorrow. Suddenly I feel a longing for the Scoundrel, for Mathias, and for Ismailov, whom the tsar has taken into custody.

Sanka spreads out her arms and runs across the meadow. I follow, though I can't run very fast. I have pains in my back and in my misshapen legs. I stop and watch as Sanka slips into the pine forest. A moment later she's gone.

Mosquitoes are dancing around me. I head toward the woods and enter the green darkness. The forest embraces me. I continue on through a curtain of needles. In the woods of my childhood the elves received me. I gathered herbs and mushrooms.

But now I don't know what I should be gathering. In front of me are five reddish-brown toadstools, spotted and with beautiful gills. They don't look like the ones in Denmark, but they speak to me, they tell me their stories. "You can eat us," one of them says, "but first you must ask permission. You must always ask permission when you eat anything from nature."

I squat down, break off a little piece, and taste it. If the mushroom is poisonous, I'll have the loveliest convulsions.

"Go ahead and take a bigger piece," says the mushroom. "Take a bigger piece. I taste quite delicious."

But I don't care to listen to mushrooms. Mushrooms are neither friends nor foes. They're simply meant to be eaten.

I wait. I'm waiting for spasms or convulsions, but nothing happens. Then I eat the whole mushroom and step into a clearing. The light is coming down in columns. The grass is tall and silky soft, the ground is swampy. I look around for Sanka. My back is aching. As I stand there, I don't understand what God's intentions were. Maybe He should have continued working on the seventh day instead of settling for all these partial solutions.

Up in the sky are hundreds of clouds. They have strange shapes. They look like animals, ships, and pieces of land. A few resemble demons, others letters of the alphabet. Blots of white ink on a blue document. The world seems a strange place, but not to me.

"Sanka?" I call.

No answer, nothing.

I could lie down in the grass and go to sleep.

I could lie down and be together with the Scoundrel and Mathias. But instead I sit on a tree stump, I bury my head in my hands, and I weep. It's good that nobody sees me. Not even God.

46.

ALEXEY, THE TSAR'S SON, HAS BEEN TORTURED FOR days. They've thrown him in irons in the cellar of the Peter & Paul

Fortress. He's lying on his stomach, his torso is bare. There are wounds and congealed blood on his back.

The executioner was told to use the cat-o'-nine-tails—ten lashes with the iron balls. Two of the tsar's servants are witnesses to the cruel treatment. They've taken off their tricorn hats, they watch the torture with the eyes of experts.

Alexey refuses to name his co-conspirators, because none exist. For a brief instant he sees his father holding the lash, perhaps in the delirium of fever. He also sees a lush garden with lilacs, a river that winds its way among willow trees and green ridges.

The executioner gets ready.

He's a stout man with the neck of a bull and kind gray eyes. He's wearing a brown cape spattered with blood. On his head he wears a pitiful wig, out of respect for the high standing of his prisoner.

The executioner reaches back. Then he swings the lash over his head and strikes the chained Alexey on the shoulder. The Tsarevich writhes in pain. A black bruise spreads over his body. The executioner steps back and looks at the stripes and congealed blood.

He pauses for a moment, then reaches back again. This time he strikes Alexey on the right side of his back, crushing several ribs. Alexey screams. He goes limp and faints.

The two witnesses make the sign of the cross and then vomit.

A commotion is heard in the corridor. The tsar enters with three soldiers and a priest. His eyes are hard, his round face is contorted with fury. A footman steps forward with a stool. Peter sits down and leans toward Alexey.

This isn't the first time they have sat like this. They sat like this the day before. When Alexey was a child. When he came home from exile.

The tsarevich is unconscious, but a little smile crosses his lips. The executioner has not struck his face. Only his body has been shattered.

Alexey regains consciousness and is given something to drink. A cup of *kvass*, but he can't keep it down. Peter looks at his son as the *kvass* runs down his chin, forming pools in his collarbone.

"I used to stand in my study and watch you playing in the garden. Your mother hovered around you. No one could tear her away from you. Not even me."

A soldier hands Peter a cloth. The tsar wipes the blood from Alexey's neck. He kisses him on the lips. Alexey opens his eyes and looks at his father. He is clearly trying to say something.

"I've never…"

Alexey looks at his father.

"…wanted…"

The tsar waits.

"…the best for you."

A shadow passes over Peter's face.

The tsarevich smiles. His consciousness is in Heaven. He is a puzzle in which the pieces are being removed by invisible hands. First his sense of smell, then his hearing, then his sight. His eyes dry out, his skin ceases to breathe.

Peter stares at his son, as if there is something he doesn't understand. There is no more Alexey on this earth. Only a single wish—that his father will forgive him his sins.

The tsar takes Alexey's hand. Peter has never held Alexey's hand before. It feels pleasant and warm.

White light sinks over the prison. Alexey's breathing gets shallower. Images from his childhood pass like clouds: the red toy soldiers, the yellow wallpaper, the sea that his father showed him in Arkhangelsk, the salty slapping of the waves against the hull. Alexey didn't care for the sea; it was too big and too intractable. The sea was not part of his country's history, or part of the Russian geography.

Now he sees the riding lessons that Peter gave him at their *dacha*. The smell of the Arabian horse, his father's praise when he didn't fall off during the ride…

Even the tsarevich's last hour is dominated by his father.

Alexey draws his soul through his body, disappears into the radiance, and dies.

The tsar remains sitting there, holding his rosary in his hand. His right arm is trembling. A spasm disfigures his face.

He is still sitting there when the soldiers carry Alexey out.

The church bells chime from the Peter & Paul Fortress, tolling out over the town, over the Neva River. Word is sent to the Church of the Ascension in the Kremlin, to Novgorod, and to all the big cities in the land.

In the neighboring cell sit Vasily Dolgoruky and his men. One of them is Ismailov.

All this I see with my dwarf vision.

From the cloister in the forest I see the world outside.

I'm not sure that I want any part of that world.

VI God's Monsters

COMMON HENBANE
Hyoscyamus niger

47.

A WORN-OUT OLD HORSE CART COMES TO GET ME. THE
wagon is uncovered, the driver is drunk, and the horse is
emaciated, with tormented eyes. In the wagonbed are vegetables,
partially frozen. There is almost no room for me, but there's
nothing new about that.

They all come to say goodbye: Danilov and the monks, but
not Sanka. She came back to the cloister after three days,
unable to remember where she had been. Now she's chained to
the wall once again. I can hear her singing in the morning, and
I listen to her laughter washing through her cell. But when I try
to go in to visit her, I'm stopped by a monk.

For the last time I go over to the chapel, bow before the
icons, and listen to the chickens cackling in the yard. Danilov
comes with me. He takes my hand. His beard has been trimmed,
his light-blue eyes bore into mine.

"Our paths are about to part, Surinka."

I nod.

"But before you leave, I want to tell you a story. When I went
into the forest many years ago, the Antichrist was standing at
the threshold. In the towns the Church of Our Lord had fallen into
disfavor. Temptations had taken over the streets. So the Lord
led me out here. He asked me: 'Which do you wish for, Danilov?
To save the soul or the flesh?' 'The soul,' I said, 'only the soul.'
But even though I answered Him with utter conviction, I had no

idea what lay ahead. I didn't realize how much it would take to stand in the sight of God. I had to live on wood sorrel to please Him, I had to whip myself twice a day, even on the holy Sabbath. God's shepherd annihilated my flesh. He taught me through the whip; he shattered my legs so that they would be prepared to obey. And do you know what happened? My body grew weaker, but my spirit grew stronger.

"So listen to what I tell you. At some point you will stand at a crossroads, and God will force you to choose: Will you go toward the Light that illuminates the sky with its warm colors and its golden glow, where God's angels are patiently waiting to receive you with hallelujahs? Or will you choose the Darkness, which at first seems soothing and enticing? It will tell you that you're headed in the right direction, but then it will consume you in the flames of Hell. The choice is yours, Surinka. Yours alone."

Danilov escorts me out to the horse cart, where he kisses me farewell. A scarred monk lifts me up into the wagon-bed. The cart starts off.

I have no idea where I'm going.

WE DRIVE THROUGH the woods, through the mud that has settled like a brown carpet over the forest floor. An ice-cold fog envelops the birches and fir trees. The wheels sink down to their hubs in the filthy muck. The driver whips the emaciated horse. The cart creaks as if it's about to fall apart.

When we get out into the country, we meet a company of soldiers. They're shivering with cold in their wet capes. Smoke from the campfires inside their tents stings my eyes. Two soldiers are washing their boots in the swamp. When we drive past, they stare at us, their eyes filled with despair.

I lean against the vegetables and think about Lukas. I wonder whether he ever got his house. Is he still the tsar's favorite, or has he been thrown in prison for his sins? No one can ever tell which way the wind will blow. It's the tsar's wind, and it can shift course at any moment.

I'm hungry, but the frozen vegetables don't tempt me in the least.

It starts to rain. Starving crows fight over a pile of garbage. We're approaching the bay and Petersburg. I catch a glimpse of the tall towers on the horizon. They're painted a gloomy black. In the ditch I see the cadavers of several children. Everything is raw and depressing. I don't know whether I'm ready for the world, or whether I have any real desire to be part of it.

There's a line outside the city gate. Tatars and boyars are patiently waiting to be allowed into the tsar's Dutch-inspired paradise. The soldiers are aggressive and drunk. After a while we drive through the city, past mud huts, barracks, and soot-covered smithies.

Petersburg is one big construction site with new canals and newly erected warehouses, with ships made of oak from Kazan and with wily innkeepers. The city is raw and unfinished, damp and lackluster, with no bridges to the numerous islands, because the tsar wants both man and beast to learn how to sail.

To my surprise we head in the direction of a huge mansion. It has a fountain and it's surrounded by trees. In the yard are several barracks for workers. I hold back a smile. When the cart stops, I jump down from the wagonbed. A little door opens, and an ancient man comes out. He has a thickset body and a sharp nose. He stands there, his legs astride, holding onto a brown cane and staring at me.

"Are you Surinka?"

I nod.

"My name is Frederik Ruysch. I'm the caretaker of His Majesty the Tsar's Curiosity Cabinet."

I grab my carpetbag and follow the man along a servants' corridor. The smell of cabbage soup hangs in the air. Big piles of firewood are stacked up along the wall.

"His Majesty the Tsar has asked me to show you around, which is a highly unusual request."

Ruysch gives me an inquisitive look.

"I'm the tsar's favorite dwarf," I tell him.

The old man tips his head back and laughs. He's wearing a lambskin coat and goatskin boots. He goes up several staircases, and I do my best to follow. My back is aching, as usual, and I'm wondering what a Curiosity Cabinet could be.

We go into several bright, cold rooms.

"Do you speak enough Russian to understand what I say? I'm a Dutchman by birth, so if that's any help, we could speak—"

"I speak excellent Russian."

"All right then. But stop me if there's anything you don't understand."

The old man smiles and goes over to a low table. I follow and find myself looking at a number of different colored stones.

"His Majesty the Tsar's Curiosity Cabinet opened a few years ago. Since you probably have no idea what a curiosity cabinet is, I can tell you that it's a collection of rarities from all over the world. The collection is open to the public. His Majesty the Tsar, in collaboration with me, is the one who decides what's to be put on display. Here in the first room we have stones and minerals from all over the world. Including fossils, petrified stones, amazonite, aventurine, and seashells from China and the Dutch Antilles. You're not allowed to touch them."

I try to look at the minerals, but the table is too high, and I can't see them.

Several visitors come in and pay a couple of kopecks in exchange for a glass of vodka.

"At the next tables you'll find a large collection of dried and pressed plants: violets, orchids, and other rare varieties that I've collected from all over the world. Many of them are used for medicinal purposes. Eventually the collection will be combined with the collection at the university, and then it will be the largest in the world. As you can see, we also have thousands of exotic insects, scorpions, and poisonous spiders. The bigger reptiles have been preserved in alcohol. Some visitors think that they might drink the contents, but I would strongly advise against it."

Frederik Ruysch places his hand on my shoulder.

"You're from Denmark, isn't that right?"

"Yes, I am."

"In our collection we happen to have a Danish viper. It has no teeth, just like most of the other animals in Denmark. You come from quite an interesting country. There are no animals that can kill any of you Danes. Both the wolf and the boar have virtually vanished from Denmark, and you would have to have a weak constitution to die from a viper bite. Yours is a country of harmony, if only you Danes would acknowledge your limitations."

Ruysch smiles briefly.

"But that's enough of that. If you come over here with me, you'll see a selection of stuffed kingfishers, golden eagles, and parrots, all of which the tsar's seamen have brought back to our country. This curiosity cabinet is yet another proof of Russia's leading position in the higher sciences."

I glance at the few visitors. They don't look especially interested in stuffed birds. They're hastily moving on through the mansion. Three children yawn and receive swift slaps from their mother.

"With regard to the larger animals, we keep them in the next chambers. We even have a trained bear from Siberia. The venerable Peter Shapirov used the bear to entertain guests, but when it killed his wine steward, he donated the bear to the Curiosity Cabinet. For that reason we keep it in a cage. It's temperamental, so I would advise you not to get too close. It might think you would make a tasty morsel."

When we enter the adjoining room I look at the bear, which stares at me with an inscrutable expression.

We go out to the corridor, where the floor is covered with fox skins that have been stitched together. Ruysch strides up the stairs, moving at an impressive speed for his age. I waddle after him, going as fast as I can. It says on a sign: *Veni, vidi et judica nil tuis crede oculis*.

"There is one area that particularly interests His Majesty

the Tsar. It's the study of human subspecies and deformities. In the old days the natural scientists believed that monsters came from the Devil, that it was the Evil One who had planted his seed in the woman. But today we know that's nothing but superstition. Everything has been created by God in His infallible way. Deformities occur during the pregnancy. Most often due to illness in the mother or because of nightmares she may have had. In many cases it's due to her fear. The results of these things you will see quite clearly in here."

I come to an abrupt halt.

In front of me is a little girl with an eye on her chin.

"We bought this girl from her parents for 15 rubles. As you can see, Liliya's eyes are not where we would expect them to be. On the other hand, she does have an eye underneath her mouth. How could something like this happen? Is Liliya the Devil's spawn? Should we cross ourselves like people did in the old days? Of course not. Because in every other way, Liliya is a perfectly functioning human being. That's why she is being carefully studied by His Majesty the Tsar's natural scientists."

I try to smile at the girl, but I can't tell if she smiles back. A few spectators toss coins at her. Pensively she gathers them up. Afterwards she puts them in her pocket and sits down on the floor with a distracted look on her face. Her little hands are covered with sores from frostbite.

I go over to the other end of the room. On top of four tables I see jars containing body parts preserved in alcohol. A hand with three fingers, intestines, a pair of feet with too many toes. They are all artistically arranged with flowers and seashells in a rainbow of colors. In the bottom of the jars the loveliest brains have been shaped into flowers.

"Visiting this place can be quite an overwhelming experience," says the Dutchman.

I nod and walk over to another display case. Inside is a skeleton holding a necklace in its hand. A sign reads in Russian:

"Why should I care about the transitory nature of the world?"
There is also the skeleton of a child kicking at a skull.

Ruysch explains to me that the skull belonged to a prosti-
tute, and that the child's skeleton is taking revenge for getting
syphilis from his mother. A sign reads: "Death spares no one."

There are many more people in this part of the exhibition,
but the Curiosity Cabinet is obviously not a big draw.

I move on to a row of open coffins with embalmed bodies.
Their eyes are glassy. The bodies are adorned with flowers,
necklaces, and little embroidered pillows. A child's body looks
as if it were made of marzipan.

"Embalming is a new art for the Russians, but with this
exhibit the tsar wishes to teach his people about a different way
of looking at death. My displays are meant to be viewed as little
morality plays."

"They're beautiful," I say.

"Thank you. But our biggest attraction is not my embalming
art. It's something that we'll see in the next room."

Ruysch places a hand on my shoulder.

"In fact, we're talking about a world-class sensation, one of
Nature's many miracles. His name is Nikolai Zhigant—a man
who was born in France as François Bourgeois. It was His Majesty
the Tsar himself, who found him in a marketplace in Calais and
brought him back to Russia."

We go into the next chamber.

In the middle of the room stands the tallest man I've ever
seen. He has short brown hair, a plump and sensitive face, and
big gray eyes. And he's completely naked.

"Nikolai Zhigant works part-time as a personal assistant
to Peter Alexeyevich. The rest of the time he lives in the Curiosity Cabinet, where he takes part in a great number of scientific
experiments. What makes Nikolai Zhigant particularly interesting is that his mother was a dwarf, just like you. We're now
trying to find out what sort of children he'll have when he mates
with women of various sizes."

I let my gaze slide over the giant's body, from the broad chest with the sparse hair to his stomach with the rolls of fat, and all the way down to his enormous cock, which is blue and swollen, with pulsing blood vessels.

I stare with fascination at the organ.

Nikolai Zhigant is shaking with cold. He has goosebumps on his legs, but he stands there without moving. A moment later I manage to catch his eye. He looks at me with the most tormented eyes that I've ever seen.

48.

FREDERIK RUYSCH'S OFFICE IS A SMALL ROOM WITH no windows. A copperplate engraving hangs on one of the walls. The writing desk is cluttered with ledgers, pressed flowers, and three raven quills. In a corner of the room is a stuffed beaver that stares at me with hungry eyes. It's a pleasant office, and the shelves are filled with books and manuscripts.

"What I'd like to do, Surinka, is ask you a number of questions."

"With your permission, my lord, I'm not really suited to standing in one place and staring at goodfolk."

"That's not your decision to make. Sit down on that chair."

Frederik Ruysch summons a servant to light the cast-iron stove. The man comes running in with firewood that he hastily stuffs inside the stove.

The Dutchman rolls the right sleeve of his shirt up to his elbow. Then he reaches for a raven quill and dips it in ink. His fingernails are yellow, his fingers thick and gnarled.

"I'm now going to query you about your background. I'd like you to answer all the questions in an honest and concise manner."

I nod.

Ruysch clears his throat.

"Were your parents dwarves or of normal height?"

"Both were normal."

"Were there ever, or are there now, other dwarves in your family?"

"I have no idea."

"What do you mean?"

"I've never known my mother's family, and my father was apparently an only child."

"You had no siblings?"

"None."

"Do you know anything about your mother's condition when she gave birth to you?"

"I wasn't exactly present."

Ruysch looks up with a stern expression. "It's in your best interest to answer the questions in as forthright a manner as you can."

I nod. Ruysch swiftly dips his pen again. Some of the ink drips on the paper, and he irritably wipes it away.

"Do you know whether your mother was ill during her pregnancy?"

"No."

"Was she sickly in any way?"

"No, but she died in childbirth."

"That is of no interest."

"It is to me."

"It doesn't matter what happened *after* you were born. As I've tried to explain to you, we're interested in the influences that had an effect from the moment you were conceived until the hours just *before* your birth. So we're interested in any stories you might have heard from your parents or a possible wetnurse. Do you understand?"

"I understand, yes."

"Good. While you're thinking about this, perhaps you could tell me whether any other dwarves were born in your area of Denmark."

"Not that I know of."

"There were no other dwarves in your village?"

"None."

"Other examples of deformities?"

"Flat feet."

"Flat feet are not of any interest."

"Harelips, cauls…"

Ruysch puts down his pen. "You're not being particularly cooperative, Surinka."

"But I'm more than happy to make myself available to science."

"It—"

"If you ask nicely, you're welcome to embalm me while I'm still alive."

Frederik Ruysch rings a little metal bell. The door opens and the same servant as before comes in. Ruysch nods wearily in my direction. The servant picks me up and carries me out the door. I sail through the mansion. We continue outside, through the slush, the mud, the horse droppings, and soon I'm tossed onto a filthy floor covered with a thin layer of straw.

Something moves in the dark. I have no idea what it is. But I don't care, either. I don't care at all.

49.

MY NEW PRISON IS AN OLD STABLE. IN THE EVENING there are thirty of us there, without blankets or other necessities. We're an army of impoverished freaks, monsters forsaken by God, with deformed limbs and twisted souls. We're the splinter of glass from the troll's mirror, sticking in the eye of the Savior. We are dwarves, hermaphrodites, and giants that have been locked up together with five-legged goats and Turkish obscurantists who believe that God rests on Friday. We've been put under lock and key so that our blood can be studied, our warts can be counted, our freckles can be entered in ledgers. There's always someone who is willing to pay to keep us alive so that they can observe us while we suffer, shit, and die.

The first night I lie there in the dark, surrounded by Eskimos. They're freezing too.

The air is thick with lice, and rats race around our legs. But my thoughts are not on the Dwarf Museum. For some reason I'm thinking about my father.

My father must have had dreams. Dreams of a better life and a better God. What went on inside of him whenever he stood up there in the pulpit? When he held court in the illegal tavern? When he comforted his parishioners? I have no idea. It's impossible to know your own parents; they are torturers who ought to have doled out fewer punishments. The family is a torture chamber where everyone knows each other's weaknesses but not each other's strengths.

So who *was* my father? Why do I remember only his malice, not his kisses on my cheek? Why do I never remember the meadow flowers he put in my hair in the morning? Or the Polish aquavit he taught me to drink? And why is it only now that I feel any fondness for him, now that he's six feet underground?

Maybe love is only something that exists at a distance. If love gets too close, it becomes warped and insincere.

Something is moving in the dark.

Something scuttles close to me, but I can't see what or who it is. I try to move away, but there's no place to go.

"Surinka? Is that you?"

"Who's there?"

"It's old Igor."

"Igor!" I cry happily, feeling his old man's lips against mine.

"Welcome to the Dwarf Museum," he says.

"How long have you been here?"

"Several years, I think."

Someone hushes us in the dark. I don't care for this hodgepodge of freaks. I feel as if I'm being strangled, as if evil is seething around me from these monsters who ought to join forces against those in power. Instead they survive by hating each other.

At that very moment some of them begin to fight. They hiss and spit and bite. I listen to the blows and the kicks. After several minutes it's quiet again. Then another argument flares up at the other end of the stable.

"What do you think is going to happen to me?" I whisper.

Igor squeezes my hand. "You're probably going to be here for a while."

"I don't want to stay here."

"Most of the guards are nice enough. You just need to remember to bribe them."

"With what, Igor? I have nothing to offer as a bribe."

Igor mutters something to reassure me and then lies down beside me. Little snowflakes filter into the stable and slowly melt. The old man smells of leather and mold, but tonight I find his smell pleasant.

A moment later Igor falls asleep. I think about Ismailov, about what might have happened to him, and about where he might be in the world.

50.

MAYBE I'M BEING NAÏVE, BUT I'M WAITING FOR THE tsar. Surely he will come soon to visit me; otherwise I wouldn't have been brought here.

But he never makes an appearance.

Maybe the tsar is too busy waging war, governing the country, and building canals in his Dutch-inspired paradise. All I know is that I miss Peter Alexeyevich, and that one day he will come for his Danish dwarf, and then my future will be secure. Then I'll move into his palace, and I'll be hot-tempered the way I'm often hot-tempered, and I'll mock those who deserve to be mocked.

But the only thing I'm allowed to become is a pillar of salt.

I have to stand at my station in the Curiosity Cabinet and stare straight ahead without meeting the eyes of the fine folk. If they ask me something, I'm supposed to answer. Otherwise

I'm supposed to keep my mouth shut. If they throw money at me, I'm allowed to pick it up. If they grope me, I'm supposed to spread whatever it's necessary to spread.

For several days I get only a cracker to eat along with a goblet of vodka. We've begged for a few blankets down in the stable, but after the hermaphrodite ran away, our circumstances have gotten worse. I have no idea where it has fled. We're questioned about the matter, but no one knows a thing. Frederik Ruysch is furious. Hermaphrodites are expensive, and it's not easy to find another in today's market. He writes to various curiosity cabinets in Dresden, Hanover, and Paris, attempting to trade a monkey man for a hermaphrodite, but no one is interested. Sometime later the old hermaphrodite is found dead in a *dacha*, apparently a suicide.

NIKOLAI ZHIGANT HAS been away from the Curiosity Cabinet for six months. He has been serving as the tsar's wine steward during a trip to the Black Sea. Peter Alexeyevich loves the Frenchman, who is a head taller than he is. But one day Nicolai is back. His situation has not improved. He still has to stand naked in those ice-cold rooms.

Several times I sneak in to have a look at him.

Nicolai is a real man. That's something that an old hag like me can appreciate. I often stare at his juicy cock, observing how it hangs like a truncheon between his legs.

Then one day Nikolai falls in love with one of the women that he's been forced to impregnate. She's a Finn and almost as tall as he is. They're a marvelous couple. They can't stand upright anywhere in the world. They have to crawl through doorways. They sit on stools that collapse like a house of cards. When they take a walk in the garden, they scrape their heads against the sky. They're perfect together, but they don't produce any children. For a year they stand side by side in the Curiosity Cabinet, hand in hand, naked as Adam and Eve. The tsar's towering favorites.

The tsar has many favorites.
I'm glad that I'm not one of them.

51.

WHY DON'T I FEEL ANY HAPPIER AFTER FINDING GOD?
I felt a peace in my soul while I lived in the cloister. I found a purpose behind my sufferings. But when I returned to the city, the world ate its way into me. It took less than a day to learn that nothing had changed. I was back where I've always been: buried deep in God's garbage heap.

I'm furious. I'm always furious. Maybe fury is the only thing that has meaning. Maybe fury is God.

52.

TWO YEARS LATER I WAKE UP SHAKING WITH COLD.
There is frost on the straw. Petersburg's snow is coming through the slats of the wall, boring its way under our skin and coaxing out wretched colds. All manner of misery drips down from the sky—the sky that I worshipped in the cloister, where I found peace and a faith in nothingness.

The tsar finally paid a visit a few months ago.

He greeted me, kissed me on the lips, and hurried onward. I'm not sure that he remembered his Danish dwarf. I'm not sure about anything at all. How long have I been here? How often have I been put on display before man and beast?

Maybe I've stood in the Curiosity Cabinet since the day I was born.

Frederik Ruysch is experimenting with me. He takes my blood, sticks me with needles, and studies my excrement. He measures my short neck with his calipers, scrapes a big slice of skin off my finger and puts it on an oval plate. I scream in terror, but Ruysch doesn't hear me. He's not interested in my screams. Instead he tells me that dwarves were once treasured in ancient Egypt. We were treated like gods. He knows this from what they've found inside the pyramids and from the excavations in the desert.

Ruysch wears an amicable expression as he manhandles me. He's always talking about an Egyptian god named Bes, the god of sexuality and childbirth, but I have a hard time listening to him. When Ruysch is done with his examinations, he locks himself in his office, where he studies both the Bible and my numbers.

One day Ruysch admits that I actually do have a soul.

"Why do you think so?" I ask dryly. "Did you find it under your microscope?"

"The soul is invisible, Surinka."

Ruysch gives me a good-natured smile.

I object. "If it's invisible, then you can't see it."

"You have human features. Your deformities were caused by your mother's fear during pregnancy. You are not a monster. You are not from the Devil. You are God's creature."

"I'm sorry to hear that."

"Why is that?"

"I would prefer to come from the Devil. That would give me a purpose."

"Is there no purpose in coming from God?"

I pause to think about his question.

Frederik Ruysch laughs. For a moment I think he's going to hug me, but then he reaches out for some papers. I look at his strange face that collapses whenever he looks down. I wonder how old the Dutchman is. Seventy? Eighty? And what is it that makes him treat us so badly? Is it the joy of humiliating those who are wretched and miserable? Is he a person that other people fear? The kind who enjoys inflicting pain in order to assert himself? That doesn't really seem to be the case. Frederik Ruysch is simply searching for the truth. Ruysch is a scientist who wants to understand the world, no matter what the cost. He wants to institute rules and laws for everything. Where others see love, he sees only mathematics.

My eyes slide over his Adam's apple, which always has a few stray hairs on it. The old man isn't very adept at shaving.

When I'm back at my station, I long for the time when I didn't have a soul.

53.

I USUALLY NEVER THINK ABOUT MY MOTHER. SHE GAVE birth to me under a new moon. After that she rushed up to Heaven's gate. But right now I'm thinking about her. In the Curiosity Cabinet there is plenty of time to think about all manner of things.

I'm thinking about how I was a perfect fetus until my mother's fear took over. About how my limbs reached for the sun, how my fingers were long, and my back was straight. But then my mother had her nightmares. What did she dream about? What was it that destroyed my body? And why wasn't it the seed that had something wrong with it? That deviltry my father pumped out whenever the spirit came over him?

Each day my mother's belly grew bigger. It grew as big as a tumor. That was how she saw me: as a monster that wanted to destroy her life. Once in a while she would talk to me: "Why do you have to come here? Why can't you stay away? I'm an adventurer, I want to experience the world, even if it's no farther than to Brønshøj. I want to travel, I want to fall in love, I don't want to take care of a child that I hardly know."

Inside her belly I listened to the world on the other side of her navel. What was out there? A playground? Endless darkness? What? Often I felt that I'd been there before, that I was simply making a return, with new worries and new anxieties.

Then one day my mother opened up.

From my place inside I saw the world coming toward me like a divine toilet—like a big white funnel, with light pouring in to punish me. Who was out there? Strangers with vapid smells— people with voices that tore apart the silence. I panicked, I wrapped the umbilical cord around my neck until I was blue in the face. But slowly I slipped out, pushed by invisible hands. It was a journey through cream. I slid past clumps of it. The world drew closer, a world that was cold as stone, with insects and filthy towels.

My mother screamed and squeezed her thighs together in an attempt to suffocate me. I remember the sweat that lashed her brow, the maggots that waited in the damp clothing. I reached out...but my mother was gone. She had slipped up to Heaven, leaving her body behind. I clenched my tiny fists, but I was lost from the moment I was born.

Lonely and lost.

The grown-ups tossed me around, drying me on discarded draperies and commenting on my sex and my silence. Was my father present? Most likely not. Father was busy spreading his seed in other parishioners. Father preached God's word in half-timbered sheds and haylofts.

Yes, that's how it was.

That's how it *could* have been.

As I envision it on that day in the Curiosity Cabinet.

FREDERIK RUYSCH HAS come by to have a talk with me. He's angry because I snarled at the visitors. A little girl patted me on the head. After that she stuck her pink finger into my nose. So I hit her. Not hard, but I did hit her. It felt good. It felt immensely liberating.

"What am I going to do with you, Surinka?"

Frederik Ruysch gives me a dejected look. I don't reply. I'm a pillar of salt. Pillars of salt don't talk.

The Dutchman clasps his hands, as if he's about to pray. His eyes are kind, but his mouth is unrelenting.

We glare at each other.

Outside it's summer. Somewhere a clock strikes. New art has appeared on the wall. A tableau of fetuses, skeletons, and the most exquisite mountain of kidney stones. Every part of the body is art. We're building blocks in the hands of the great master, Frederik Ruysch.

I'm hustled back to my station.

Igor is standing next to me. We're supposed to hold each other's hands whenever people are present, but no one feels like visiting the Curiosity Cabinet. Occasionally there are seven or eight visitors, most of them foreigners. The Russian church regards the Curiosity Cabinet as something demonic. And the church is quite right about that.

The Russians don't care to see children's bodies embalmed. They'd rather not look at severed limbs artistically arranged in display cases. They take no pleasure in collections of eyeballs or bladders. The Russians believe that the dead turn into vampires if they're not put into the ground at once.

Igor and I are surrounded by vampires.

ONE DAY I'M given some paper so that I can draw whenever I'm bored. There's something soothing about drawing pictures of my life. I examine my hatred as I sketch my enemies: people from my childhood, Count Rosenkvist, and the old man Frederik Ruysch. Afterwards I burn the drawings, letting the flames creep over their faces. Revenge is sweet, but there's never enough of it.

I also draw the tsar: his tall body, his round head with the birthmark, and his narrow shoulders. I sit with that drawing for a long time. Behind me the guard has fallen asleep. Sunlight is coming in through the small windows.

Someone ought to burn the Curiosity Cabinet down to the ground. Someone ought to free these wretches and turn this Sodom and Gomorrah into ashes. I ponder whether I could lead a rebellion, but I know that I'm too small. Instead I try to make new acquaintances. I'd like to be friends with Liliya, the girl with the eye on her chin, but she refuses to talk to me. Each time I approach, her whole body starts to shake, as if she thinks that I intend to harm her. One day I try to lend her my coat, but she just stares down at the straw with her melancholy eyes. Why doesn't she understand that I only want the best for her?

No one wants to talk to me. Everyone closes up around their own hatred.

That's what life is like in the Curiosity Cabinet.

ONE WINTER MORNING something happens. Frederik Ruysch walks through the mansion wearing his fur coat. He's making sure that everything is in order, that the Eskimos are standing ready with their spears, that the goat with five legs has been tied up properly. Ruysch enjoys playing God in his own paradise. He has his hands behind his back. He has an arrogant expression on his face with the sharp nose. But he has a kind word for all of us: "Excellent." "Good job." And the like.

When he comes over to me, he moistens his lips.

"Surinka?"

"Yes, my lord."

"How is our Danish dwarf on this divine morning?"

"As good as you wish me to be, my lord."

"You have a visitor."

"A visitor?"

"A gentleman who says that he knows you."

I fight to stay calm.

"Don't you want to know who it is?" he asks.

"I thought I wasn't allowed to have visitors."

"You're not."

"I'm hardly allowed even to fart without your written permission. Isn't that true, my lord?"

A vein starts to throb in the Dutchman's forehead. Today he does look like he's eighty. Maybe it's because of all the embalmings. Maybe he should embalm himself so that the rest of us can be free of his experiments.

At that moment Lukas comes in.

We stare at each other.

Then I clench my fists.

54.

THE FOG IS LIKE AN ICE-COLD EMBRACE. IT COMES rolling in from the sky, it clings to the skin, and it erases the coastline and the birds. Even the boat that we're sitting in has vanished. We're in the middle of a world wrapped in clouds. One fog bank after another buries us. At one point I can't even see my feet. I can't see Lukas or the man who's steering the barge. It's marvelous to get lost in one's own life. I suddenly have an urge to dive down into the water, to let it carry me wherever it likes. But fate demands that I stay seated where I am.

There is no longer any wind. Just fog.

We're not making any headway.

I can sense that Lukas is getting nervous. He barks out a few commands to the bargeman, but no one answers him. The fog glides through me and through Lukas. We're floating through a world like black fairies.

Suddenly I catch sight of a patch of grayish-blue water.

Anything could happen. The surface of the water could be breached by a sea monster with fins and a trident. Monsters could grow out of the sky and drift down to the barge. Maybe I'll never have to go back to the Curiosity Cabinet. Maybe I can just stay here in this boat.

The fog lifts.

A veil slips aside. It gets warmer and brighter. I can see a stretch of gray coastline, a small bridge, a few scrawny trees. Slowly a house comes into view, a house with a red roof, an ornamental garden, and a well.

"Welcome to my home," says Lukas.

IT'S A WONDERFUL two-story stone house with a chimney and four bay windows. The door is painted green, the timbered ceiling in reddish tones, and all the chairs have high backs and golden leather cushions. Lukas has even been given a butler, who coaxes my carpetbag away from me with an impeccable nod. He's a dwarf from the Siberian steppes.

Lukas shows me around the small rooms.

"My house was finished several years ago. The tsar attended the ribbon-cutting. He was in high spirits and promised to take care of me until the end of my days. Take a look at the beautiful tile stove with the Biblical scenes. It was made by a master Italian craftsman. I was allowed to choose the scenes myself. And believe me, I browbeat the man."

Lukas has put on weight. His hair is almost all gray, and his paunch has gotten much bigger.

"Prince Menshikov gave me that picture on the wall. It shows the Russian double eagle, holding the tsar in its claws. I'm very happy here, Surinka. I really am."

I smile.

"But I've missed you, Surinka. Quite a lot, actually."

He tries to hug me.

"What happened to Natasha?" I ask.

"Natasha is gone. But let's not talk about her. Would you like something to eat? We don't have much, but there's always a little soup and some fish."

Lukas barks an order. Then he turns to face me again.

"But I'm hoping that you'll tell me about your stay at the cloister. How was it there? Tell me the whole story with as many details as you can remember, so I can picture everything for myself. You've always been such a fabulous storyteller."

Lukas looks at me with anticipation.

"It was quiet," I tell him.

"Quiet?"

I nod.

"Yes, but was it ... edifying? Didn't your stay there help you?"

"What do you mean?"

"With all your various ... problems?"

"I don't really know what you mean, Lukas."

"With the devil that crept into your mouth? You weren't always yourself, Surinka. You really weren't."

"What do you mean by I wasn't 'myself,' Lukas? I'd certainly like to hear what you mean by that."

"Yourself, Surinka. Yourself, when you're normal and loving."

"No one has ever accused me of being loving."

"I have," says Lukas, beaming.

I get up and go over to the windows with the leaded panes made of mica. I can't see the water through the panes. I can't see anything at all. If I lived in such a beautiful house, I would have big windows so the light could bake all the rooms. Nature would seep into the house, ivy would climb up along the high-backed chairs, water plants would twine around the clothes tree. But Russians never wish for light. They cultivate melancholy, even inside their houses.

"Do I have to go back to the Curiosity Cabinet?"

"That's not up to me, Surinka."

"But you've just taken me out."

"I got you out because I pleaded with the tsar."

"Why?"

"I told him that I had a use for you."

"What use do you have for me, Lukas?"

At that moment the butler comes in. He seems bad-tempered, maybe because of his hideous hunchback. He looks at me with suspicion as he sets a tureen of soup on the table.

"I have decided . . . "—Lukas looks into my eyes—"that I love you, and that I can't live without you, Surinka."

I laugh joylessly. "And when exactly did you 'decide' this, dear Lukas?"

"Over the past couple of years."

"I don't believe you."

"It's true."

"You're in love with love. You have a need for grand emotions in that little body of yours."

"Stop insulting me, Surinka."

"Then stop talking about your feelings for me when you haven't seen me in years."

"Surinka, you've tried to insult me from the very first day we met. But I don't care. You can't insult me any longer. I love you too much to feel offended."

"We'll have to test that out," I say.

"Surinka, I have an offer to make: move in with me."

The little man gives me an imploring look.

"Look, this is how it is. We can live in sin, of course, the way you're used to in your own country, in Denmark. But if things go well for us, then I think that we—"

"Can't we eat the soup instead of bothering with all this nonsense?" I beg.

"It's not nonsense. I promise you that I can get the tsar's permission."

"You know what? I'm sick of you and your tsar. You send me off to a cloister to find God, but the only thing I find there are lashes from a whip. Then you rescue me from the Curiosity Cabinet with a snap of your fingers. But just as I'm starting to enjoy my freedom, you start talking about a new prison."

"I haven't said a word about a prison."

"Oh yes, you have. You just can't hear it, because you're the guard."

Lukas gives me a downhearted look. A fly lands on his hand.

"I don't know what to say, Surinka. I'm not as smart as you are."

I stroke his cheek with my hand.

"That may well be, but you do have power."

"And what's wrong with that?"

"Nothing. I'm just jealous."

Lukas looks at me with big eyes. Then he starts to cry. I go over and sit on his lap. Tears are streaming down his face. I stay where I am, pressing his adorable face to my bosom.

And that's how we sit as the soup grows cold.

There's so much that I'd like to tell Lukas. About Terje, who treated me so badly, although I deserved it. About Mathias, who sank down to the bottom of the sea with his adorable harelip, but

210 PETER H. FOGTDAL

who still won't leave me alone. I'd like to tell Lukas about my father, whom I loved more than I ever loved anyone else. About how I nursed him when he was dying, how I held his hand as he cursed his inconsiderate Creator. I'd like to tell Lukas that my father and I were closer to each other at the hour of death then we ever were in life. I'd like to tell him about all of these things, but I don't. I don't know why. But I can't.

We make love in Lukas's little bed with the silk pillows, the green canopy, and the scent of expensive perfumes that aren't suited to a *karlik*, a dwarf. Our lovemaking is different than it used to be. Lukas keeps his eyes open as he burrows between my legs. He's on top, and he sits there like an emperor, studying me. His hands are loving and gentle. His kisses me tenderly and smiles. There is something so familiar about Lukas's body— its sweet smell, the tiny hairs around his navel that look like a thicket on a mountain ridge.

Outside, the moon is shining with its silvery sheen. A wolf howls in the woods. It's beautiful. The world can be so beautiful, if only it would just leave me alone.

I turn to face Lukas and kiss him in the glow of the candles. We hold each other until dawn. Then we fall asleep.

I've never been so utterly bored.

55.

IT'S NOT A BAD LIFE. IT'S LOVELY ON THIS ISLAND OUT-side the city. I can see the towers and the building sites of Peters-burg. I can sense all the hustle and bustle without being part of it. The world is a poem. It's possible to write yourself into it once in a while, but it's even more beautiful to write yourself out.

It snows at Christmastime. The phantoms merge with the trees, the birds fall frozen to the ground. We can't even stay warm if we sleep on top of the stove. There is frost on every single object in the small rooms. At least twenty icicles hang from the eaves of the house.

Ismailov has been taken to Siberia in the flatbed of a cattle wagon.

Lukas tells me about this one evening.

In Siberia it's even colder than in Petersburg. That's where the tsar sends his enemies. Siberia is a wasteland. Siberia is like a cloister where human beings encounter God in all His rawness. In Siberia a person can obtain forgiveness, but only if he manages to survive.

I think about Ismailov, about whether he's suffering more than he usually did. The Russians love to suffer. It's happiness that makes them nervous.

That evening I say a prayer for my gloomy friend. I picture him before me: his melancholy eyes, his stooped body, the abscess in his tooth.

It's the first time that I pray since my days at the cloister. I pray into an empty space. But I feel that I do get something in return. A nearness and a sense that someone is listening.

One evening I ask Lukas, "What ever happened to that idiot Dolgoruky?"

We're sitting as close to the stove as we can get. I'm burrowed under a red blanket and my squirrel-skin coat. On my feet I'm wearing three pairs of wool socks, but my teeth are still chattering.

"I wish you wouldn't talk about the prince like that."

"He was Ismailov's superior, wasn't he?"

Lukas nods and fixes his eyes on the stove.

"Was he also taken to Siberia? Or is he now shorter by a head?"

"Rumor has it that Dolgoruky has been banished to Kazan."

"Why?"

"Because he participated in Alexey's coup attempt."

"I don't think there ever was a coup attempt."

"How would you know that? You're a foreigner."

"Contrary to what you may believe, Lukas, a foreigner is actually quite capable of thinking."

The little man shakes his head and looks at me without a trace of humor.

"Why are you always so negative with regard to the fine folk?" he asks.

"Why? Because someone has to be negative."

"I don't understand."

I tilt my head and try to sound less annoyed than usual.

"The fine folk are born for only two purposes: to be fine folk and to go to war. If there isn't any war, they have to settle for being fine folk. That's why they hope for war—so that their lives will have some meaning."

Lukas looks at me pensively.

"And for what purpose were you born, Surinka?"

"To be a stone in their shoes."

I get up from the little table. At that instant one of Lukas's icons topples to the floor. He gives me a frightened look and crosses himself three times. There are deep furrows on his brow. His ears are as red as copper.

I feel an impulse to kiss him, but I don't. I think about Ismailov in Siberia, about how his legs are chained to a hedge, about how he has to eat bark from the trees in order to survive. I think about Alexey, who was tortured to death in prison because he didn't want to be tsar—or at least not on his father's terms.

It's always a matter of choosing sides.

Of backing the right man.

That's all that matters in the world that men have created, the world that very soon must go under.

OVER THE NEXT few days I pump Lukas for information about Ismailov—about why he doesn't like Ismailov, about the political situation in Russia, about everything between Heaven and Earth. I know that I'm getting on his nerves. But I have a real urge to get on his nerves.

Lukas goes for walks in the woods to escape my questioning.

But one day he comes down with a cold. He goes to bed, coughing. Now I have him right where I want him.

I sit down next to his bed while he sleeps.

I want to take away your sunshine, Lukas. Not because I'm evil but because the sun can't exist without shadows. I want to examine the lie that keeps you afloat—the idea that it's wonderful to be Lukas, that it's splendid to be the tsar's favorite dwarf, that there's nothing better to do than to bring crackers to Menshikov like some kind of dog. When does it hurt the most, Lukas? That's what I'd like to know. What hurts you more than anything else? Is it when the tsar mocks you? Or is it when he can't remember your name? Is it when he forgets all about you for a year or two? When are you going to curse Peter Alexeyevich to Hell, Lukas? That's what I'd like to know. I want to get behind that smile of yours, and your clown's heart. And then I'll console you when you fall apart—I'll console you when you realize that you are infinitely unloved.

At that moment I'll be at your side, but not before.

Not a moment before.

56.

TIME SLIPS AWAY.

Lukas has been in bed for several weeks. He raves in delirium. It's beautiful. One morning he wakes up and asks me to heat up a pitcher of beer for him. The little man is lying under a brown wool blanket embroidered with flowers. He coughs. His mucus is yellow. I take some of my dried herbs out of my carpetbag: mushrooms, henbane, and swallowwort. Then I make a couple of signs over him and place the twig of an ash tree on his chest as I say a few prayers.

Lukas watches me with a gloomy expression. "Where did you learn all these rituals of yours? At the cloister?"

"In Denmark."

"It's not black magic, is it?"

"Not everything that comes from abroad is black magic, Lukas."

"Almost everything."

I caress his cheek. "What do you think your beloved tsar would say, if he heard you say that?"

"Peter Alexeyevich no longer travels abroad."

"Rumor has it that he's ill."

"You shouldn't listen to rumors."

I place a wreath made of plants on Lukas's head, I put mustard plasters on his wrists. Lukas is freezing one minute and sweating the next. His eyes are dull, his nose keeps running. He's not a pretty sight.

"I'm not going die, am I, Surinka?"

"You have a head cold, Lukas."

Lukas coughs so adorably. I hold his hand and say another prayer. Then I lie down beside him.

"We're going to live here together, aren't we, Surinka? Then we can go into the city whenever the tsar needs us. And after we've conquered the world, we'll go back to our house, feed the chickens, and take pleasure in each other's company. That's how it will be. We don't even have to get married, if you don't want to. I'm not a stern taskmaster. You know that, don't you?"

I nod. Lukas slips his hand into mine.

"I know that you love me. You don't even have to say it," he says.

I smile and give him a drink with herbs.

"I can see it in your eyes, Surinka. It's wonderful. That's exactly what it is."

Lukas swallows the mixture of herbs and smiles at me. There are still a few leaves in the bottom, but I'm satisfied—satisfied and sad.

Lukas starts to tell me a story. As usual, he spits as he talks. His lips are slightly blue, but the blue color suits him, even though he's more ill than he knows.

I run my hand through his hair. There are gray hairs at his

temples. And I whisper to him that he's going to feel tired, very tired. And soon.

Lukas is still telling the story, but his eyelids are getting heavier. Several spasms slide across his face, but he seems happy and content. I kiss him on the lips, I rub his little copper-red ears, and I tickle his Adam's apple, which is still bobbing excitedly.

I start the countdown. I'm counting down over Lukas. His eyes become remote and lackluster. He's asleep now, and no one can do him any harm in the dream that he's dreaming.

I look out the little window.

Outside I see the island and the sea disappear.

I put my arm around Lukas and feel his delicate breath against my cheek. There is a full moon. The full moon is speaking.

57.

SHE WAS A WITCH WHO LIVED NOT IN THE FOREST BUT in a house in Husum. I met her when I was about ten years old. She was young, with broad shoulders, and her hands were as rough as a man's. When she looked at someone, it was as if she were reading an invisible book. At first I was afraid of her, but after she invited me in, I was no longer scared. I asked her why the elves had forsaken me, why I couldn't be friends with them anymore. And then she explained that I was supposed to be in this world, that it was here I should live. "But once in a while you'll be able to look inside," she said. "Once in a while you can open your eyes to the spirit realm, and then you'll discover the will-o'-the-wisps that dance through the forest. You'll catch sight of the merman who guards the waters from rubbish and foolishness. But only in brief glimpses, Sørine. It's important that you control the spirit world, or else it will control you. That's why human beings are born with a hole in their memories. So that we don't allow ourselves to be sucked up to Heaven."

I didn't understand what the wise woman meant, but she

set me on top of her table, closed her eyes, and removed what needed to be removed.

At one point I saw a light all around her, as if she were on fire. Then I fell into a long and dreamless sleep. I was walking in a vast landscape. I saw that everything had a soul, that everything had a voice, even the humblest little thistle. There was a hidden harmony in the woods and the meadows. For the next few years I worked for the wise woman. I learned to protect myself with herbs, I learned to trust in Thor and Odin instead of the Christian chatterboxes. I read in the book of nature and trusted in the thoughts that found their way into my mind. But it didn't make me any happier. I was still looking for an explanation for why I was the way I was, why my body refused to grow along with my dreams.

During those years I used to stare at myself in the mirror. If I stood there long enough, something would change. Slowly I became covered with tiny hairs, like an animal. My breasts were two black holes, my stomach a shaggy mat. Through my skin it was possible to see my skeleton, the churning of my blood, the beating of my heart. I was a human being, and yet not a human being. And I was little, oh so little.

There was something about the transition from child to youth that I couldn't comprehend. I didn't understand why blood ran out of my body once a month. Where did it come from? Where did I come from? There were so many questions in my head, so many things that I had to figure out. But I had no idea where to start.

One day something happened to the wise woman.

She started getting headaches that felt like iron bands around her skull. She took to her bed, and when she recovered, she wasn't the same. A light had gone out, and something else had taken its place. She still helped her fellow creatures, but she was angrier and less patient. On Sundays she took me to the marketplace, where she forced me to drink the blood of those who had been executed. "It will give you strength," said Anja, because Anja was her name. "You need strength so that you can tell the difference between good and evil."

A dark figure often stood behind her. It whispered its messages, but only the witch could hear what they were. In town they saw her riding a broomstick as she howled at the moon. Rumors began to spread: Anja had assumed the shape of a snow hare; she killed firstborn children with the evil eye; she poisoned the river water with her spit. She had to be stopped.

One morning they came to get her. They were city fathers: black-garbed, pious, and grim. She was driven to the prison in Copenhagen. What happened to her after that, I don't know. Maybe she flew up to Brocken in the Harz Mountains, maybe she's still sitting in her cell in Copenhagen.

They left me alone because I took up so little space in the world, because I was endearing, because I couldn't hurt anyone even if I tried.

A year later my father sold me to Count Rosenkvist. But I never forgot Anja and her herbs. They stayed with me, they were part of me. I couldn't live without them.

58.

EARLY ONE MORNING I LEAVE, TAKING WITH ME MY carpetbag, my deer-antler cane, and my worn, squirrel-skin coat. The ice stretches out before me like a white carpet. The moon is shining and it follows me as I move across the ice toward Petersburg. At any moment I expect the ice to give way, but it's like a carpet of cobblestones.

Slowly dawn arrives. There are no birds in the sky. All of Nature has a solemnity and stillness about it, like before the Creation. The ice has blue streaks, patterns, and shadows.

Lukas is still asleep in his bed. He's feeling better after I gave him my herbs.

For the first time in a week he's sleeping peacefully. His hands are folded on his chest. His face is pale. He's getting better.

Petersburg wakes up. The trees are white with frost, the

sky is the color of raspberries. Several families have settled near
the river. They've built log huts and they've tethered goats.
Everyone is stretching, letting the frost escape from their mouths.
When they speak, their words turn to ice. Everything is ice.
Maybe it's always been that way.

For a change I'm feeling lonely.

Not because I'm alone, but because the horizon is so white.
I have no future. Everything is uncertain and fragile. I once
thought that life would bring me peace, but there is never any
peace.

I remember one time when I walked through the blackest
of nights. It was an evening in March. I was about twenty. There
were no stars in the sky, no moon, only darkness. At one point I
took a shortcut through a cemetery. I could make out the grave-
stones all around me, a single poplar tree, and the church walls.
There was no wind and not a sound, just an infinite emptiness in
the sky above me and in the earth underneath. But I wasn't
afraid. I felt protected by the nothingness. I had a feeling that
there wasn't anything out there that could threaten me, and I
hoped that dawn would never come.

It's dawn now.

A horse-drawn leather sleigh glides past me. The horses
have rime on their manes. The city's church bells chime.

I have no idea where I'm going.

Preferably to Ismailov's Siberia.

Or to my own Denmark.

THE CEREMONY STARTS at midday. I have no idea what it's
about.

I'm standing on a flatbed wagon when I see the procession
coming down the road. In front march soldiers in red uniforms
with fluttering silk banners. After them come priests carrying
glass crucifixes, icons, and missals adorned with diamonds. One
of the priests is holding a golden pitcher in the air. It looks idiotic,
but the holy ones have always been idiotic.

The procession continues. I don't know which are the priests and which are the metropolitans; they're all dressed in the finest attire, with tall hats, beautiful kirtles, and wild beards.

"What's going on?" I ask a woman.

She glares at me and then turns back to watch the procession. As it passes, everyone hastens to bow down. A few throw themselves onto the snow; others place their hands on the ice-covered ground. I catch sight of a red canopy, but I can't see who is walking beneath it. The crowds get thicker. People come swarming out of houses, factories, and chapels. Along the way the soldiers try to keep order with drawn sabers. All of them are heading toward the Neva. I decide to follow along, as I fight for my life among the legs of the goodfolk. The sun peeks out for a brief moment, but even the sun is difficult to see.

When we reach the river, I climb up into a tree. Out on the ice an area has been closed off with a white fence. It's covered with Persian carpets. Suddenly I catch sight of the tsar. He's sitting on a tall chair, the only one on the ice. Against my will, tears come to my eyes. Peter Alexeyevich has grown old. His movements are slow and frail. He's wearing a powdered wig, a sable fur, and shiny boots. I've never seen him look so elegant. He seems ponderous and solemn, as if the flesh might fall off his bones at any moment.

Three of the metropolitans are standing next to a hole in the ice. A monk uses an oar to stir the water and keep it from freezing. Others are swinging censers reeking with incense. A priest reads aloud from an enormous missal. The metropolitan who is most beautifully dressed dips a huge crucifix into the hole in the water and lets the drops drip into a gilded silver dish. A sigh passes through the crowd. Some people murmur prayers. The tsar goes over to the hole and dips his fingers in the silver dish.

I know that he's going to die a few months from now. He can dip his fingers in as much holy water as he likes, but he's going to die soon. And he will never see his dwarves again.

The tsar looks up at the sky as he rubs holy water around his eyes.

I'm tired, thinks Peter Alexeyevich. Catherine has her lovers, and Menshikov is stealing from the treasury. The world is filled with peace; things have never been worse. Human beings are not made for peace. They can't bear such an unnatural state. My Russia is falling back on old habits. Even a tsar feels powerless.

Peter sits down on his chair and coughs. The other fine folk are given some of the holy drops. The water hole freezes over. The big Bible becomes covered with snow crystals: first the Old Testament, then the Book of Job, then the Gospel according to Matthew.

The world is coming to an end in a vacuum, thinks Peter. At night I am haunted by Alexey. He's paler than ever before, his back is covered with welts. I condemned myself to death when he breathed his last. We humans always condemn ourselves; we don't need God for that.

The procession heads back to the city, but without the tsar.

The tsar gets into his sleigh. It looks like an elegant coffin with black cushions and a big bear-skin rug. Peter gazes out over the citizens standing along the road. His face has caved in, it's a mask devoid of any humor or warmth.

For a brief moment our eyes meet, but the tsar doesn't recognize me.

By the time I climb down from the tree, I am forever cured of Russia.

I once thought that it would be my new country, but it's not. I belong somewhere else. But where?

Where?

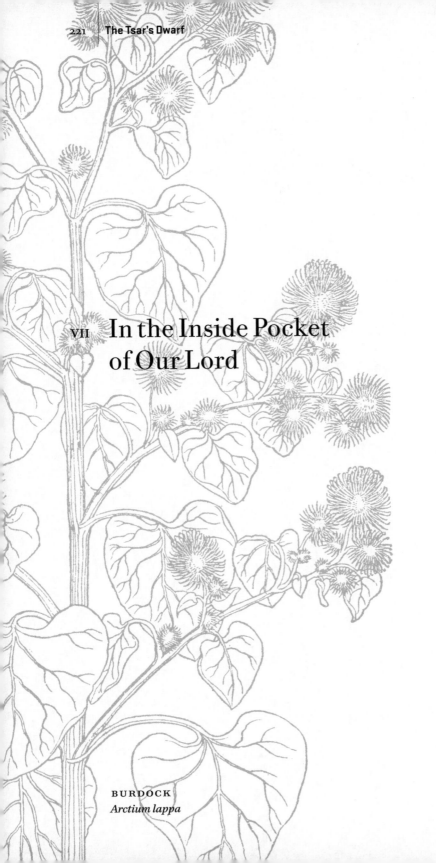

VII   In the Inside Pocket of Our Lord

BURDOCK
Arctium lappa

59.

THE DAYLIGHT LASTS ONLY A FEW HOURS IN PETERS-
burg. The light seems to know that it should stay away. There
is too much to fight against: too many gloomy nooks and
crannies, too many frozen hearts. Darkness settles over the city,
not like a blanket, but like a lullaby that soothes the Russians
into a deep sleep.

I walk through a marketplace with three kopecks in my
pocket. All around me vendors are selling fish, padlocks, and
walrus tusks. The merchants tear the hats off the heads of goodfolk to get them to stop. A thief steals a beaver skin and flees
through the market on his old nag. Several soldiers start hooting,
others make the sign of the cross. Not to protect themselves but
because they're siding with the thief.

I consider putting on a little show, but I don't feel like performing anymore. I wander around and steal a frozen loaf of
bread from a few Kirghizes. At night I sleep inside a church. It's
ice-cold. I feel sick and helpless. Isn't there a life for me somewhere? I want to have a life.

I wonder if Lukas is sleeping right now.

I don't want to think about him. There are things in the
world that you shouldn't concern yourself with. Once upon a
time there was an island. It no longer exists.

I'M AWAKENED BY the merchants who come to get their wares from the church. They've locked them up for the night, and I was given permission to sleep on a few cushions in exchange for certain favors.

Three Cossacks have arrived at the marketplace to sell sable furs. They laugh at me, but I can't understand what they're saying. One of them invites me to a *kabak*. We sit down on a long bench and order a few tankards of vodka. The Cossack's hands are a little too eager. I give him a slap, but he finds that amusing. He lifts me in the air with one hand and flings me over to a few other boozers. They toss me around the room until they get tired of the game.

I totter out into the snow, grateful not to have broken any bones. It's dusk. Two Russians are standing there, spitting into each other's face. At that moment I catch sight of four sleighs. They look like little huts with horses hitched to the front. The horses are adorned with foxtails and golden harnesses. They're stomping vigorously to keep warm. A groom is seated on one of the sleighs, sound asleep. Several soldiers are talking on the other side of the caravan. For some reason the door to the second sleigh is open. I try to climb up to the hatch, but it's too high. I try jumping up again. This time I make it.

The traveling sleigh is empty but beautifully furnished with blankets, cushions, and a peephole. There's room for two or three people to sleep inside. A saint looks at me sternly from the wall.

Suddenly I hear voices. I crawl under the blankets. Several children climb inside. The hatch door slams shut. With a lurch the sleigh sets off. The children are eagerly talking. One of them tells a joke and then laughs. One of them sits down on top of me and gives a start.

"What's that?" says a boy's voice, sounding nervous.

Silence falls over the sleigh. For a moment I think about what I should do. Then I lift the blanket aside and look into the eyes of three frightened children wearing fur coats and caps.

They look at me, their mouths agape. The youngest, a little girl, starts to cry.

"Who are you?" asks a boy with freckles.

"My name is Surinka."

"What are you doing in our traveling sleigh?"

I give them a reassuring smile, but all of a sudden I have no idea what to say.

"You're not supposed to be here," says the older boy, trying to sound brave.

I sit up and smile again. The children stare at my little torso and my short legs. Outside I can hear the snow thudding against the sleigh.

"How ugly you are," says the second boy sheepishly.

"Thank you."

"Are you a real midget?"

"Yes. I'm a present from your parents."

"A present?"

The three children stare at me.

"For your journey. So you'll have someone to play with."

"Are you going to Poland with us?"

The little girl is still crying. The two boys stare at me in awe.

"Our father didn't say anything about you."

"He wanted it to be a surprise."

"Why...why do you talk so strange?" asks the younger boy.

"Because I was born in a hole in the ground."

"Were you really?"

"Yes, dwarves are always born in holes in the ground, and when we turn six, we learn to fly. That's why I flew off and came all the way here to Russia."

"I'm six," says the younger boy with freckles. "Can you teach me how to fly?"

"First you'll have to buy yourself a broomstick, and they're very expensive in Russia."

The older boy laughs. The other two hasten to laugh with him.

"You're both funny *and* ugly. We accept you as our present."

"Thank you."

"You're lucky, because we're a very fine family."

"Are you really?"

"My father buys wine for the tsar. We've lived all over the world."

"Is that right? Where?" I'm trying to act as if I like children.

"In France and in the Austrian Empire."

"Have you ever been to Denmark?"

"What's Denmark?"

"That's where I come from."

"But you said you came from a hole in the ground."

"Yes, a Danish hole in the ground."

The older boy puts on his most grown-up expression.

"Do they make good wine in Denmark? If they don't make good wine, then we haven't been there."

"We make cherry wine."

"Cherry wine isn't real wine. That's what my father says."

The older boy is a handsome, dark-haired lad around ten. His name is Fyodor. He doesn't look like a Russian. The younger boy, Kristopher, is just as blond as his older brother is dark. Kamilka is the spitting image of her oldest brother. She has brown eyes, and she looks like a real charmer—a spoiled one at that.

Kristopher leans forward and pulls my hair.

I smile.

It's going to be a long journey to Poland.

FYODOR, KRISTOPHER, AND Kamilka tell me about their life, about the pleasure trips when they were pursued by wolves, about their rich boyar parents who were married by the tsar twelve years ago, and about how they have lived in Paris, Vienna, and Heidelberg. The two younger children take turns sitting on my lap as the sleigh sways and glides through the snow.

Darkness sinks over the frozen landscape. We're probably

going to spend the night at a mail-coach inn. Even with soldiers, it's too dangerous to be on the road at night.

For a brief moment I wonder what's going to happen to me when the parents discover that they've brought along a little *karlitsa*. But I don't want to think about that. I'll simply make up a good lie. Fine folk can always be bought with lies. Their entire existence is based on lies.

Kamilka has fallen asleep. She's adorable, with her long dark hair slipping out from under her cap. Her hands are clenched into fists. Her legs stick out from the blankets. She's dreaming about butterflies and silk gowns.

The sleigh slows down.

"It's time to eat," says Fyodor. Suddenly there's a look in his eyes that I haven't noticed before.

THE MAIL-COACH INN is a dilapidated building surrounded by snowdrifts and traveling sleighs. A thin column of smoke rises up from the chimney. Beyond the building is a barn with a tiled roof. A pine forest looms like a white wall.

A servant opens the sleigh door, and the children tumble out. At first I don't know what to do, but then I climb out after them. Outside stands a coachman and a distinguished-looking man wearing a sable coat.

"We really like Surinka, Father."

Kristopher beams as he hugs the distinguished-looking gentleman. The boy's father stares at me, his mouth agape.

"Who are you?"

"That's Surinka," says Kamilka with a smile. "She talks funny because she was born in a hole in the ground."

"Your name is Surinka?"

"Yes, my lord. At your service."

"What on earth are you doing in my sleigh?"

"I'm the children's new governess."

The man keeps on staring at me.

"You've been traveling with my children?" he says.

"Yes, my lord."

"You're quite impertinent, aren't you?"

"I'm good at taking care of little folks, your grace. And I can entertain the family at dinner."

At that moment the mother approaches. "What sort of horrid creature is that?" she says.

The mother looks like Kamilka, though her features are darker. She's wearing a big gray fur coat with peculiar patterns. Her leather boots look as if they're too small for her.

"She's our new governor," says Kamilka.

"Governess, silly."

"Where did you find such a hideous little *karlitsa*?"

Fyodor is indignant. "We didn't find it. It was hiding under the blankets in our sleigh. The others thought it was a present from our noble father, but I knew it was lying."

I bow to the mother. "Your grace, I've taken care of children at the court of His Majesty Frederik IV. With exquisite skill, I might add. I come to you with the best of references. I can cook, I can perform, and if you agree to take me on, I will crawl into the hearts of your children and not come out until I have your permission."

"It's all true, yes it is," says Kristopher, nodding emphatically.

The gentleman picks up Kamilka and kisses her cheek. Then he turns to me.

"I should give you a good beating."

"As you wish."

"But you've clearly made an impression on my children."

"Not on me," says Fyodor, shaking his head vigorously.

The gentleman looks at Kamilka. His voice becomes cloying. "Shall we hire the stowaway, Kamilka?"

Then the gentleman looks at me.

"You're a lucky *karlitsa*. A few days ago our old governess took ill, and we didn't have time to hire another, so you can travel with us for a few days. But now it's time to eat. You can sit with us, provided you have proper table manners."

Kristopher and Kamilka shout with joy and hug their parents. We go inside the inn. Piled up on the floor are heaps of furs and felt boots. People are sitting on several long benches and eating. They look up as we come in. They fill their pipes and hastily shovel down the food, as if it were their last meal.

The postmaster is obsequious and offers the family a private room for the night. Later we're served a plate of cabbage soup with a goblet of vodka. I help Kristopher drink the soup as I tell jokes and draw attention to myself without wishing to do so.

Fyodor stares at me the whole time. I stare back and make faces that prompt him to laugh. Before the evening is over, I've won at least at little respect from him. But it's hard to be charming. I hope it's not going to become a habit.

60.

MY NEW FAMILY IS NAMED MAXIMYCH. EVERY ONE OF them snores. I lie on a blanket and listen to the symphony. It sounds as if each of them has a cloudburst in his mouth. Occasionally a spout spurts up, like it does from baleen whales. First from my lord, then from Fyodor, and after that from Kristopher, my lady, and Kamilka.

They're a family of beautiful baleen whales.

I've dared to light a candle so that I can read for a while. I've emptied my carpetbag out onto the floor. There isn't much inside: a blouse with slashed sleeves, my old Bible, a few herbs and dresses. In the bottom of the bag is the letter from my protector, Rasmus Æreboe.

I unfold the fragile piece of paper. Some of the writing has been erased by the ravages of time. Other words are quite clear, formed by ornate and kindly letters:

Our Lord has filled you with purpose. He has given you a task, so that you, with God's help, will survive … I often felt myself lost among the Russian barbarians, and there were times

when my blood was so agitated that it refused to calm down.
So, Sørine, beware of...

I can't read anymore of the letter without tearing the
paper. I fold it back up and carefully put it away. Rasmus Æreboe
always makes me happy, maybe because the *notarius* was a
decent man.

Occasionally I've actually been lucky. Occasionally I've
felt protected. Should I thank God for these gifts? And will I have
the same luck with the Maximych family?

I lie down under the blanket, letting my life pass in review.
I would prefer to keep thinking about Rasmus Æreboe, but my
thoughts return to Sanka, Danilov, and those peaceful days at
the cloister.

To my surprise the cloister gave me a sense of security—
a sense that the evil was out there, never inside myself. I was in
Paradise, after all. And in Paradise there are no temptations;
that's why it's Paradise.

What was it Danilov told me before I left? Something
about how one day I would stand at a crossroads where I could
choose the Light, which illuminated the sky with its warmth
and golden glow—or the Darkness, which at first seemed soothing and inviting, but which would consume me in its flames.

But do I have to wait for that crossroads? Isn't it present at
every moment of my life?

I turn over. I can hear the sounds of a brawl downstairs.
After a while I hear laughter and singing. I don't understand Russians. Maybe they don't understand themselves.

IT'S MORNING. FYODOR goes out into the snow to examine
the sleighs with the air of an expert. He stops next to a merchant's wretched sleigh. There is a hint of contempt in his eyes.
Then he continues on to a more magnificent vehicle: a leather
sleigh shaped like a swan.

I follow him, although it's difficult for me to make my way through the snow. When he notices me, he stops.

"So I see that you have an interest in sleighs," I say.

"Yes, but only if they're pulled by eight horses, otherwise they don't move fast enough."

"Have you ever ridden in a sleigh with eight horses?"

"Of course. My paternal grandfather has a sleigh made of gold. It has a team of ten. He's quite rich, you see."

"But your parents are rich too, aren't they?"

"My grandfather is richer."

Fyodor watches the stable boys who are getting the horses ready. Some of the animals are thin and emaciated. They have bald spots on their coats and tormented eyes. It's as if they're saying: Why should we work in this cold? We would rather eat grain in the warm stable than trudge through the heavy snow.

All around us the guests are making preparations for another day of travel. Servants carry out traveling trunks from the inn as they loudly complain about the frost. I look at Fyodor. He has a solemn expression on his dark face. Someday he's going to break the hearts of dozens of girls, that little shit.

"I'm slightly taller than you. Are you aware of that?" Fyodor gives me a triumphant smile.

"The whole world is taller than me," I say.

"So you were about the size of a pissant when you were born, right?"

"I was the size of a toenail."

Against his will, Fyodor laughs.

"That's not true," he says.

"Oh yes, it is."

"Wasn't your mother sad when she saw that you were so small?"

"She was so sad that she croaked."

Fyodor looks at me in astonishment. "Did she really?"

"Almost."

"You're quite funny sometimes."

I reach for his gloved hand. "We're going to be good friends, you and I."

"My brother and sister like you. They've never seen a dwarf before."

"But you have?"

"I saw one of the tsar's dwarves, but it wasn't as ugly as you are."

"That's because it wasn't a real dwarf."

"You never know," says Fyodor, sounding wiser than his years.

A dog barks angrily at the horses. A stable boy gives it a kick. The dog runs back to the stable with its tail between its legs.

Fyodor studies me with a grown-up expression. "My mother thinks that you're wanted by the authorities."

"For what?"

"I'm not sure. Why did you hide in our sleigh?"

"Because I saw all of you, and you seemed so nice."

"I don't believe that, but I'll still give you a cracker."

I thank him and take a cracker that has been too long in Fyodor's glove. The boy turns around and goes over to the family caravan. Beyond the sleighs one of the soldiers has stripped off his shirt and is washing his chest with cold snow.

The light is about to take hold. It latches onto the white landscape, but only for a fleeting moment. Shortly thereafter we continue on with fresh horses.

MRS. MAXIMYCH HAS joined us inside the sleigh. She has a dark complexion like her older son, with high cheekbones and watchful eyes. I can tell that she doesn't trust me. And why should she? I've finagled my way into her life, and I'm going to finagle my way out.

Mrs. Maximych is a Kirghiz from a part of the realm that is close to China. She may have slanted eyes, but it's difficult to tell because of her bloated face. We're sitting next to each other.

She watches me carefully as I play with the children and help Kristopher pee into a goblet so the caravan won't have to stop.

"You've never taken care of children before, have you?"

Mrs. Maximych stares at me hard.

"I've taken care of children at Copenhagen Castle."

"What children?"

"One of the king's illegitimate daughters."

"You're a liar, Surinka."

"As my lady wishes."

"But Kamilka is quite fond of you, and when Kamilka is fond of someone, her father doesn't have the heart to say no."

"I'll wait on your children hand and foot, my lady. You won't regret your decision."

Mrs. Maximych laughs scornfully.

"And maybe there will come a day when I'll win your trust. The mistress of the Danish monarch used to confide in me. And after she had confided in me, she would fly across the floor like a fairy. In all modesty I can tell you this: I am very wise. In fact, my ugly body is so filled with wisdom that I have to poke a hole in myself several times a day so that the wisdom has a way to escape."

Kamilka is thrilled. "When do you do that?" she asks.

"Do what?"

"Poke a hole in yourself."

"Every morning when I wake up. I poke a little hole in my scalp, and then all the learning that I can't use comes pouring out."

"What do you put in its place?"

"Good stories."

Kristopher stares at me in awe. "Do you know any fairy tales?"

"I know all the best fairy tales in the world."

"Tell us one now."

Kristopher takes my hand, as if he wants to give me courage.

"First tell me if you want it to be a Danish story."

"No, Russian. Otherwise we won't understand it."

Mrs. Maximych puts her arm around Kamilka and looks at me with a mixture of anticipation and mistrust. I look at the faces of her children. They haven't yet been marked by life's torments, but it's just a matter of time. Then I open my mouth, eager to see what comes out:

61.

ONCE UPON A TIME THERE WAS DOG THAT COULDN'T wag his tail. And that was very strange, because he had a big, bushy tail. All the other dogs wagged their tails, but not Tristovich. Tristovich was a Russian doggie, you see, and he loved to drink vodka from his bowl. Tristovich also had a sweetheart. She didn't like the fact that he gallivanted around so much.

"You need to stay home instead of running around with your tail between your legs," she said every evening when they sat in their doghouse and ate cat meat in spicy sauce.

Tristovich nodded. He wanted to be a good sweetheart. But it was because he was much *too* good that he couldn't wag his tail. In fact, he couldn't even wag his tail when he went to see his secret girlfriend, a luscious bulldog who slobbered all over him every chance she got.

Well, one day Tristovich was walking down the street in the town where he lived.

"Woof woof," he barked at everyone he met, because Tristovich was a fierce mutt who didn't care for people. He would often leave little doggy droppings outside the doors of the rich, and then the people would slip and fall full-length to the ground. Tristovich loved it when the fine folk got doggy droppings in their powdered wigs. Then he would clutch his dog tummy and bark with delight. But not even the sight of the rich people's ill luck could make Tristovich wag his tail. That's why he sat down in a cabbage patch to have a good look at it.

"Come on and wag, you stupid tail," he snarled. "Or else I'll cut you off and feed you to a rat."

But his tail just hung there between his legs like a drooping plant. And no one was able to change that. Not even the wise woman in the marsh who once made a guinea hen speak Polish.

So Tristovich walked the long way back home to his sweetheart. There he lay down to sleep, until he was so tired that he couldn't sleep anymore."

"WHAT A GOOD story," says Kristopher.

"Shhhhhh." Fyodor throws a pillow at his brother.

ONE DAY TRISTOVICH had a dream. He dreamed that he was walking around blue mountains and wagging his tail. Not only that, in his dream he was wagging so wildly that he won a tail-wagging contest. When Tristovich woke up, he knew that he was supposed to gallivant around the world. It's important to listen to dreams. They are what make holes in the sky so that angel-poodles can send messages down through the clouds. And so Tristovich said to his sweetheart, "I've just had a lovely dream in which I went gallivanting around the world."

His sweetheart looked at him with her inflamed dachshund eyes.

"Only dogheads take their dreams seriously. Everyone else takes out the trash."

And then she wept for two years and twenty-three days, because dogs always weep for two years and twenty-three days when anything bad happens in their lives.

Tristovich packed up a knapsack, kissed his sweetheart on her moist snout, and headed off to gallivant around the world. It was fun. Tristovich met all sorts of exciting animals that he never would have met if he'd stayed home. He met a gigantic tortoise that had a map on its shell so it could find its way through the ferns. He met a clan of zebras who sentenced to death any animal with spots. And Tristovich made friends with a flock of parrots who poked out the eyes of anyone who stole their stories. Oh yes, the world was a vast and marvelous place. There was love, and there were bones that could make any dog drown in his own saliva.

KAMILKA AND KRISTOPHER snicker.

ONE DAY TRISTOVICH heard about a valley that lay on the other side of the blue mountains. In that valley lived a clan of dogs that wagged their tails so much that they actually earned money by doing so.

"That's where I need to go," said Tristovich, who was not nearly as sad anymore. But his tail still hung down like a drooping plant.

Tristovich set off on the long journey. He traveled through a jungle where dangers lurked under every palm tree. Look: there was a boa constrictor eating a marmoset. And wasn't that a scorpion spraying poison at a leopard cub? But Tristovich was brave. He climbed up on rocks where he found spiders the size of his fist. And after forty days and forty nights he arrived in the valley of the wagging dogs.

Tristovich gaped as he walked among the handsome doghouses. He'd never seen so many doggies with wagging tails. They were so frisky, and they wagged so much that other animals hired the dogs to fan them with their tails in the midday sun. Look, there sat a rhinoceros, enjoying the cool breeze from a dog's tail. And farther on was a giraffe surrounded by twenty dogs, all of them wagging so hard that there wasn't even a drop of sweat on the giraffe's long neck.

On the first night Tristovich slept in a meadow soft with flowers. He had lovely dreams about squirrels and Siamese cats roasted on a stick. But all of sudden he was awakened by something tugging at his behind. Tristovich peered along his back in fright, and there he saw that his tail was moving. Cautiously at first, then harder. His tail moved up and down, as if it had always done so. Right and left, toward all corners of the world. Tristovich leaped up and ran around the valley.

"I'm wagging, I'm wagging," he shouted. And the other dogs stopped to stare, because no one had ever seen a dog with such a beautiful tail.

His tail stuck straight up. And Tristovich wagged and wagged, not just for hours, like the other dogs. He wagged for days, for several months in a row. And the beautiful girl dogs looked at Tristovich with admiration, because there weren't any other doggies who could wag as long as he could.

"How clever you are," they each told him. "Why don't you come home with me to my doghouse and we can wag together."

Tristovich didn't want to hurt anyone's feelings, so he said yes to all the girl dogs, and he'd never been so happy in his life. "If only my life will keep going on like this," he thought. And then he closed his eyes and prayed to Our Dog in Heaven.

For many mornings after that Tristovich got up early, and sure enough: his tail was still wagging. The sun came peeking through the peephole in his doghouse, and Tristovich went strutting down to the river to drink some water. It was a crystal-clear morning with a warm breeze. In the trees sat hummingbirds and kingfishers, admiring the handsome dog. Even the flies had a kind word for Tristovich.

Tristovich began to drink from the clear water. The drops quenched his thirst, and on the river bottom he saw little fish playing tag with a crab. But all of a sudden a mountain lion appeared. It came leaping out of the jungle and struck Tristovich down with a single swipe of its paw.

"Oh no," thought Tristovich as he collapsed into the river. A few hours later he died. And so that's what happened to Tristovich, who had all of his dreams fulfilled but still was eaten by a mountain lion.

I LOOK AT the children and smile.

It's completely silent inside the sleigh. Mrs. Maximych and the three children are staring at me. A little tear trickles down Kamilka's cheek.

"Is … is that the end of the story?"

"Yes."

Mrs. Maximych comforts her and gives me a peeved look.

"I refuse to let Tristovich die," says Kristopher. "He's a fun dog. I like him."

"But the ones you love often die."

"No, they don't," says Kamilka angrily.

I smile as I look at the children.

"Well, maybe Tristovich didn't die all the way," I suggest.

The children look at me eagerly and nod.

"Since this is a fairy tale, we can just bring Tristovich back to life and see what happens on his journey. Shall we do that?"

"Yes!"

Kristopher takes my hand. I pat him on the head and give Kamilka a smile. She wipes away a tear with her little hand.

Fyodor makes himself more comfortable on the seat. Mrs. Maximych gives me a look that is both uneasy and filled with anticipation.

WELL, THERE LAY Tristovich, bleeding on the rock, but strangely enough he didn't feel any pain at all in his dog-body. "How can that be?" thought Tristovich. "My whole dog-head should hurt, but I've never felt better."

The mountain lion was still bending over him. Tristovich thought, "You'd taste good in sweet-and-sour sauce, but you're much too big for my little dog bowl." Then the mountain lion trotted back to the jungle, and Tristovich felt as light as a feather. He slid out of his dog-body and up to Heaven. "Oh, how fun this is," thought Tristovich as he looked down at his body on the ground. "I've been split in two, and now the best part of me is flying up to the clouds so that I can see the world." And it was quite true: Tristovich could see the valley. He could see his town in Russia, he could see the Emperor in China, who was just about to change his trousers because he had eaten something that didn't agree with him. And suddenly Tristovich was met by angel-poodles. They took him by the paw and flew up to Heaven, past lavender lagoons and the most beautiful waterfalls made of silk. All of a sudden an ugly little dwarf terrier was standing in front of him.

"Who are you?" asked Tristovich, who wasn't the least bit fond of dwarf terriers.

"I am God," said the dwarf terrier, and Tristovich was just about to start barking loudly because the dwarf terrier had squinty little eyes and bad breath.

But gradually something happened. Tristovich's eyesight changed, and suddenly he could see that the dwarf terrier was not a dwarf terrier at all but a big and beautiful Great Dane who filled up the whole world. Over his body he wore a magnificent cloak with numerous pockets, and in each one lived dozens of dogs. If you looked closely, you could see little heads sticking out.

"Woof woof," they barked.

Tristovich knew that he belonged in one of those pockets, but he didn't know which one.

"Have you lived a good dog-life?" asked the big Great Dane, looking at Tristovich with infinite love. Tristovich nodded and thought about his sweetheart with the dachshund eyes. He also thought about his tail, that had wagged with such pleasure until a mountain lion had arrived.

"Yes, I've lived a good dog-life," said Tristovich as he started with fascination at the big cloak.

Only now did he discover that there were differences in the size of the pockets. The pockets on top were the most beautiful. They were adorned with diamonds and gold. Farther down there was less space, and not much of a view. And the closer you got to the ground, the worse the air was. Several dogs were living down below in between the paws of Our Dog, and in that place there was a divine stench.

"To be perfectly honest, I'm not sure whether I've been a good doggy or not," said Tristovich, feeling guilty. He thought about all the dog droppings he had left so that the fine folk would fall. But the Great Dane didn't care. He licked Tristovich with his big tongue, up and down, along his fur, even inside his ear. And suddenly Tristovich felt so happy that he didn't know what to do with himself.

At that moment one of the angel-poodles appeared to take him to where he was going to live. On the way to the cloak, they passed hundreds of pockets. There was one for Russian Orthodox dogs, with dog-icons and vodka crackers. There was one for pietists, where it was forbidden to play the violin. Yes, even the false god of the Turks had a beautiful pocket with virgins and splendid carpets that were so deep that paws would sink into them, never to appear again.

Tristovich was starting to get tired. It had been a long journey. When he reached his pocket, he met countless old friends. They barked with pleasure when they saw him, and they sniffed at all the places where dogs always sniff. After such a long day, Tristovich lay down to sleep next to his mother, who had died when she was run over by a carriage. And if you look very closely, you'll see that he's still asleep.

But after a moment Tristovich wakes up. The sun is peeking through the peephole, and Tristovich struts down to the river to get some water to drink. The drops quench his thirst, and on the river bottom he sees little fish playing tag with a crab. And when the mountain lion comes leaping, he makes it stop, and then kisses it on the snout. And Tristovich says: "Go ahead and eat as much of me as you like, but I'm not the least bit afraid."

Now you see, that was the story about Tristovich. Where he is now, no one knows. But his tail is still wagging as if it had always done so.

I LOOK AT the children's happy faces. At that moment the sleigh slows down. Darkness rolls across the white landscape. I'm tired, more tired than I've been in a long time. Inside the next mail-coach inn, I fall asleep next to a big stack of firewood.

62.

THE NEXT FEW DAYS ARE FILLED WITH SNOWDRIFTS
and fairy tales. At the Polish border, we get in line to show
our travel documents and bribe a guard. But the six sleighs in the
caravan are searched all the same. Goods are tossed out: barrels
of vodka, crates of caviar, all sorts of things from all over the world.

Suddenly the snow begins to melt. Wheels are put on in
place of the runners, and we drive through the landscapes which
start to lose their white color. On the hills stand fortresses with
huge moats. Springtime sun dances on the village rooftops. Everything is better kept in Poland than in Russia. Including the
homes of the townspeople, the streets, and the small chapels.

Our first stop is at an elegant estate. Maximych knows the
owner, who receives us at the manor house. I'm installed in a
room with the children. All of them are restless. Kamilka cries,
while Fyodor teases Kristopher about his freckles. I have an
urge to give them a few slaps, but that will have to wait until I've
become even more indispensable.

It's my plan to be indispensable.

The fireplace doesn't warm up the room. There's a cross-
bow on the wall.

THE NEXT MORNING the master summons me to the library.

Vasha Maximych is an even-tempered and plump man
with nice blue eyes. He's a head shorter than his wife, and he
limps a bit on his left leg. Right now he's sitting at an oak
desk with a pile of papers in front of him. When he sees me, he
gets up absentmindedly and then smiles.

"We need to have a little talk, Surinka."

I bow humbly and wait.

"Well, how should I begin? I've discussed you with my
esteemed wife, and we've agreed that…well, what exactly have
we agreed? That certain things just won't do."

He tries to give me a stern look.

"You have an excellent way of dealing with the children.

They're very fond of a poppet like you, but I have to think about their upbringing. You understand that, don't you?"

"Yes, your grace."

"That fairy tale you told to the children…did you make that up yourself?"

"Yes, my lord."

"My wife said that it was very enjoyable, although not particularly edifying. As I understand it, you described Our Lord as a sheep dog?"

"A Great Dane."

"A Great Dane? Well, who knows what that is. But I presume it's a dog from your homeland?"

"Yes, your grace."

"You have to understand, Surinka, that it just won't do for you to turn God on High into a mutt. In fact, that's blasphemy, and in certain countries you'd be sentenced to death for such things."

"In certain countries, my lord?"

A glint of anger appears in Maximych's eyes.

"The fact is that neither my wife nor I wish for our children to listen to heathen stories from the ungodly Europe, no matter how amusing they might be. Is that understood?"

"I most sincerely ask for your forgiveness. I don't always know what's going to happen when I open my mouth."

Maximych gives me a pensive look. Then he bursts out laughing.

"What was it the dog was called? The one you told the story about?"

"Tristovich, your grace."

"Tristovich. Who can't wag his tail. That's priceless. You seem to be quite fond of dogs, is that right?"

"I can't stand them, my lord."

"Why not?"

"Because they're stupid and ingratiating. I prefer cats. They'll tear you to shreds if they're hungry."

"You're so refreshingly honest. I think we'll keep you for a little while longer. Shall we agree that you will tell a story every evening to our little family?"

I bow. "Thank you, your grace."

Maximych nods curtly and then sits down behind the desk again. I head for the door.

"Oh, Surinka..."

Maximych's kind-hearted eyes look at me. "I'm making you responsible for my children. They're my dearest possessions, of course. So if anything should happen to them, you'll be hanged from the nearest gallows... Is that understood?"

I swallow hard. "Of course."

"Good. Then we understand each other."

He smiles amiably and returns his attention to his papers. I go upstairs to join the children in their room. As soon as I step inside the door, Kristopher throws a pillow at me. And then we're in the midst of a pillow fight that rages until late in the evening.

At night I sleep in the same bed with the children, but my thoughts are foolish and gloomy.

63.

THE NEARBY TOWN IS A PLEASANT ONE, WITH ITS SHOPS and its chapels containing Papist idols. The local people gawk when I waddle along the main street with my small cane. But the children protect me. Fyodor is especially considerate. He lashes out at the beggars and he sends the townspeople scattering with his most authoritative expression.

Whenever I have any spare time, I go for walks in the woods. I gather herbs and mushrooms. On rare occasions Kristopher comes with me. He holds my hand, chases after squirrels, and hides from the warthogs that crash through the underbrush.

One day we sit down on a toppled tree trunk. The sunlight is filtering through the trees. In the distance we can see several deer grazing. An owl stares sagely from a branch.

"Surinka, can I ask you something?"

I nod.

"Do you believe there's a God up in Heaven?"

"I don't know."

"I believe it."

"Aren't you a little too young to be filling your head with such things?"

"I'm the only one in my family who believes in God. Fyodor doesn't, and my mother and father are more fond of wine."

I laugh loudly.

"My paternal grandmother died a year ago. Do you think she's living in one of the pockets that Tristovich talked about?"

"I'm not sure about that, Kristopher."

"Sometimes I dream about her. Then she smiles at me and says that I'm going to have a long life. I miss her, but she says that she has to stay where she is, and I'm not supposed to try and bring her back."

I look at the buttercups and a little stream running between several larch trees.

"Did you ever have a grandmother?" he asks.

"I suppose I did."

"I think everybody should have a grandmother."

Kristopher starts to cry. I kiss his hair, which is soft and fair. The tears make his cheeks shine.

I get up from the tree trunk. I suddenly wish that I was alone.

Maybe I should tell the young man that his grandmother is waiting for him deep in the woods. "Go on, Kristopher. Off you go. Your grandmother wants to talk to you." But I don't have the heart to say that.

The forest is beautiful with flowers and with the light that falls gently between the branches. I catch sight of a few poisonous mushrooms. They're perched on a toppled tree trunk. They're yellow and inviting.

The most poisonous mushrooms are always the most beautiful.

I pull out my little knife. Kristopher has caught sight of a fox, and he's stalking it like a hunter. I approach one of the mushrooms. I pause to look at it. For some reason it doesn't speak to me.

Then I slice off a piece and place it carefully inside my carpetbag. There are lots of mushrooms. I pick a few more, enjoying the smell of them in the damp forest with all its secrets. In the distance the fox has disappeared. Kristopher comes back, his face radiant, as if he had killed the fox with his bare hands.

I smile, take his hand, and we walk back to the estate. I'm in the inside pocket of Our Lord.

That's what the Russians call it when life is going well: to be in the inside pocket of Our Lord.

VIII   Königsberg

AGRIMONY
Agrimonia eupatoria

64.

I LOVE LOOKING AT THE CHILDREN WHEN THEY'RE ASLEEP.
I see them grow right before my eyes. Even in the dark it's possible to see how their legs get longer, how downy hair spreads
over their arms. They are perfect. Not a hair is out of place, not a
spine is out of joint.

I sit there for years.

Kamilka gets new teeth. Fyodor an Adam's apple. Their
navels expand, yawning over more than they can cover. Their fac-
ial features mature, their voices deepen, as if brought from
some distant well. One day they'll be grown up. I know that. It's
horrible, appalling.

The children have lessons with a castigator. They have to
know God by heart, they have to memorize all the rivers in
Siberia. They have to demonstrate their cleverness in botany and
the art of fencing.

Kristopher shows a particular skill with the rapier. In the
evening he counts his scars. He likes to boast about how many evil
people he's going to kill before he turns fifteen.

Kamilka receives almost no tutoring. All she's supposed
to do is find a husband. But Kamilka demands to have the same
lessons as the boys. It's as if she knows that a prison awaits her,
and that's why she needs to have a key. I think she's marvelous.
She's taller than I am by now.

All the children are taller than me.

FYODOR TURNS THIRTEEN. He's been given a uniform, and he drinks vodka like a boyar. The girls can't take their eyes off him. If he were older, I'd want to copulate with him myself.

It's a good life. We stay at the estate while Maximych travels around with his wine and furs. Sometimes he comes back from Dresden with gifts. He had a meeting with the king of Poland and tried to drink him under the table.

"But I couldn't," The master sighs. "No one can drink August II under the table."

It's a beautiful family. And I'm part of it.

MRS. MAXIMYCH HAS sewn a wardrobe for me: summer clothes, winter clothes, a cap and socks. She's an excellent seamstress. She often sits at her loom into the wee hours of the night. She has a look of utter concentration on her face, almost angry, while she works. And she always drinks a glass of cherry wine.

"You must look decent, Surinka."

She studies me critically as I try on the clothes. It's clear that she regards sewing clothes for a dwarf to be a challenge. She tugs at the fabric with a look of annoyance and tells me to walk back and forth to see if the dresses are too tight. I'm especially pleased that my boots are made of wolf skin. I've never had such warm toes before. The warmth spreads through my whole body whenever I put on those boots.

Every Sunday we go to church. Then she drenches me in foul-smelling perfumes as she tells me how bored she always gets during the liturgy. But my back aches, and there's nothing she can do about that.

Mrs. Maximych and I have become friends. She tells me about when she came to Moscow from Kirghizia: how big the city seemed to her; how she met her husband, who has always treated her with love and respect. But Mrs. Maximych does not initiate me into her secrets.

I would love to hear her secrets.

ONE DAY THE door opens to the master's library. He comes out, looking gloomy and sad. On his head he has a fur cap, but his tunic is open so that a gray leather shirt with white buttons is visible.

"Come into my office, Surinka."

I nod. There's something about my master's expression that I don't like.

Maximych sits down, and to my surprise I see that he has been crying. For a moment he studies his hands. An empty decanter is on the table. A large goblet has toppled over onto the floor.

"Our highborn monarch, Peter Alexeyevich, is dead."

I swallow hard. "When, your grace?"

"Less than a week ago. I've just received word."

I nod and let my gaze sweep over the office. A deer's head looks down from its place above the fireplace. An orange glow fills the room.

Maximych snaps his fingers and a servant takes a piece of firewood from a stack that is as tall as I am.

The tsar is dead. Four such strange words—words that don't belong together. They seem unreal.

Maximych buries his face in his hands and tells me about the time the tsar came to visit him at his home. How they drank together all night, how Peter had called him his son. That was the start of a warm friendship and some lucrative transactions for my master.

I nod and listen attentively. I know that it's important to let Maximych talk. And maybe there'll be some information that I can use. The squire talks for an hour. Afterwards I go upstairs to Kamilka's room. She tells me about some trivial experience that she's had. Then she shows me her drawings. They're beautiful and violent, full of death and destruction.

Kamilka talks about a gallows that she visited with her mother.

"I saw a real corpse. Have you ever seen a corpse?"

I nod absentmindedly. "I've seen many," I tell her.

"Not as many as I have."

I nod again and start to draw along with Kamilka. She's very skillful at using color. Her brown eyes are focused. Now she's drawing a city on fire. The flames are yellow and orange. They're consuming a family that is seated in a sleigh with all their belongings. Behind them a church crumbles to the ground.

I have a strange feeling in my stomach.

Kamilka looks up. "Surinka?"

"Yes?"

"How long are you going to stay with us?"

"I don't know."

"Forever?"

"That could be."

She frowns. "How long is forever? Is it a long time?"

"A very long time."

"Longer than a year?"

"I think so, yes."

I pat Kamilka on the head, but my thoughts are with the tsar.

It feels as if death doesn't suit him. I can't think of any other way to say it. Death doesn't suit him.

I HAVE SO many memories of Peter Alexeyevich. So many stories about that man who filled my world. The tsar was a master of fourteen different trades. In the field he acted as the royal barber-surgeon. If anyone needed an operation, the tsar took care of it himself. I saw him do it in Copenhagen, when one of his officers was wounded. The tsar placed him on a cot and then went to get his instruments. They were in a leather bag. He took them out and studied them carefully. After that he closed out the rest of the world. He cut into the Russian with his sharpest knife. Blood gushed out, spurting at his face. The patient begged for his life, but the tsar continued the operation with the utmost concentration. When the soldier died, Peter kept on sewing him up— he pulled out the stitches and then sewed the wound up again, in order to train himself.

Afterwards the tsar wiped his instruments on an admiral's uniform. Then he asked for aquavit and eggs, and he caroused with the same attentiveness with which he had performed the operation. When he went to bed in the early morning hours, he still had blood on his eyebrows.

And now he's dead.

The tsar has no heirs. Catherine will undoubtedly take over his reign.

Catherine and Menshikov.

I go to a church to light a candle for the tsar, but the wick refuses to burn. I light another, but someone blows it out. A cold wind gusts around me. I look at the Poles in the church and wish that I had their faith. But maybe I do.

65.

THE YEARS PASS. ONE SUMMER DAY WE LEAVE.

I have no idea where we're going. Our caravan consists of six carriages. The Polish landscape is beautiful, but ravaged by war. The farms have been burned to the ground, the forests have been felled. We drive north to the sea. The children get restless. Kamilka and Kristopher are fighting. Fyodor stares out the window in sullen silence. Is he dreaming about a girl or about a life without siblings?

The children have begun to treat me differently. I'm no longer their governess. No one wants to listen to my stories, but they do want me to read their fortunes in the tea leaves, as dwarves have done from time immemorial.

"But that's all a lot of nonsense," I say indignantly. "Do you want me to fill your heads with nonsense?"

"Yes, please," says Kamilka.

"You all have a brilliant future ahead of you," I predict, looking over the tops of my new steel spectacles. "Fyodor is going to be a very rich merchant, Kristopher will be the best fencer in all of Russia, and Kamilka is going to marry a rich prince. Is that the sort of thing you want to hear?"

254 PETER H. FOGTDAL

"Yes."

The children nod and look at me with enthusiasm. I go on with my crude fortune-telling, as if I were a Tatar at a flea market. When I'm done, Fyodor smiles.

"And what about you?" he says.

"Me?"

"Yes. What's going to happen to you?"

"But I'm just a dwarf."

"Yes, but—"

"And dwarves have no future," I say, gulping down the tea leaves with a grunt.

Kristopher and Kamilka laugh heartily. I press my hands to my back. A moment later the children are busy with something else.

WE ARRIVE IN Königsberg one evening when the clouds are crimson. We move in to a mansion in town. It was here that Rasmus Æreboe stayed on his way to Russia. But whatever it was that he told me about the place, I can't remember.

Königsberg is a port city. It has stylish castles and small marketplace squares with beggars and Jews. All manner of people can be seen in the streets. A prince from Latvia is here for a state visit. The harbor is adorned with banners and triumphal arches. It reminds me of the time when the tsar came to Copenhagen—back when my king thought that his fortune was made. But Scania continued to be only a dream or a thorn in his side. And now it's Russia that is the great power in the North.

Not Sweden. And certainly not the Kingdom of Denmark and Norway.

I walk out along the wharf and look with fascination at the Baltic Sea.

How long ago was it that I last saw open water? Ten years? Twelve? The air is different here than it is in Petersburg. You can scrape the salt from your skin with a straight razor. From a balcony I watch a few skiffs rocking on the waves. There's no doubt about it: I have missed the sea. There is nothing more dreary than bays and landlocked territory.

Shortly after we arrive, Kristopher and I take a walk around the harbor.

There's a great commotion going on: crates of freight, horse-drawn wagons, and drunken seamen. A Swede picks me up and gives me a smack on the lips. I give him a slap. He laughs and puts me down on a pile of scrap fish. Kristopher doesn't dare come to my aid, but afterwards he hauls me back to my feet.

We continue our stroll past the warehouses and customs buildings. It starts to rain. Autumn is in the air. Yellowish-brown leaves and goosebumps.

I take the lad to a filthy pub. We order vodka and borscht. Kristopher looks around, his eyes wide. He's not used to such a harsh atmosphere. A little old woman is singing a lewd ballad. As she sings, a seaman tries to assault her, but she just gives him a pinch in a spot where he'd rather not be pinched. It's always the girls who have the power. Men just haven't discovered that yet.

"Do you like being in a pub?" I ask Kristopher.

I pour more liquor into his goblet.

"I'm not sure."

"One day I'll teach you to drink."

"I know how to drink."

"But you can't drink real vodka, can you?"

Kristopher nods half-heartedly as he looks at a man with a harelip. The man has scabs on his hands and eyes, which are red and inflamed. Kristopher shrinks inside himself; he suddenly seem little and scared.

Some time later we go outside and sit down on the wharf. The harbor is crowded with vendors. Many of them make the sign of the cross when they see me. A beggar spits in my direction, as if I were something that has to be warded off.

Kristopher is still acting pensive. He's frowning hard. A moment later he turns to me and says, "Surinka?"

"Yes?"

"Isn't it hard being a dwarf?"

I look at him in surprise. "No one has ever asked me that before."

"Well, is it?"

"Yes, I suppose it is, Kristopher."

"If someone threw me onto a garbage heap, I'd be mad."

"I would be too."

"So what do you do when you get *really* mad?"

"I curse them to Hell."

"You're not supposed to do that."

"That's why I do it."

Kristopher studies me solemnly. Then his face lights up with a grin. A moment later he slips his hand into mine.

"Do you know what I think?"

I shake my head.

"I think you're a good person."

I gaze out across the sea. Then I stand up and reach for my small cane. Kristopher is still holding my hand, but he's a big boy now. He needs to take care of himself.

That evening I dream that the children all perish. Terje and Lukas are standing next to the children's beds. In my dream they're both the same height and equally pale. Lukas is the angrier of the two. He has no eyes, merely empty sockets that give me an accusatory stare. Terje laughs and turns into a bird that flies away.

Sorrowfully I watch him go. He has become a beautiful swallow that disappears into the blue sky.

Then Lukas flies off in the same direction. Far away. Away from me.

66.

AFTER THAT I KEEP TAKING WALKS DOWN TO THE HARBOR. I tell myself that it's because I want to look at the sea, to watch it change color. From my vantage place on the wharf I enjoy the first of the autumn storms. Walls of foam rise up horizontally. Barges are splintered into kindling wood. The sea has no mercy; it's beautiful and unrelenting.

One day a Danish ship puts into dock.

I see the Dannebrog flag waving from the mast. Out tumble thirty seamen. They're not in uniform; only the officers are elegantly dressed with their tricorn hats and their buttons gleaming like suns. I fall into conversation with a ship's cook from Helsingør. His name is Sylvester. We talk about the Danish capital and about how pleasant it is to sit at Torvet, the marketplace square. I feel like crying. I never thought that I would miss something as ridiculous as Copenhagen.

Sylvester is a bald old salt with an earring in one ear and a scar on his neck. When he laughs, he has the biggest mouth that I've ever seen.

"We're here in Königsberg for a few weeks," says Sylvester. "Come out to the ship and visit us."

"No, thank you."

"Why not?"

Several sailors are coming toward us. As soon as they see me, they start laughing very loud. I say a hasty goodbye to the cook and walk home to the mansion in the pouring rain. A servant lets me in the kitchen entrance. It smells of beets. I go upstairs, past the servants' quarters to the family's residence, where only a few of the servants are allowed in.

The atmosphere seems very strange.

I go into the children's room, but no one is home. For lack of anything better to do, I take out my father's old Bible and read a few passages. It still makes for dreary reading. Not even Judas can make me smile.

In my carpetbag are the mushrooms that I gathered in the woods. With two fingers I pick up a piece and look at it. Then I take a bite and wait for my body to react.

Now I'm in a better mood.

In a short time I'll be dead.

Or alive.

I'm not always sure that there's any difference.

67.

THE SQUIRE HAS PUT ON WEIGHT, MAYBE BECAUSE HE has started drinking the wine instead of selling it. Now he's standing behind his desk, which is covered with papers, as usual. His blue eyes rest on me. For a change he gets right to the point.

"Kristopher told me that you took him with you to a tavern."

"Yes, your grace."

"What was the reason for that?"

"There was no reason."

"I don't care to have my children mixing with commoners."

"With your permission, your grace, I thought that it would be healthy."

"Healthy?"

"Yes, for Kristopher to see how poor people live."

"Why would it be 'healthy' for the son of a boyar to visit a miserable public house with sailors and prostitutes?"

"You're right, as always. I sincerely beg your pardon."

Maximych frowns. "Surinka, don't you think that we've treated you decently?"

"A watchdog couldn't have it any better, your grace."

Maximych doesn't hear me. "My wife and I have begun to have doubts about your judgment."

"The gallows are too good for me. Maybe I should be broken on the post and wheel?"

Maximych's fat fingers are drumming on the top of the desk. In a moment he's going to have a fit of temper. He has three such fits each year; they're like gusts of wind and no one takes them seriously. There isn't a scrap of malice in Maximych. That's why it's so hard to respect him.

Now he takes a deep breath, trying to control himself. I watch him with curiosity, following the path of the blood rising up to his face—the way it floods into his cheeks, the way it spreads over his neck and ears. But the squire doesn't explode.

I consider what I might say to annoy him, but I can't think of anything.

So I smile.

"Out!" shouts Maximych. "Out!"

MORE DANISH SHIPS dock at Königsberg: warships, frigates, and old tubs with ragged sails. There are Danish lads all over town. I hear more Danish than German or Polish.

One afternoon I leave the children to visit the city's taverns. Sitting in the first one is a group of Danish cadets, eating bean soup. They're rowdy and vulgar. I feel right at home in their company. In front of them are some soggy playing cards that look as if they've been doused in a tankard of beer.

Suddenly I catch sight of Sylvester. The ship's cook greets me extravagantly, giving me a big hug. He has acquired a black eye since we last talked. And he smells of something that I can't identify.

"Buy me a dram, Sørine?"

I nod and reach into my pocket for a few coins that I've stolen from Mrs. Maximych. At the far end of the room two sailors have started brawling. I ignore them. I want to know what's been happening back home.

"Ask me whatever you like," says Sylvester as he pours the first dram into his enormous mouth.

I order another.

"Who's the king of Denmark now?" I ask. "Is it still Frederik?"

"Yes, but His Majesty has gotten so damned holy."

"So His Majesty is no longer enjoying himself with Anna Sophie?"

All the seamen laugh boisterously.

"Anna Sophie is our queen. She's been queen for years."

"But she doesn't have royal blood."

"His Majesty married her long ago. When was the last time you were in Denmark, Sørine? During the time of the Vikings?"

I grimace, thinking about my encounter with Frederik's

mistress: her naiveté, her scandalous immaturity. Anna Sophie was stupid as snot, and yet irresistible. And now she is mistress no longer, but rather Queen of Denmark and Norway.

We drink a toast to the health of the royal couple. The longer I sit in that tavern, the more I enjoy speaking my native language. Danish fills my body in a different way than Russian. It's as if the words are happy to come home to my mouth, as if they're celebrating being back inside my filthy jaws.

More lads show up, order beer, and pour some for me. They want to see how much a poppet can hold.

The seamen tell me about places that they've visited. One of the lads has been to the Gold Coast, another to Portugal and Spain. They talk about black girls and snakes in the jungle. Our ships sail to all corners of the world. I listen with fascination; I can't get enough of the stories, as long as there are Danes in them.

"Listen here, Sørine..." Sylvester puts his arm around me. "If you'd like to go home, why don't you come along with us? You take up hardly any room, anyway."

"Where are you headed?"

"Falster."

"And what would I do to pass the time on the island of Falster?"

"From there we'll be sailing to Copenhagen."

"No, thanks. I'm a servant in the house of a fine gentleman."

"A damn Polack."

"He's Russian, and he treats me decently."

The seamen shrug their shoulders, as if they can't imagine that a Russian could be decent.

A while later they start talking about Lækkerbidsken, the best pub in all of Copenhagen. It's on Vestergade, close to the western gate. The Scoundrel often went there; he was always good for a fiery witticism. In his prime he dominated the parties. He was funny and he had a quick wit. The only one quicker than him was me.

"And what would I have to pay if I go with you?"

"You can take care of Rufus, the ship's cat."

"And?"

"Well, us boys, too, of course."

One of the seamen sticks his hand between my legs. I swat it away and laugh along with the lads. Even the worst vulgarities sound poetic if you haven't spoken your own language since time immemorial.

Three whores in swaying skirts come in to offer their wares. One of them sits down at our table. She's beautiful but haggard. She offers to take care of the lads in the nearby boathouse.

I suddenly think of Kristopher and his little family. All my belongings are back at the mansion: my father's old Bible, the clothes that Mrs. Maximych made for me, and all my herbs.

I'm going to stay in Königsberg. How could I do anything else?

Sylvester puts his sweaty arm around me again.

"So, what do you say, you little turd?"

"When do you sail?"

"In an hour."

A Pole is playing the fiddle. Two rats are fighting over a meat pie. When we leave the tavern the sea is gleaming, and the sky is heavy with drizzle.

BACK AT THE mansion Kristopher is practicing his fencing. The muscles of his body are tensed. Maybe there will be a scar for me today, he thinks. I'd like to have a deep scar so that everyone can see how valiant I am.

Fyodor is in the library. He lights up a clay pipe and looks into the fireplace. Then he starts talking about the rising price of Rhine wine. His voice is changing. A pimple glistens on his chin.

Kamilka has been given a swing, but she would rather fence with Kristopher. The tutor tries to explain to her about the Bible and the tower of Babel. When Kamilka yawns, a fly flits into her mouth.

None of them is thinking about their dwarf, not one of them.

I look at the seaweed floating heavily on the sea.
I've never felt so small.

IX The *Wolfhound*

GOOSEBERRY
Ribes grossularia

68.

THE *WOLFHOUND* ISN'T A FRIGATE; IT'S A TOWN. HUN-
dreds of people live on board: sailors, cadets, and officers. It's
teeming with stockpiles of lines, canvas, and ship parts. There
are labyrinthine crew quarters, officers' cabins, and supply
holds. And last but not least: on deck are countless cannons that
can be aimed at pirates and others with hostile intentions.

The *Wolfhound* was once used during the war with Sweden.
At one time it came under the command of an admiral named
Tordenskiold. It won an important battle at Fehmarn. But now
the Swedes are no longer our enemies. Now it's important to
trade and bring in money for the dwindling state treasury. The
Wolfhound carries salt and stockfish between Poland and
Denmark-Norway. It has also been to the Gold Coast; it has been
to most parts of the world.

I watch the life on board the frigate with cutiosity. I see the
cadets swab the deck in the morning. I admire the young sailors
who clean the cannons and clamber up the sails like spiders.
I acquire a new vocabulary: shallop, gale wind, and the rank of
schoutbynacht. The frigate is a whole little world, filled with
cursing and swearing, but the mood is good. The captain is from
Jutland; he has a broken nose and cold sores. There's no end
to what he will do for his crew. He has even allowed a dwarf on
board, to the joy and merriment of all.

The *Wolfhound* is part of a squadron of warships, frigates, and sloops. I've been assigned to work with Sylvester, who amuses himself by spitting in the food when no one is looking.

RUFUS, THE SHIP'S cat, is lying next to me on the floor. He's a red forest cat with stripes on his chest. His fur is bushy, and his paws are as big as potholders. Once in a while he lifts his head and speaks.

"This is a good life we have here. You just have to be careful not to fall overboard. The air is salty and fresh, the seamen are hardy. There's often a scrap fish or a dried mackerel bone. I have no complaints."

I turn over. I'm feeling seasick. When you're seasick, you don't feel like talking to a cat.

"Go up and get some fresh air, Sørine."

That's Sylvester. He's grumbling at me.

He's more irritable on board than he was on land. The title of "cook" is a bit of an exaggeration. Sylvester makes thin soup, which he serves with stale bread and aquavit to wash it all down. I can't stand to be around him today. It's impossible to be around a cook when you're seasick.

I turn over again and try to sleep, but my thoughts keep whirling around. If I hadn't been so stupid I could be sitting in Maximych's library right now. I could have been living a good life with my Russian family. But instead I'm on my way home to a country that I don't even miss.

"I understand you so well," says the cat with a nod. "I never dreamed that I'd end up on a ship. What good is a cat on a ship? The last five cats were washed overboard. One after the other, down into the waves. But they were stupid and careless. The old cats puffed out their chests; they strutted about as if they owned the entire Baltic Sea. But I have a different temperament. I stay down here in the cabin. I let everyone pet me and spoil me. But one day I'll get reckless. One day the sun will shine. And I'll go up to the bridge. Everything will seem so safe. But then a swell will appear. I'll try to hold on, but I'll land in the drink. It's just a matter of time. It's only a matter of time before we all end up with our paws in the air and a belly full of salt water."

The next second the cat starts licking his paws, as if he were an ordinary forest cat.

I turn over on my blanket.

I don't want to go home. I don't want to do anything at all.

THE FIRST TIME I ever sat in a boat was on Sortedam Lake in Copenhagen.

It was a warm day in July. My father had taken me along to the woods. We drank a tankard of goat milk, ate stockfish, and then sailed around in an old tub. Sortedam Lake was like an ocean. In the distance were the city ramparts and the tall towers. It was magical and terrifying. In the old boat I realized for the first time that I could disappear in the world, that it would outgrow me the older I got. Beneath me was the bottomless lake; above me stretched the sky. Everything was so immense, so boundless.

But a dwarf learns to adapt.

That's what you have to do when the world refuses to cooperate.

You defend yourself, you become hot-tempered—otherwise you don't have a chance.

"I understand you so well," says the cat with a nod. "But right now I choose to lick my paws. Look, I'm totally focused on grooming my fur, I couldn't care less about the past. Right now my left paw and me are all that exist. I'm not even worried about how hard it could be to lick my right paw. That's how I look at the world, but it's enough because I'm a cat."

I turn over again.

I miss Kristopher, Kamilka, and Fyodor. May they burn in Hell.

69.

I'M NOT THE ONLY ONE FEELING NAUSEATED. NOW THE others are too. The wooden plates slide off the table. A rat scurries around in confusion, hoping to be eaten by the cat, but the cat isn't interested. We ride up one side of a swell and down the other. Water is coming in through every crack, creeping into every bodily orifice. All the corners of the world flow together, the horizon disappears. The more we pray, the more the waves pound against the hull. It's like being surrounded by anger. The only thing to do is lie down and wait. My life passes in review: I think about Lukas and how he died. When I left him, the life was seeping out of his body. He was so pale, so adorable. I comforted him and sang him a lullaby in Danish. The song soothed him. That's how it is with languages that you can't understand. Either they scare you or else they're a solace.

Afterwards I took my carpetbag and walked across the ice to Petersburg. The world was infinitely white. Everything merged into the whiteness; everything became sharper. Since then I've done my best not to think about Lukas. I've decided that he never existed. He was just a dwarf, after all, nothing more than a damn dwarf.

What is it the poets say? That love makes you strong? But that's hogwash. Love makes you weak. I am infinitely weak.

70.

I THINK IT'S GOOD THAT I FORGOT MY HERBS BACK IN Königsberg.

I don't care about them anymore.

Sometimes I feel like I'm not the one mixing the herbs—the herbs are mixing me.

71.

ON THE FOURTH DAY WE FIND OURSELVES SOMEWHERE between the new moon and Poland. The swells subside, and we have a tailwind. All the mollycoddled boys get out of their hammocks and go up on deck. Some of the seamen speak the strange dialect of the Norwegians, a few speak Dutch. Sylvester's good humor has returned, and he gives me a hug. The world is in its place once again, the sea is calm.

After I recover, I tell the boys stories.

We sit around a small table with soup and aquavit. The stories have to be bawdy or the lads start yawning their heads off. The more stories I tell, the better I get at holding their interest. They sit there gawking as they listen to the story about the big dwarf wedding when more than sixty dwarves were married off against their will. They listen to the tale of the mighty tsar who kept his soldiers' molars in a leather pouch. And they shudder at the story about the sinister Curiosity Cabinet, where the tsar exhibited human fetuses in blue alcohol that wasn't fit for drinking. Sometimes I tell stories until early morning, and the more I talk, the calmer the sea becomes.

Sylvester is bending over the pots of meat. Surprisingly enough, he has a handsome profile. It's only from the front that his innate stupidity is evident.

"You tell good yarns, Sørine. Where did you hear them?"

"At the tsar's court."

"You mean a little turd like you has been to the tsar's court?"

He blinks.

"Not only that," I brag. "I've performed there any number of times. I've even performed for His Majesty Frederik IV."

"That must have been a long time ago."

"Why do you say that?"

"Because the king doesn't care for amusements. He's only interested in prayers and sermons."

"So you think His Majesty has no use for a dwarf?"

"Not on your life."

"What about the Crown Prince?"

"Everyone says he's even more boring than his father."

I sigh and try to imagine what it will feel like to walk down Vintapperstræde again. What if it looks the same? What if everything has changed? Which is worse: when life stands still, or when it's pulled out from under you like a rug?

I go back up on deck. The captain is standing on the bridge. On the horizon I can see a streak of green. But they tell me that it's not yet Denmark.

To my surprise I discover that the cat has followed me. I consider tossing the animal overboard, but then I remember that his name is Rufus. It's hard to drown a cat named Rufus.

We sleep together for the next few nights.

The cat thinks I'm a pillow. Maybe that's why I can't kill him. Because he thinks I'm soft, because he has a use for me.

Sometimes the cat looks at me in a way that makes me shiver.

"You're lying here, looking forward to seeing Copenhagen," he says. "But a big surprise is in store for you there. Sometimes you may think that you have a city, but suddenly you don't have that city anymore."

A moment later the cat falls asleep. There are dreams behind his eyelids—dreams of thick cream and balls of yarn. Rufus jerks his paws back and forth. He shakes his snout and smacks his lips with pleasure.

Maybe I could be fond of a cat, if somebody forced me. Maybe.

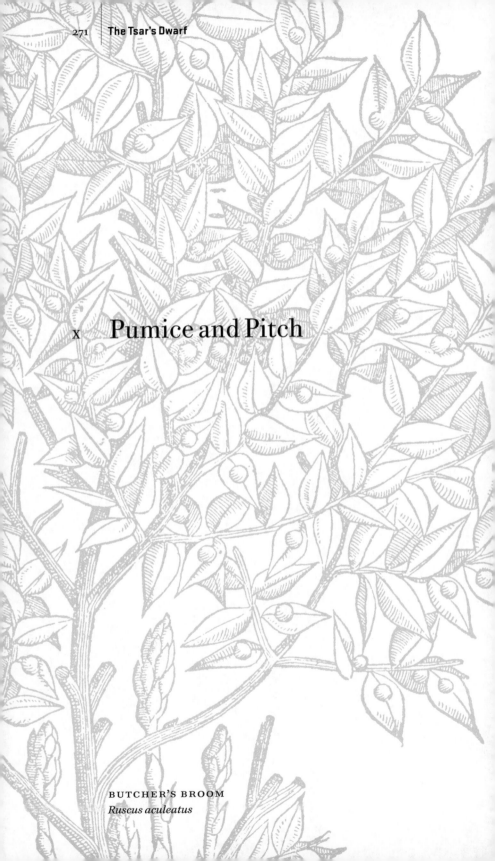

x Pumice and Pitch

BUTCHER'S BROOM
Ruscus aculeatus

72.

NYKIØBING IS A DRIED-UP PROVINCIAL TOWN IN DEN-
mark with a couple of ugly churches that God wouldn't dream
of frequenting. There is a marketplace square and an old castle
that hasn't been properly maintained. There is a dreary strait
between Falster and Lolland that plays host to hungry seagulls
and rotting skiffs.

Peter Alexeyevich stopped here when he came to Denmark.

He moved into the inn and said no to a banquet with the
town's noblemen. In the evening he grabbed a petty officer and
slept with him in the bed. Peter never could stand to sleep alone.

The tsar's soldiers pitched camp near Guldborgsund,
using the farmers' fences as firewood and making soup out of
weeds. After that Peter sailed up the coast to meet with the
king. That was twelve years ago, but everyone in Nykiøbing still
remembers him. It's impossible to forget Peter Alexeyevich,
utterly impossible.

The more misfortune you cause, the more alive you are.

I still love him. Do I love Denmark too?

I'M STANDING OUTSIDE the inn, which is on the marketplace
square in Nykiøbing. The residents of Falster are staring at me.
They've never seen a dwarf before; they had never seen a tsar
before either. Peter Alexeyevich hated the way they stared at him.
It wasn't beyond him to raise his executioner's sword and give

the culprits a good thrashing. The tsar always did whatever he pleased.

I walk around the square and look at the wares for sale. There's a sad-looking selection of beets, cabbage, and rhubarb. But the islanders are kindly; they sing when they speak. Even when they threaten each other, it sounds like they're reciting nursery rhymes.

I fall into conversation with a shopkeeper. It's a very strange feeling: to be here in my own country, speaking my own language. The shopkeeper asks me why I've come to town. I tell him a pack of lies. When he glances away, I swipe a few apples and flee through the crowd. After that I go back to Sylvester, to the cat, and to the good ship *Wolfhound*.

I have to pinch myself on the arm.

I'm back in my home country. I'm back to my native tongue.

THE NEXT DAY we arrive in Copenhagen.

I see the king's city from a distance: all the towers, the spires of the Stock Exchange and Vor Frue Church. Copenhagen Castle looms from its place on Holmen. The walls have been whitewashed, and it has a new roof. A flock of seagulls follows in our wake. The waters of the Øresund are turquoise and turbulent, with occasional patches of green.

The city comes closer: the rope works, the sports hall, and the hospitals. I catch sight of Holmen Church and scores of rotting huts along the harbor. Did I really once live in Copenhagen? That seems so long ago, but also like it was just yesterday. I suddenly have a feeling that my years in Russia were only a dream, that now I've awakened—that reality has caught up with me.

Heavy clouds hover over the Øresund. It's impossible to see Sweden. Only a few skiffs and shallops are visible. We glide through the seaweed and quagmire. There is something mournful about our approach from the sea.

Have I missed the city? To my surprise I don't feel much of anything. Maybe because Brønshøj is my home town, not

Copenhagen. The only reason for living in Copenhagen is to survive; there is no other reason.

I don't miss Russia either. I am where I'm supposed to be. It's a strange feeling, but that's how it is.

I am supposed to be here. Now.

THE SAILORS ARE restless. They can't get ashore fast enough. I wait on deck so as not to be trampled. Everything is a great tumult around me. Several sailmakers dash past me. I hear men speaking the dialects of Jutland, Fyen, and Norway. A shot is fired from somewhere in the harbor. The wharf is swarming with sailors and merchants.

On deck I say goodbye to Sylvester and Rufus. I was just getting used to them, and now we have to part.

"Where are you headed?" asks Sylvester.

"I don't know."

"You can sleep in my lodgings in Nyboder."

I shake my head and give him a hug.

"Sørine, do you have any money?"

"Plenty," I lie.

The cat looks at me and shakes his head. He watches me as I disembark. He stands there on deck for a long time, small and melancholy.

It starts to drizzle. I have a feeling that something has been punctured. That the world can now flow into me; I can no longer stop it.

I exit the customs building and walk toward town. There is more traffic on the streets, more coaches and sedan chairs. The fine folk are wearing shorter wigs. On a street corner a crowd of wenches gathers to have a look at me. I lash out at them. I want to be left alone.

"What a tiny turd you are. You could fit in my hand."

I snort scornfully. I'm able to understand all the insults people are hurling at me—every single curse that flies toward me. But that's not really an advantage.

A farmer from Amager picks me up and hands me to his wife. I kick her in the chest. The man flings me to the ground. Two fine gentlemen take pity on me and help me to my feet. One of them hands me my cane and then bows.

I limp along Norgesgade, past the elegant mansions. A fine lady gets into a sedan chair. I watch it disappear into the crowds of citizens and livestock.

Later I end up on Kongens Nye Torv. The square has been paved with cobblestones, and it looks more stylish. The statue of the old king towers up in the center. One of the mansions has been spruced up. The rain has become a downpour.

I sit down and close my eyes.

When that man threw me to the ground, I hurt myself more than I wanted to admit.

I always hurt myself more than I want to admit.

73.

MY MOTHER USED TO FOLLOW ME.

I realized that when I was little. Someone was holding their hand over me. When things went well, it was because someone was protecting me. But we were separated by the sky. My mother couldn't protect me the same way my father could. My mother was with God; she was no more than a void that could be filled with meaning.

I used to be furious at her. But it was a vexing sort of anger. Because who was she? Where did she come from? I knew only the stories about my birth. Otherwise I knew nothing about my mother, not even her first name. "Her name was Anna," my father told me when I turned seven. "Her name was Hannah," he said when I was nine. She came from Valby, Islev, and Hvidovre, by turns. Often she was the daughter of a baron, occasionally a poor orphan that he had taken under his wing. My father was the charitable Samaritan; he protected women with his cock.

At one point I considered going through the church records, but what business did a dwarf have with church records?

Dwarves have no right to the past; it doesn't belong to us. That was the attitude I encountered when I asked.

When I moved to Vintapperstræde, I had the peculiar feeling that my mother had once lived there. That she might have guided me there from the invisible world. One evening I was stupid enough to mention this to the Scoundrel. He laughed at me and said I was crazy and dumb. So I invented a mother for myself. I called her Hanne, and I gave her features that appealed to me. It had been Hanne's greatest dream to give birth to a dwarf, because a dwarf has more use for a mother than anyone else. That was my story.

The truth is something that you should keep to yourself.

What is the truth about Copenhagen? That I've come back. That's all I know: I've come back.

DARKNESS COMES SLOWER than in Russia. Everything is more gentle and hazy. It's as if the light wants to say: I'm leaving you slowly, do not despair; I will be back tomorrow.

Otherwise I haven't thought much about the differences. Danes aren't as robust as Russians, or as brutal. In Copenhagen there is a different atmosphere, a different type of despondency.

In the insulting book that he wrote, Robert Molesworth said that Danes are mediocre, that we have no real talent for anything, that we are a peculiar gray mass of people resigned to the way things are. A pack of grumblers, yes. But a pack of self-satisfied grumblers convinced of our own superiority.
I don't know whether that's true. But a book can only be insulting if there's some truth to what it says.

Slowly I approach my neighborhood.

Only a few things have changed in the adjoining street. A bay window has been torn down, a little hovel has collapsed. Otherwise people are cooking supper, as usual. The livestock are being fed inside the small half-timbered houses. A calf peeks out through a hatch door. Everything is quiet.

I sit down on a filthy doorstep. I'm tired. My back is aching terribly. It no longer wants to hold me up. I'm only a few steps away from Vintapperstræde, but I don't have the strength to go on. I have to sit on the doorstep for a while.

Maybe I returned home too fast. Maybe my soul hasn't caught up with me.

I have to sit here until I start to yearn.

I close my eyes and take a deep breath. At that moment I sense something in the air.

An autumn wind sweeps through the street, under the doors, under everyone's clothes. Trash whirls up from the gutters. Two watchmen approach, wearing top boots and carrying morning-stars. One of them is missing an eye. When he sees me, he opens his mouth, but not a sound crosses his lips.

The watchmen light the copper lamps and disappear, slouching under their fur caps.

The wind grows stronger and takes on sharp edges. No one is out on the street except me. I stand up. I know that I shouldn't stand up. The wind picks up even more force, rattling hinges and eaves. A man hurries down the street. He holds onto his cap and disappears through a barn door.

Then I see the rats. There's a whole army of them, nearly a hundred. They're wet and disgusting and running straight toward me. At first I don't know what to do. But they're not after me. A few run over my feet, the rest dash through the sewage on the street and vanish around the corner.

An infant cries, and several dogs bark in the distance.

All the animals are nervous.

I start walking, but every step is painful. At that moment I notice the sky. It's lit up and red. It's on fire.

74.

IT STARTS AS AN ACCIDENT ON LILLE KLEMENS STRÆDE.

The chicken-seller's son is only a boy. A stupid little boy who doesn't know what he's doing. He goes up to the attic with his little sister. They have a ball with them, and they happily start playing with it. The boy has brought along a candle. He sets the candle on a barrel full of chicken fat. The candle topples over. Flames ignite the barrel, then the grain, the cask of aquavit, and the thick layer of wood shavings. Suddenly the thatched roof is ablaze. The fire runs along the tar-filled gutters of the roof, it keeps on going down the street. The flames are merciless. The fire spreads faster, much too fast.

The chicken-seller's son is a stupid little boy, but not that stupid. He has always had a weakness for fire. Now he stands in the midst of it. Children can be quite wicked; grownups don't always see it, but there is wickedness in boys. He is thrilled by the flames, he is bewitched by them. But they're too big. Now they whirl around and come toward him with yellow teeth. The boy is nailed to the floor. He tries to scream, but he can't. At that instant the flames catch hold of his pants. His sister has run downstairs; she takes the fire with her in her hair. Her father douses her with water. The sparks take hold in the bedstraw. The girl stands frozen in the middle of the room. She watches the fire. It burns through her blouse. It doesn't hurt. Not yet. But it will.

The fire ignites everything.

Outside the wind is diabolical, seeming to move wherever it can do the most damage. As if it were guided by the Evil One himself. The houses stand close to each other, like indecent lovers. The flames speed along. Now they reach Helligkorsstræde, Badstuestræde, and Vestergade. The soldiers' drums start up, heavy and portentous. A moment later the tocsins begin to toll, sounding the alarm. The city is filled with a great clamor: terror-stricken cries and children sobbing. The smoke is black. Everywhere there's the stink of sweet flesh.

The rats return with the same sinister silence. The fire spreads, settling like a red dome over the city. Sparks ignite mansions, brew-houses, and the hovels of the poor. The firemasters try to get through with their water wagons, but they're blocked by all the onlookers. The fire is now in Lille Lars Bjørns Stræde,

Studiestræde, and Sankt Peders Stræde. By midnight it's nearing
the student lodgings and the churches.

I KEEP ON walking. The fire hasn't yet reached my part of the
city, but it's only a matter of time. The mood is peculiar. People
are talking and glancing up at the red sky as if it has nothing to
do with them. Children are playing in the street while the smoke
forms a thick cloud in the air.

I pass some livestock. Færgestræde is teeming with goodfolk. Flatbed carts are filled with possessions: furniture, tankards, and ships' compasses. Two horse-drawn wagons are plun-
dered by street urchins. One of them runs off with a chamberpot,
another with a little travel trunk. Several men chase after them,
but they can't make any headway because of the crowds.

"It's burning on Nørregade too."

A few soldiers march through the city with their bayonets
raised. Their faces are stern and solemn.

I change direction and walk along Kiøbmagergade. The
city is lit up as if it were midday. People are dragging their
belongings inside the churches. An old woman collapses in front
of me. She doesn't get up. She just lies there, resigned.

"Arson. It's arson."

"The Jews are to blame."

I creep along the wall of the buildings, nervous and
frightened. The fire is coming from all directions, pouring over
the buildings like a raging flood. The tocsins toll louder. Panic
spreads through the narrow streets.

It starts to rain. Drops land on my cheeks, but a few minutes later the rain stops. I'm approaching Nørreport, the north
gate. Hundreds of people have gathered there. The gate is closed.
People are shouting and cursing the guards. Several shots rip
through the air. A man falls to the ground, struck in the neck. His
body twitches, blood trickles onto the cobblestones.

Brawls start up everywhere. I seek refuge in a back courtyard, but a soldier chases me out. Smoke settles in my throat,

making me cough. Huge embers fly through the air. The heat is fierce and oppressive.

I have no idea where I should go.

A dog barks angrily and sinks its teeth into the ankle of a guard. He slits the animal's throat and then gives the head a furious kick. I sit down on the ground and cry.

I'm in Hell. This is Hell.

THEN I SEE the figure up on the rampart.

He's sitting astride a beautiful steed. He's staring down at the city gate. Only two soldiers are with him. It's His Majesty the King. When the crowd catches sight of him, the commotion stops. Several citizens sink to their knees, others say a prayer and smile.

"His Majesty."

"Long live King Frederik!"

The king has grown old. His face is wrinkled, his eyelids are heavier than twelve years ago. He's wearing a broad-brimmed hat and a coat made of lambskin. The king seems lost, as if he can't fully comprehend the flames and the smoke.

It's God punishing me, he thinks.

First the towns of Tønder and Viborg and Saxkiøbing burned. Now it's my city's turn. I'm paying the price for the sins of my youth. God's punishment is righteous. God's punishment is always righteous.

Frederik assumes all of the blame.

Eight of his children are dead. All that were conceived in love have perished. Those that were born of indifference are alive. Eight children have been laid to rest in the earth. Five cities are in ashes.

Such is the will of God. And now Copenhagen is burning.

A FIGURE APPROACHES the king. I can't see who it is, whether it might be Anna Sophie, the Crown Prince, or an advisor. The king listens and then vanishes, riding wildly across the embankment. I watch him go with tears in my eyes. At that moment a deafening explosion is heard. A tower of flames rises up over the city. Thousands of sparks fall onto the rooftops, embers fly and rise up into the sky. The tocsins toll louder. Judgment Day has come.

Judgment Day has come.

75.

THEY'RE TRYING TO BLOW UP BLASENS TAVERN. THEY want to save Vor Frue Church. The plan is to bring down a row of houses in order to stop the blaze. They bring eight cannons and set out the dynamite—twenty sticks in the tavern's cellar, fifteen sticks in the eaves. The dynamite explodes before the soldiers manage to get out. Sparks from the explosion catch hold of Vor Frue Church and spread with the speed of lightning. Smoke billows out of the tower windows. The fire is working its way through God's house, through the altars and the organ loft. Flames light up the chapels and leap for the cenotaphs on the altarpiece. The fierce heat makes the beautiful spire melt. Nørregade is blocked off. The city holds its breath. I hold my breath.

Everyone is waiting and praying.

God will protect His church.

Everyone is saying a prayer and watching the flames against the black sky.

Everyone is waiting.

The night fades. Morning arrives. The sky is gray and a smoldering red. The city is strangely silent. People are grim and resolute. Around ten o'clock the spire begins to melt. For a moment it hangs in the air. Then it topples to the street with a deafening roar. The smoke is suffocating, rising up in the sky like a mushroom. Nørregade is covered with ash and bricks. A sigh passes through the spectators. The melted church bells lie in a glowing heap along with furniture, chairs, hymnals, and everything else.

I hurry on, weaving my way between carts and goodfolk.

Suddenly it's nice to be small. I find shortcuts and continue on, moving between the legs of the poor who are stealing to their hearts' content. My back feels better; it no longer hurts. A man falls over, foaming at the mouth. I crawl over a corpse lying in an awkward position. Several boys search the pockets for coins and then dash off to find more loot. I feel like singing. I'm going crazy. And why not?

THE GARRISON IS called out, but only to protect Rosenborg Castle. The water bearers abandon their work. They are dejected and resigned. The whole city is burning. It's like Sodom and Gomorrah. At last God has His revenge. Evil takes up residence in the flames, blocking up the water hoses so the fire can rage. The wind does its part, blowing in the right direction, igniting the orphans' home and the soap factory. I continue my wandering through Hell. Fire flares up from empty cellars; it catches hold of stacks of hay, barrels of tar, and larders. The student lodgings are in ruins, the professors' houses in ashes. But Ulfeldt's pillar of shame on Gråbrødretorv is untouched. Only two of the letters have melted off.

Hundreds of citizens have fled to Trinitatis Church. Their belongings are piled up on the altar and tombstones. Everyone is praying. The children's sobs are heart-rending. But the flames spare no one. They eat their way through the walls, set fire to the altarpieces and the people's possessions. The vapor is poisonous, the floor is white-hot. Now the flames are approaching the Round Tower, licking along the walls, taking hold of the observatory and the astronomical instruments. Part of the roof caves in. Everything is melting. The city is melting.

I laugh like someone possessed. I find shortcuts and run the gauntlet through the crowds. I feel better than I've ever felt. Why do I feel better than I've ever felt?

A boy runs into me. He's about six years old, with blond hair, a nose pressed flat, and an adorable harelip. I grab his hand and race through the street, away.

"Don't worry, we'll find your family," I say.

The boy nods and squeezes my hand. I think about Kristopher, Fyodor, and Kamilka. I want to save this boy from the flames. I want to save his life. He starts to cry. I stop to tell him the story about Tristovich, but I can't remember how it goes. All I can do is laugh.

I laugh and laugh. The flames are chasing us, working their way through a row of houses, licking along the windowpanes, which shatter into thousands of pieces. I cast a sidelong glance at the lad. There is something familiar about the boy's flat-pressed nose and harelip. His hand feels nicer than Kristopher's. It's not as sweaty.

"What's your name?" I ask with a smile.

"Mathias."

I stare at the lad.

"Mathias?"

He nods. I start to shake all over, violently and uncontrollably. Then I take a swipe at him. The boy gives me a frightened look, tears his hand away, and runs into the crowd.

"Mathias!" I yell. "Mathias!"

A few sparks strike my cheek. It's getting hotter. The flames make a wall collapse in a deafening roar. Where is Mathias? I have to find Mathias. I stop to catch my breath and get knocked to the ground. Someone steps on my face, but I manage to get back on my feet. People are lugging jewelry boxes, prayer benches, and travel trunks. The smoke is billowing toward us in black and gray waves. The city vanishes, it has already vanished. I gasp for air, and for a moment I black out. Then onward, onward...

A fine gentleman runs into me. An instant later he's sucked into the throng and vanishes. A kitten darts between my legs. I try to pick it up. It looks like Rufus. Everything is getting brighter and clearer. The smoke disappears down the side street and through the gates.

"Sørine?"

The fine gentleman who ran into me is back.

"Sørine Bentsdatter?"

I stare at the man. He has big, guileless eyes and a sensitive mouth. His nose bears witness to a fussy temperament. An ugly scar on his forehead lends him a certain gravity. I push him away. He can leave me alone.

"Don't you recognize me, Sørine Bentsdatter?"

I shake my head and start to cry, but the man has taken hold of my arm. I have an urge to chop off his hand. I struggle, but I can't pull myself free. Suddenly I laugh.

"Mr. Æreboe...the esteemed Mr. Æreboe."

The *notarius* lets his hand drop and looks through me.

"It's a catastrophe, Sørine. The university library has gone up in flames. Our entire whole history has been lost, the whole history of Denmark. Do you understand what that means?"

I nod.

"Do you realize what was inside there? *Atlas Danicus*, the most priceless manuscripts...Tycho Brahe's calculations... Do you understand? We tried to save them, Sørine, but there was nothing we could do."

I nod again and tug at my sleeve. Æreboe's eyes are shiny.

"Everything has gone up in flames. Why would God want this to happen? Can you explain it to me?"

Only now do I see that the clothes of the *notarius* are covered in soot. He wears no wig. There are cuts all over his scalp. His voice has a beautiful but brittle quaver to it.

"I don't know, sir."

The *notarius* has grown older, but his complexion is still that of an angel. The city has disappeared around us: the houses, the beautiful squares, everything. An orange glow settles over the sky. It's so lovely that I can't stop crying.

I stare at Æreboe. I can't get enough of looking at him. And it's as if he's seeing me for the first time.

"You've come safely home from Russia?"

I nod and keep on crying.

"I'm glad to hear that."

Æreboe lets his hand slide down his soot-covered coat. The smoke slips right through him. We're in another landscape. His voice sounds bright and warm.

"Well, I have to go home to my wife. She'll be worried. She's always worried."

I nod and stand there, nailed to the spot. I hear a great crackling sound, but it's far away. A roof falls in, sparks are hurled through the air and strike my face. I gasp with pain, but I can't move because of the angels. The light gets stronger, more transparent.

"Come with me. You need a place to sleep."

Behind us the carillon of Saint Nikolaj Church comes to an abrupt halt. The barking of the dogs stops. The city is silent, infinitely silent.

I look at the *notarius* and then gaze down the burning street. To my right the flames reach all the way to the sky. The horizon is lit up with blazing colors and a golden glow. To my left it's dark and cool. The sky is calm and enticing.

I have to choose. Rasmus Æreboe looks at me. And then we set off.

Author's note

I LOVE PSYCHOPATHS.

Not in real life but in fiction.

The Russian Tsar Peter the Great was a charismatic psychopath but he was also an unparallelled genius, a violent visionary, a ruthless reformer, a shrewd politician, an obnoxious drunk, a capable carpenter, a delightful dentist, a skillful sailor, and a leading dwarf connoisseur. I wanted to write a novel about this enigma, so I started to work on a story about Peter's disastrous 1716 visit to his Danish ally Frederik IV in Copenhagen.

But after a few months I got bored. Other people had written books about Peter Alexeyevich. Why should I do the same? Then one day, out of the blue, I got the idea that the king should give the Tsar a Danish dwarf as a gift. After all, Peter collected dwarves as others collect stamps. I continued to write—and out of me grew this obnoxious, funny female dwarf who hated God and the world for the way she was treated.

I spent a year and a half of my life with Sørine Bentsdatter. The more I wrote about her, the more I loved her. When we had to part, I cried like a baby.

The Tsar's Dwarf has been published in Denmark, France, and Portugal. I hope my American readers will love my dwarf as well.

Yours,

Peter H. Fogtdal
Copenhagen, Denmark, and Portland, Oregon; February 22, 2008

Current Titles

Hawthorne Books is committed to independent publishing. While our interest in American literary fiction and narrative nonfiction shapes our catalog, one of our goals is to discover more international titles and books in translation. All of our titles are published as affordable original trade paperbacks, but feature details not typically found even in case bound titles from bigger houses: acid-free papers; sewn bindings which will not crack; heavy, laminated covers with double-scored French flaps that function as built-in bookmarks.

Core: A Romance
Kassten Alonso

Fiction / 208pp / $12.95 / 0-9716915-7-6

This intense and compact novel crackles with obsession, betrayal, and madness. As the narrator becomes fixated on his best friend's girlfriend, his precarious hold on sanity deteriorates into delusion and violence in this twenty-first-century retelling of the classic myth of Hades and Persephone.

"Jump through this Gothic stained-glass window and you are in for some serious investigation of darkness and all of its deadly sins. But take heart, brave traveler, the adventure will prove thrilling."
Tom Spanbauer Author of *Now is the Hour*

501 Minutes to Christ
Poe Ballantine

Essays / 174pp / $13.95 / 0-9766311-9-9

This collection of personal essays ranges from Ballantine's diabolical plan to punch John Irving in the nose during a literary festival, to the tale of how after years of sacrifice and persistence, Ballantine finally secured a contract with a major publisher for a short story collection that never came to fruition.

"My soul yearns to know this most entangled enigma. I confess to Thee, O Lord, that I really have no idea what Poe Ballantine is talking about."
St. Augustine

Decline of the Lawrence Welk Empire
Poe Ballantine

Fiction / 376pp / $15.95 / 0-9766311-1-3

Edgar Donahoe is back for another misadventure, this time in the Caribbean. When he becomes involved with his best friend's girl and is stalked by murderous island native Chollie Legion, even Cinnamon Jim, the medicine man, is no help—it takes a hurricane to blow Edgar out of the mess.

"This second novel ... initially conjures images of *Lord of the Flies*, but then you would have to add about ten years to the protagonists' ages and make them sex-crazed, gold-seeking alcoholics."
Library Journal

God Clobbers Us All
Poe Ballantine

Fiction / 196pp / $15.95 / 0-9716915-4-1

Set against a decaying San Diego rest home in the 1970s, *God Clobbers Us All* is the shimmering, hysterical, melancholy account of eighteen-year-old surfer-boy/orderly Edgar Donahoe, who struggles with romance, death, friendship, and an ill-advised affair with the wife of a maladjusted war veteran.

"Calmer than Bukowski, less portentous than Kerouac, more hopeful than West, Poe Ballantine may not be sitting at the table of his mentors, but perhaps he deserves his own after all."
San Diego Union-Tribune

Things I Like About America
Poe Ballantine

Essays / 266pp / $12.95 / 0-9716915-1-7

These risky personal essays are populated with odd jobs, eccentric characters, boarding houses, buses, and beer. Written with piercing intimacy and self-effacing humor, they take us on a Greyhound journey through small-town America and explore what it means to be human.

"Part social commentary, part collective biography, this guided tour may not be comfortable, but one thing's for sure: You will be at home."
Willamette Week

WINNER, 2005 LANGUM PRIZE FOR HISTORICAL FICTION

Madison House
Peter Donahue

Fiction / 528pp / $16.95 / 0-9766311-0-5

This novel chronicles Victorian Seattle's explosive transformation from frontier outpost to metropolis. Maddie Ingram, owner of Madison House, and her quirky and endearing boarders find their lives linked when the city decides to regrade Denny Hill and the fate of their home hangs in the balance.

"Peter Donahue seems to have a map of old Seattle in his head... And all future attempts in its historical vein will be made in light of this book."
David Guterson Author of *Snow Falling on Cedars*

Clown Girl Introduction by Chuck Palahniuk
Monica Drake
Fiction / 298pp / $15.95 / 0-9766311-5-6

Clown Girl lives in Baloneytown, a neighborhood so run-down that drugs, balloon animals, and even rubber chickens contribute to the local currency. Using clown life to illuminate a struggle between integrity and economic reality, this novel examines issues of class, gender, economics, and prejudice.

"The pace of [this] narrative is methamphetamine-frantic, as Drake drills down past the face paint and into Nita's core ... There is a lot more going on here than just clowning around."
Publishers Weekly

So Late, So Soon
D'Arcy Fallon
Memoir / 224pp / $15.95 / 0-9716915-3-3

An irreverent, fly-on-the-wall view of the Lighthouse Ranch, a Christian commune the eighteen-year-old hitchhiker D'Arcy Fallon called home for three years in the mid-1970s, when life's questions overwhelmed her and reconciling her family's past with her future seemed impossible.

"What would draw an otherwise independent woman to a life of menial labor and subservience? Fallon's answer is both an inside look at '70s commune life and a funny, poignant coming of age."
Judy Blunt Author of *Breaking Clean*

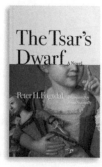

The Tsar's Dwarf
Peter H. Fogtdal Translated by Tiina Nunnally
Fiction / $15.95 / 0-9790188-0-3

A Danish dwarf is given by Denmark's king to Peter the Great, who, smitten with her grotesquerie and intelligence, takes her to his court in St. Petersburg. Her wit helps her forge an existence amid the squalor of early 18th-century Russia. A masterfully translated novel – a bawdy, deeply human tale.

There's potent mix of heartbreak and hilarity in this vividly imagined novel. The dwarf Sørine fixes her keen gaze on history's tangled events and misses nothing. She is completely spellbinding.
Joanna Scott Pulitzer Prize finalist for *The Manikin*

September 11: West Coast Writers Approach Ground Zero Edited by Jeff Meyers

Essays / 266pp / $16.95 / 0-9716915-0-9

The events of September 11, 2001, their repercussions, and our varied responses to them inspired this collection. By history and geographic distance, the West Coast has developed a community different from the East; ultimately shared interests bridge the distinctions in provocative and heartening ways.

"*September 11: West Coast Writers Approach Ground Zero* deserves attention. This book has some highly thoughtful contributions that should be read with care on both coasts, and even in between."
San Francisco Chronicle

Dastgah: Diary of a Headtrip
Mark Mordue

Travel Memoir / 316pp / $15.95 / 0-9716915-6-8

A world trip that ranges from a Rolling Stones concert in Istanbul to meetings with mullahs and junkies in Tehran, from a cricket match in Calcutta to an S&M bar in New York, as Mark Mordue explores countries most Americans never see, as well as issues of world citizenship in the twenty-first century.

"Mordue has elevated *Dastgah* beyond the realms of the traditional travelogue by sharing not only what he learned about cultures he visited but also his brutally honest self-discoveries."
Elle

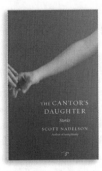

FINALIST, 2006 OREGON BOOK AWARD
WINNER, SAMUEL GOLDBERG & SONS
FICTION PRIZE FOR EMERGING JEWISH
WRITERS

The Cantor's Daughter
Scott Nadelson

Fiction / 280pp / $15.95 / 0-9766311-2-1

Sympathetic, heartbreaking, and funny, these stories – capturing people in critical moments of transition – reveal our fragile emotional bonds and the fears that often cause those bonds to falter or fail.

"These beautifully crafted stories are populated by Jewish suburbanites living in New Jersey, but ethnicity doesn't play too large a role here. Rather, it is the humanity of the characters and our empathy for them that bind us to their plights."
Austin Chronicle

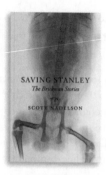

Saving Stanley: The Brickman Stories
Scott Nadelson
Ficion / 230pp / $15.95 / 0-9716915-2-5

These interrelated short stories are graceful, vivid narratives that bring into sudden focus the spirit and the stubborn resilience of the Brickmans, a Jewish family of four living in suburban New Jersey. This fierce collection provides an unblinking examination of family life and the human instinct for attachment.

"Focusing on small decisions and subtle shifts, *Saving Stanley* closely examines the frayed ties that bind. With a fly-on-the-wall sensibility and a keen sense for dramatic restraint, Nadelson is … both a promising writer and an apt documentarian."
Willamette Week

Seaview   Introduction by Robert Coover
Toby Olson
Fiction / 316pp / $15.95 / 0-9766311-6-4

This novel follows a golf hustler and his dying wife across an American wasteland. Trying to return the woman to her childhood home on Cape Cod, the pair are accompanied by a mysterious Pima Indian activist and shadowed by a vengeful drug dealer to the novel's apocalypse on the Seaview Links.

"Even a remarkable dreamer of nightmares like Nathanael West might have been hard-pressed to top the finale … Unlike any other recent American novel in the freshness of its approach and vision."
The New York Times Book Review

The Well and the Mine   Introduction by Fannie Flagg
Gin Phillips
Fiction / $15.95 / 0-9766311-7-2

In 1931 Carbon Hill, Alabama, a small coal-mining town, nine-year-old Tess Moore watches a woman shove the cover off the family well and toss in a baby without a word. The event forces the family to face the darker side of their community and seek to understand the motivations of their family and friends.

"Gin Phillips is the real thing. *The Well and the Mine* is a stunning triumph: haunting, lyrical, a portrait of the southern family, a story of the human predicament."
Vicki Covington Author of *Gathering Home* and *The Last Hotel for Women*

Leaving Brooklyn Introduction by Ursula Hegi
Lynne Sharon Schwartz
Fiction / 168pp / $12.95 / 0-9766311-4-8

An injury at birth left fifteen-year-old Audrey with a wandering eye and her own way of seeing; her relationship with a Manhattan eye doctor exposes her to the sexual rites of adulthood in this startling and wonderfully rich novel, which raises the themes of innocence and escape to transcendent heights.

"Stunning. Coming of age is seldom registered as disarmingly as it is in *Leaving Brooklyn*."
New York Times Book Review

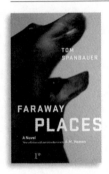

Faraway Places Introduction by A.M. Homes
Tom Spanbauer
Fiction / $14.95 / 0-9766311-8-0

This novel marks the end of childhood for Jake Weber and the beginning of trouble for his family. An innocent swim ends with something far beyond anyone's expectations: Jake witnesses a brutal murder and is forced to keep quiet, even as the woman's lover is falsely accused.

"Forceful and moving ... Spanbauer tells his short, brutal story with delicacy and deep respect for place and character."
Publishers Weekly

FINALIST, 2005 OREGON BOOK AWARD

The Greening of Ben Brown
Michael Strelow
Fiction / 272pp / $15.95 / 0-9716915-8-4

Ben Brown becomes a citizen of East Leven, Oregon after he recovers from an electrocution that has turned him green. He befriends eighteen-year-old Andrew James and together they unearth a chemical-spill cover-up that forces the town to confront its demons and its citizens to choose sides.

"Strelow resonates as both poet and storyteller. [He] lovingly invokes ... a blend of fable, social realism, wry wisdom, and irreverence that brings to mind Ken Kesey, Tom Robbins, and the best elements of a low-key mystery."
The Oregonian

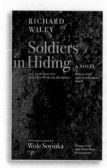

Soldiers in Hiding Introduced by Wole Soyinka
Richard Wiley
Fiction / 194pp / $14.95 / 0-9766311-3-X

Teddy Maki is a Japanese American jazz musician trapped in Tokyo with his friend, Jimmy Yakamoto, both of whom are drafted into the Japanese army after Pearl Harbor. Thirty years later, Maki is a big star on Japanese TV and wrestling with the guilt over Jimmy's death that he's been carrying since the war.

"Wonderful ... Original ... Terrific ... Haunting ... Reading *Soldiers in Hiding* is like watching a man on a high wire!"
The New York Times